The Fa

Owen came face to face with the fierce muzzle and flashing claws of a great red bear, and stared deeply into fearsome blood-red eyes that promised death to all who came near. Owen fell backward, trying to hold the Sword of Skye to ward off the terrible image who lumbered toward him.

"Stearborn! To me! Help!" Owen was crushed by the weight of a snake-man hurled at him by the advancing bear. "To me," he cried again, as he looked upward into the cavernous maw, rowed with long white fangs that dripped blood. It occurred to him that he might be about to die, but the thought came to him of Seravan and Gitel, and the way the two horses had talked of their other animal friends . . .

"All hail, Bruinthor," he called, his voice choked with fear.

"All hail, little brother," replied the huge animal politely, swatting away the body that held Owen captive. "Come up! We have more work this day than to lie about watching the others do our fighting for us!"

* * *

"Has everything a lover of fantasy wants in a book."
　　　—John Morressy, author of *A Voice for Princess*
　　　on *The Fires of Windameir*

*

A WANDERER'S RETURN

BY NIEL HANCOCK

POPULAR LIBRARY

An Imprint of Warner Books, Inc.

A Warner Communications Company

POPULAR LIBRARY EDITION

Popular Library ®, the fanciful P design, and Questar ® are registered
trademarks of Warner Books, Inc.

Cover illustration by Tim Hildebrandt

Popular Library books are published by
Warner Books, Inc.
666 Fifth Avenue
New York, N.Y. 10103

🅦 A Warner Communications Company

Printed in the United States of America

First Printing: November, 1988

10 9 8 7 6 5 4 3 2 1

Once more older hands
    follow the border of scars
        that healed, and no eye nor ear
        can find those wounds
      that killed the apple-cheeked kid
       from Moline,
shot through his heart
    with the grief of a country
      which could not open its arms
      for a wounded child
        sent to do the hideous work
          of bitter, mindwrecked men.

For all of us who have survived the war,
and the long years after.

NH
Co. "C"
716th MP Bn.
RVN 1967–68

A WANDERER'S RETURN

EARTH AND SEA

1. Voyage to the Coast 3

2. News of the Sacred Thistle 12

3. A Mysterious Grotto 21

4. Daughter of the Altar 32

5. Rewen's Promise 44

6. The Quays of White Bird 56

7. Tales of the Red Mountain 62

8. A History of the Flying Snakes 68

9. The Whirlpool 81

10. The Chain of Orlan 94

VOYAGERS ALL

11. Death on the River 109

12. In Blor Alhal 121

13. The Heart of Stone   *128*

14. At the Crossroads   *135*

15. The Conductors of Quineth Rel   *145*

16. Broached   *150*

17. Spindrift   *154*

18. Man Overboard   *160*

19. The Apprentice   *163*

THE WELINGTRON

20. A Student Once More   *173*

21. The Black Mist   *180*

22. Another Gale   *185*

23. The Billows   *191*

24. A Voice of Blor Alhal   *196*

25. Storm Signals   *202*

26. The Welingesse Fal   *205*

27. Torch of Darkness   *210*

FIRE AND AIR

28. The Chalk Caves   219

29. A Visitor from the Sea   224

30. A Light in the Forest   228

31. The Gray Wastes   232

32. The Sons of Aranas   241

33. The Great Salt Pit   244

34. A Messenger of Doom   250

35. In Norith Tal   253

TEACHINGS OF THE MASTER

36. The Curtain of Fear   267

37. The Death of Master Flit   270

38. Flames of Baluven   274

39. Partings on the Quay   277

40. The River's Edge   285

41. The Forge of Roshagel   288

42. A Thread of Light   295

Earth
and
Sea

Voyage to the Coast

The sky hung like a blue dome above the river in the chill of the golden-red dawn. Small water birds left shimmering wakes behind them as they flapped their wings and raced across the smooth surface to become airborne. The soft splashing they made reached Owen as he slept in his cabin, on the Hogan Mag. He lay wrapped in a warm cloak that the Archaelian Findlin had found in the big chest in the Hulin Vipre captain's quarters. It was inky black, and bore the brass insignias of Deros's enemies, but it was warm, and there was no need to lose sleep for fear of them. The raiding parties of the Hulin Vipre and the dreadful Olgnite spidermen were nothing at this moment but a nightmare from the past. His village, Sweet Rock, was gone, but he would soon journey to Eirn Bol, Deros's island home, to aid her besieged father.

Owen stirred in his sleep, dreams of the recent fighting giving way to memories of Stearborn, his commander, telling him which ship he'd sail in. He had given Owen sage advice, delivered with a sharp cuff on the back. Never trust a stranger when your back's to a wall, and the devils are over you like molasses on travel cake! That's when you'll want a lad that's known your name for more than a week!

"Then why put me with Ulen?" he'd demanded. "He would be better if he were left in White Bird. It would be one less danger for us to worry about on this voyage."

But the old warrior had only said, "You'll find he'll fill a need nicely one day. Maybe not in a way you would have thought, but mark me, he'll stand us a good turn yet."

So Owen turned his attention to trying to convince Findlin and Lorimen to keep Ulen with them once the vessels reached Fionten.

"That would be a wery difficult task, lad. Findlin and I have our own hands full with the young Carinbar. He's taken a set to his sails that since you hawe flown the skittle and are taking this woyage, maybe he should go too! No, no, these two old fools don't owe you much in the way of thanks for setting his mind off on a wery dangerous course of action!" Lorimen tried to look grim, but could not conceal a smile that brightened his features. "If he keeps on at this pace, we will be scouting around for another Carinbar soon."

"I'd rather have him aboard than the Gortlander," argued Owen.

Findlin looked out over the flowing silver water, his eyes narrowed. "It won't do to say who it would be best to hawe. I'm an old tar who's been back and forth over these parts enough times that I should hawe hung up my oars a long time back. I can't ewer recall knowing ahead of time who I would want with me on a woyage, and who I wouldn't."

"Then you follow common sense," Owen had persisted.

"If you have a known enemy, you don't give them opportunity to give you a hurt."

The Archaelian laughed lightly. "The enemies I hawe in my time would account for a list as long as my arm, and ewery one of them had their chances to hurt me, whether I gawe them the opportunity, or they found one on their own."

Owen awoke with his words ringing in his mind, and tried to fashion another approach to the problem. It was galling to have Ulen Scarlett aboard the same vessel, and he hated to see the arrogant young Gortlander speaking to Deros. She didn't discourage him, and often acted as though she enjoyed making Owen uncomfortable. Emerald and his new bride had gone with Famhart and Linne, Owen's parents, on the overland march to White Bird, and because Owen had had no one to ask for advice, he tried to lock his feelings tightly within himself, and rose to face the day. As he came through the companionway hatch, he heard Ulen Scarlett talking to Deros.

"We've a course laid," he said, tapping the big chart spread out in the cockpit of the boat. "First downriver to White Bird, of course, to meet whatever survivors there are."

Owen crept closer, trying not to be seen. He felt shame at his behavior, but the overpowering urge to hear what was being said won out. The Gortlander was still speaking: "With any luck, we'll be to the coast in another day. After that, they say the weather is our only enemy. The gales blow now, and it wouldn't be wise to sail in them."

"I came here in the autumn gales," replied Deros. "The ship was sound, and the captain was a seaman of Eirn Bol. It would take more than a stormy sea to keep him from making landfall."

Ulen sneered cruelly. "But the good captain has probably ended up a meal for the Olgnite, or killed by the Vipre.

Findlin says that we'll wait in White Bird until he's sure the weather will hold long enough to try to make a run outside to reach Fionten."

A fresh breeze from the water blew Deros's hair back from her face so that Owen was able to see her more clearly. She turned to face the rail, and looked in the direction of the coast. "He may have reasons for creeping so slowly, but my heart is burdened with worry for my father. Every day we linger here he is in greater danger."

Owen could stand it no longer, and strode forward to stand beside Deros. "We shall be in time," he said. "Even without Gillerman and Ephinias, we shall have enough help to reach Eirn Bol."

The young woman reddened at the sight of Owen, and looked down at her hands. "I didn't see you," she said softly.

"Helwin is very clever at being where he is unseen," said Ulen. "It seems he is becoming very adept at the role of skulking about. Maybe the Olgnite curse lingers."

"I sometimes find it suits my purpose," Owen shot back. "When you deal with those who present two faces, you must sometimes find ways to see what is on the other side."

"I won't have you spying on me," snapped Deros angrily. "I will have you put with your friends on the other ship!"

They were interrupted by the young Archaelian.

"We're to get under way today," Enlid reported cheerfully, speaking to Deros and ignoring his two rivals.

"The sooner we're away from this place, the better I'll like it," said Ulen. "There is a stench in my nostrils."

"It's probably the smell of a stoat," said Owen, smiling slightly. "They have a way of fouling their own nests."

Ulen stepped forward angrily, but before he could speak,

Findlin came on deck, and Enlid turned to his uncle. "Tell Lady Deros how soon she'll see her father."

"I'm not sure we will reach Eirn Bol," replied Findlin. "We'll be the luckiest two Fionten men who hawe ewer walked aboard a deck if we clear these waters before the Werges. The gales in autumn are so fierce here, they'we been known to blow a wessel clean away to the Belgrate Reefs, and that's a piece beyond any waters known to a liwing soul!"

"We still hawe a few weeks before the marking of the Werges on the calendar, uncle. That will giwe us time to be well clear."

"What are you speaking of?" asked Owen. "What are the Verges?"

"That's the time of year before the winter," explained Enlid. "We mark our calendars by the four changes of the year. The hot part is the Awerges, then there comes the Werges, followed by the Wolwerges, with the snow and ice, and finally, Palwerges, when the bloom comes back to the earth."

"There's an old slate that you'd do well to mind, nephew," said Findlin.

> "Sailors brawe
>   may find their grawe
>   by woyaging in the Werges,
> While old salts wise
>   may keep their liwes
>   by porting in the Werges."

Findlin was about to elaborate on the wisdom in the verse when a small punt poled frantically by two men rounded a bend in the river. A horn blew in alarm.

"Snap to it, lads!" barked Stearborn, who had come on deck in response to the horns. "Stand to, any who wear the

Steward colors!" He strode to the railing to see who their visitors were, and what they might want.

"Ahoy, ships!" one of the men cried, when they were within hailing distance of the two boats. "Lend a hand, for pity's sake! Throw these two pilgrims a line, and pull us away from our enemies!"

The men were dressed in poor rags, and appeared gaunt and dirty. As they came nearer the boat, Owen could see the metal collars at the men's throats, and was at the point of telling the others this when riders appeared on the far riverbank, their animals blowing hard and dancing about impatiently as they were drawn up hard at the water's edge.

One of the horsemen dismounted quickly, and drawing a longbow from his saddle scabbard, he carefully notched an arrow and sent it winging toward the two men in the punt. The shaft struck the water a foot from its intended target, and the archer drew another arrow back to shoot.

"Look out!" bellowed Stearborn. "Pull for your life!" He uncoiled a line that was lying on deck next to the anchor rope, and with a powerful cast, threw the rope to the men, striking one of them on the shoulder. "Pull yourself in, lads! Pull for your lives, or you'll soon be a pincushion!"

The two men dropped their poles and hauled on the line with all their might just as the archer across the river loosed another shaft, which snapped through the air with an angry hiss, burying itself with a loud thunking noise into the railing next to Stearborn's hand.

"Bring my bow!" thundered the old commander, his face a fierce red. "And get my Leech shafts! By the Bowstrings of Earolin, I'll prick these jolly louts to teach them better manners than to bandy with a Steward."

A younger Steward had come from below decks with the bow and quiver Stearborn had asked for, and quickly handed them to his commander.

"Stand by, Morlin! And have the other lads muster!"

"Sir."

"There has to be a start to this somewhere, and if these ruffians have a chance to play while the Line Stewards are absent, we'll find this a rough chore, trying to bring law and order back here when we've regrouped and returned."

"If you return," said Ulen. "The tide has changed all over these lands, and what has been may be gone forever. The Olgnite hordes have seen to that."

Stearborn studied the young horseman a moment, his hand poised to release his arrow. "You have a very slack way of regarding things, Master Ulen! Perhaps a bout of good training at the hands of the Stewards will brace you up a bit!" He took careful aim and released his shaft, which flew straight and true toward the mounted men on the far shore, and buried itself in the earth at the archer's feet who had shot at the two men in the punt.

"You missed," jeered Ulen, exulting in the failure of the old commander.

"I didn't intend to hit the blighter," said Stearborn softly. "I believe in giving anyone a fair warning."

The mounted party across the river dismounted, and a half dozen of the men now had their bows out, and loosed a volley of arrows at the two Hulin Vipre vessels. One of the shafts struck the deck of the boat where Ulen stood, sending him ducking backward to seek cover. Another of the arrows pierced one of the men in the punt at his shoulder, and he toppled backward into the water with a stifled cry of pain. Owen was over the side in a flash, pulling the man to safety on the protected side of the boat, and calling out for someone to help him lift the wounded man aboard.

"Come on! We is here! Hand him up so's we can haul him up!" encouraged McKandles. "Push him up a bit so's Lofen and I can grab ahold of his flipper!"

"Be careful! The shaft's broken in him!" As Owen

struggled with the injured man, a figure leapt over the rail into the water beside them and helped hoist the man high enough for Lofen and McKandles to heave him onto the deck. Only then did Owen see that Deros was with him in the water.

"He is a man from our crew!" blurted the excited girl.

"We'd better get back aboard," Owen said. "It looks like those men in the wood have help!" He treaded water and looked cautiously around the stern of the Alogan Mag. There were a dozen more riders now, sending volleys of arrows toward the two moored boats. At the front of the line of archers, two bodies lay unmoving, struck by the long Steward shafts of Stearborn.

Deros grabbed hold of the rope Lofen dangled over the transom. "Get hold of it, my lady! Kandles and I will tug you up!"

Deros did as she was told, and was hauled roughly aboard by the two Gortlanders. Arrows whistled about them, but they threw the rope back in for Owen.

"This here ain't no time to be awadin' in that there fish soup! Hang on!" shouted McKandles, and Owen felt his arms almost pulled out of their sockets by the two strong yanks that pulled him hastily onto the deck. As soon as he was safely up, Lofen and McKandles darted for cover beneath the companionway amidships. "Come on," they hissed. "Them blaggards is ashootin' right down our throats!"

Stearborn was crouched behind the stern railing, notching another shaft. "Come up, lad! I need another bowman here to help me keep the beggars off their pace. They've had new numbers since you've been in the drink."

"Who are they?" Owen gasped.

"I can't tell what banner they fly, but it looks to me to be that bunch we chased out into Lachland during the border campaigns the winter that the burnings happened up toward Clover Hill."

"They must be very strong, to risk running against us again."

"That's always the way of hunting packs," said Stearborn. "They strike only when they outnumber you. The curs probably saw the Olgnites attack, and followed behind to pick the bones of what might be left! And they know the rest of the Stewards are gone on to White Bird, so they may think they have a tasty prize here."

"Deros says these two here were part of the crew on the ship she came on," said Owen, looking at the wounded stranger who was being tended by his friend.

Stearborn looked away from the riders across the river and whistled. "That's a strange piece of news. I wonder if there are any others?"

A crew member brought Owen a bow, and he joined Stearborn in shooting at the horsemen on the opposite bank. Jeremy, Judge, and Hamlin on the other boat also sent volleys of arrows when they noticed a flanking movement had sent other riders farther downstream, where they hurriedly scouted the banks for a place to ford.

"Look to the two Archaels," shouted Stearborn. "We need to make way here quickly, or we'll be pinched off and plucked like a game hen! Get these lines in, and help get under way!"

Men hurried to raise the anchor and ran to the rowing benches. Others hauled in the anchor.

The two vessels coasted slowly out into the current. Then the red sails were raised and caught the frail morning breeze. In another instant they filled and pulled the boats into the center of the broad river, and away from the raiders on the shore.

News of the Sacred Thistle

Findlin, at the helm of the Alogan Mag, laid out the large chart before him. Stearborn was beside him, and Owen could see the two deep in conversation, with the old Steward commander driving his fist into his palm to make a point. The Archaelian shook his head vigorously, pointing to something on the map, then arguing heatedly before having to tend to his steering in a tricky part of the river. Owen was dying to leave his rowing bench to go find out what was causing so much dissension between the two, but the current was now quite strong, and the boat constantly threatened to broach in the treacherous parts, so he was forced to keep pulling. Over the noise of the oarlocks and sails in the wind, he could hear Lorimen in the other boat calling out cadence in a voice that echoed plainly from both banks, which had grown narrower and steeper as they went.

At the next bend, Owen saw the high walls of the canyon on both sides, and over his shoulder he could see the stretches of white water that boiled down the center of the river. Findlin steered the boat close to the edge of the sheer rock walls where the water was almost like a lake. He seized the opportunity to ship his oar, and go back to hear what Findlin and Stearborn were talking about.

"These narrows run on for another bit, but it's safe

enough for a wessel like this. Our own boats hawe done this stretch of water enough times to tell me that!"

"But what next?" asked Stearborn.

"We shall hawe enough water to continue on The Line all the way to the coast, and on the course we hawe shaped. We shall sawe a full day's sailing by going this way."

"The other branch of the river looked better," persisted Stearborn. "Saving a full day means nothing to a drowned man. I don't pretend to know oats from barley about all this business with the water and boats, but I can see by that chart it isn't a wise choice to try to squeeze boats of this size through a thread of water that wouldn't float a bug!"

"It's a thread for a time, but it's deep and clear of rocks. I know it looks crooked and dangerous, but we may hawe need of the time we gain. These bandits at our backs will try to catch us unawares somewhere along the riwer before we get to White Bird. You can set a wager to that, and pay yourself double! They will search the other channel first, and that's all the more time for us to wanish out of their reach."

Stearborn nodded, his eyes a fierce blue. "They haven't had enough, I can tell. You're right about that news, Findlin. They won't rest until they have another shot at us, now that they have reinforcements."

Owen used this opportunity to ask again if anyone knew who the raiders were, or where they had come from.

"The lads we picked up said they're come from Lower Lachland. They were part of the crew on Deros's ship when she first came to these parts. They said they managed to elude the Hulin Vipre and the Olgnite, but were tricked by this bunch. They said they pretended to be merchants and traders, and then fell on everyone in the dead of night and took them for slaves. It was a long while that way, but they found one of the punts from the boats left by the Hulin

Vipre, or by Findlin's bunch, and were going to try their luck on the river. It was better to die that way than to live as dogs, they said. And then they saw us, and that's that."

"But who are the bandits? I thought we'd seen all the worst with the Olgnite and that lot from where Deros lives."

"They sound as though they're a mixed lot," growled Stearborn. "The Stewards have had a run in or two with that lot beyond the Lach boundaries. Some of them were renegades from The Line, and others came down from the Plain of Reeds. There is always mischief up there. Rogue priests starting up their own following, or warrior kings from the old days of the dragon. There were a lot of those scattered out after the trouble began again with the Dark One."

"Has Deros had a chance to talk to the two from her old ship?" asked Owen.

Findlin nodded. "She's tending to the wounded one now. Says his name is Rulon, and was the captain's mate."

The river became more violent suddenly. Owen ran to the oars to help drive the wildly rolling boat to the next patch of calm water, which ran right up against the high rock wall of a canyon that seemed to rise into the distance above them so far the sun was blocked out, leaving them in a shadowed slit of earth, with the noise of the river deafening to their ears.

Stearborn called out, and pointed at something that caused Findlin to veer aside, steering straight for a high, white rock that loomed out of the darkened shadow like a great animal raised on its hind paws.

Behind the rock, the canyon walls formed a cave. Before it stood calm water that was crystal clear.

"I hawe sailed many a time on strange stretches of water, and seen a dozen kinds of mysteries that kept me up at nights to think of them, but this is one of the strangest! We hawe come up and down this riwer more times than I like to remember, but I hawe newer seen this trick before!" Findlin said.

The Alogan Mag was barely inside the calm haven when Lorimen brought the other Hulin Vipre craft gliding silently in behind, his crew as wide-eyed and disbelieving as those aboard Findlin's boat.

"Ahoy," came a shout. "Let's anchor and find out what secrets this cawe might hold!" It was Lorimen, now standing in the bow of his boat, hailing his friend.

Stearborn's eyes were wide in wonderment as he looked around the quiet grotto. Outside, they could hear the roar of the water, but in the recess among the canyon walls, the water was almost like a pond, deep and clear, with small, colorful pebbles on the bottom reflecting light that shone out of the roof. Owen looked up to find the source of the light and saw in the distance over their heads an opening which let in a bright patch of sunlight that flooded the cavern with a pale, golden light.

He was joined by Deros at the rail, as the crew dropped anchor and began lowering their sails.

"What do you make of this?" asked Findlin, addressing the gruff Steward commander. "This is your riwer. Hawe you ewer heard of anything of this nature?"

Stearborn shook his head. "This is old," he said at last. "I don't think anyone from The Line was around when this was made."

"There was a bear in the front," offered Owen. "The big white rock. I'm sure it's the form of a bear."

Findlin was lost in his thoughts for a moment, looking at his new surroundings. "It's unbelievable that we newer saw this before."

The boats were securely anchored, and Lorimen came alongside in a skiff, as wide-eyed as his friend. "We hawe come a long way today toward making me a believer in impossible things," he said, scrambling aboard. He was followed by the young Stewards, who were looking about in awe.

Findlin and Lorimen conferred, and after talking with Stearborn, decided to split the groups to explore, in order to find out more about the hidden grotto, and to leave some time after dark, in case their pursuers were still abroad.

"It will be safe enough here," agreed Findlin. "No one could come on us from any direction but the riwer, and we'll leawe a guard to cower that. We know the renegades behind us hawe no boats, or they would hawe used them by now."

"They have no boats," confirmed Tombin, one of the escaped men. "They are afraid of the water, unless their horses can ford it."

"Then that's a point in our favor," said Stearborn. "Most of our travels from here on will be aboard boats, so they will have to be content with the barrens of The Line, and the other settlements that have been driven out by the spidermen."

"They were marching to the sea," went on Tombin. "That's how we were caught. They came on our vessel where we had her moored, and pretended to be merchants on a trading journey. Our captain caught on to them after he saw they carried no goods to trade. There was a fight then, and we managed to escape, Rulon and I, but they came on us again in the woods and caught us. We'd had no food or sleep for two days, and it was over in a flash. They had us chained to their pack animals, and were going on toward the sea, when they got wind of a big battle going on. They had scouts all up and down both sides of the river, and that's how we found out about the webbers. There were too many to count, according to one of the scouts, so they laid back to watch what would happen, and to take anything that was left."

"That must have been the attack on Sweet Rock," said

Stearborn. "I thought I'd heard signals then that didn't belong to the squashers or the Stewards, or even the Hulin Vipre."

"It was a large settlement. The night was like daylight, there were so many fires. I thought for a time we'd all be fried in the woods, but we were able to loose our bonds and got away. That's when we found the punt on the river."

Stearborn laughed, removing his cloak and wrapping it about a packet of his belongings he was leaving on deck. "Your bad luck has held true. First captured by the raiders from Lachland, and then here you are with a merry crew that's lost in their own way, with enemies on all sides howling for their blood."

"They will be sore put to it, when the time comes for repaying the deed," said Jeremy. "They'll be out of their wits, with one foot in the stirrup and the other in an early grave."

"These crass fellows tease you overmuch," put in Hamlin. "Don't pay them any mind. You'll soon be at the coast, where you can decide as you want whether to go on with us, or to stay to rest and make other plans."

The young stranger shook his head, looking earnestly around at his rescuers. "My Lady Deros has said this ship is returning to Eirn Bol. Rulon and I will be on it! It has been a long while since I've seen my homeland, and my heart aches to return."

"You'll have your chance," promised Stearborn. "But first we have to see what we have here. If there are any caves, they may be the very thing we need when we return to The Line. It would give us a place to cache arms and stores for a prolonged campaign."

"There may be no need for that," suggested Owen.

"Don't fool yourself, lad," growled the old commander. "The Lachs have seen they have a clear field here. They'll be on it like dogs to a deserted kill!" Stearborn's jaw set into a grim scowl. "They'll be here when we return, and it will be good to have all the help we can muster. These caves will give us secret meeting points, and places where we can build our supplies."

Findlin had gone ashore with the first of the skiffs, and beckoned for the others to hurry. "There are paths here that lead on into the cliff. Some of them smell like they may have an opening topside!"

Deros waited next to her injured countryman, who was pale and weak, but seemed to be in good spirits. She stopped Stearborn as he readied to board the skiff to be rowed to the rocky beach that ran around the grotto's interior. "Don't be gone too long. We can't waste our time here."

"It's not a waste of time for me, my lady. It's my responsibility to know everything I can about the lay of the land. This might mean the difference for us someday."

"Look at the stones," said Tombin, peering over the rail into the shallows.

"That one looks almost like the one I have." Ulen held out his hand and looked again at the red stone in the Hulin Vipre prince's ring. The eye of the gem glimmered and moved in strange patterns as the thin ray of sunlight hit it, and it did seem to echo the fire from the stones that lined the bottom of the shallow water. "I shall have to have one of those before we leave."

"Come on, then," shot Owen, already clambering down into the skiff. But Ulen Scarlett stayed aboard with Deros. Owen protested, "I don't feel right leaving her there with him! The last time, he lost her to the Olgnites, and then when she was safe from the spidermen, he turned her over to the Hulin Vipre without even striking a blow!"

Stearborn finally convinced him that it was well. "The boats are safe, and the lass can handle herself," he said.

"There's no need riling yourself into a dither about it, for we'll be back in short order."

"I don't see why she doesn't tell him to stay away," Owen muttered with poor grace.

The old Steward chuckled, rolling his eyes. "There is never logic where the heart is concerned." Owen reddened.

Meanwhile McKandles clung to the small boat with all his might, his color drained. Lofen waited his turn above, calling out encouragements to his friend. "It ain't deep, Kandles! Even if that splinter you is aridin' tips you in, it ain't knee-deep to a foal nohow!"

"It ain't no deeper'n nothin'! I don't wants to see nothin' no more watery than a dipper full when I is thirsty! You is mighty free with your thinkin' now, Lofen Tackman, but we'll see how you sings when you is asittin' here in this tippity bucket!"

"Stow your noise," chastised Findlin. "There's no one around who hates a dunk any worse than me! As long as you're sailing with Findlin, you can count your blessings, for here's one Archael waterman who only likes to sail on it, and not swim in it!"

"A man that's arter my own way of athinkin' about it," agreed McKandles, although he didn't let go of the gunwale of the skiff until it ground noisily onto the pebble beach and he was on solid ground. The stony shore widened. The water now lapped the rock floors, which had replaced the pebble beach. The light was still quite bright, and they could see in the three directions where the caverns extended farther into the heart of the cliff. Findlin led their group along the low path that ran right into the face of the rock. The path was carved out of the smooth stone in such a way that it must have taken the moving water hundreds of turnings to have formed the elaborate pattern of bends and twists.

As they passed the first curve of the cave wall, they saw the great figures hanging from the ceiling, looking like jagged fangs, and marveled at the hidden pools where an underground river surfaced to form ponds of still, crystal water, icy to the touch and refreshing to drink.

"This here don't look like no water I has ever seen," muttered Lofen. "It would freeze you to the bone if you was to fall in!"

"Looky here," said McKandles suddenly. "There ain't no bottomside to this here hole!" He pointed to a circular pool, about ten feet across, with smooth sides and a faint glimmer from the depths that pulsed slowly, making the surface seem like ripples of light washing the rock sides of the pool.

"Careful," warned Findlin. "You'll be in there in a flash if you miss your footing."

"There isn't a bottom that I can see," agreed Stearborn, peering hard into the clear, pale blue water.

"There is more holes like this up ahead here," cried Lofen, looking over his shoulder and edging nearer the smooth, cool surface of the cavern wall. His foot slipped on the wet stone floor, and after a brief struggle to regain his balance, his horrified companions watched him tumble headfirst into the icy waters of the pool.

"Help him," cried Owen, leaping forward. "Grab my feet! I'll try to pull him up!"

McKandles held the young man's legs, and Owen leaned forward into the water. His breath was taken away by the cold, and he had to force his eyes open to try to spot the Gortlander, but to his great surprise, the pool was empty. He struggled back to the surface, blowing out his breath in agitation. "He's gone," he spewed. "There's no one there!"

"Impossible," blurted Findlin. "We all saw him go in!"

"But he's not there now!"

"He's gone straight to the bottom of that fish hole," lamented McKandles. "I was always atellin' that lout that he was full of potatoes! Now he ain't got no hope of afloatin' to the top! Poor old Lofen! I never thought I was agoin' to has to be the one to be aputtin' a flower on his poor old remains."

"We need a swimmer," said Findlin. "Maybe there's a ledge under the rock here. Sometimes that happens."

"The water's too cold," protested Owen. "Even if you could swim, you couldn't last for long in this." But he put his head under for another look.

This time he noticed stairs and someone or something moving on them in a glimmer of pale light that shimmered in the frigid water. He came up for air, shouting, "There's a stairway there under the ledge! It's carved out of the stone, and seems to lead back away from the water!"

A Mysterious Grotto

Owen gulped in another lungful of air, and put his face back into the water, trying to find again the moving forms he had glimpsed momentarily on the stairs. The color of the water had gone to a deep golden pearl, and there was a whirling motion toward the center of the pool that seemed to gather speed as it turned, whirling faster and widening its circle. He pulled his head up then, calling out to the others, "Here! Quickly, Stearborn! Findlin! Look!"

When they had decided to explore the caves, Stearborn had suggested they bring rope and a block and tackle.

Findlin grabbed the rope and began to lay out a harness to wrap about his body. "One of you lads bear a hand here! You must lower me in here so I can hawe a look."

Stearborn had knelt beside the pool again, and was preparing to lower his head beneath the surface, when the water began to swirl and ripple, making small whitecaps, and the level began to rise slowly, until it was almost head-high to the stunned onlookers.

"Flood!" cried Findlin. "Make for the boats!"

"No time," shouted Stearborn. "We're cut off from the tunnel!"

Owen and McKandles, who stood closest to the whirling water, were snatched into the maelstrom and were gone from the others' sight so quickly it was another few heartbeats before they were missed.

"It's got the lads!" cried Findlin, struggling to reach the spot where they had disappeared.

"Get back," warned Stearborn, but too late, and he fell back helplessly, watching the Archael vanish into the whirling column of water. The old Steward drew his sword, and calling out his war cry, he charged headlong into the churning, frigid waters, determined that if he could not save his friends, then he would join them in their moment of death.

In another heartbeat, he stood bone dry and face to face with the equally startled Findlin and Owen. McKandles and Lofen were slapping each other on the back in high spirits, and looking about in awestruck wonder.

"I never knowed it would be so easy to get drownded," Lofen was saying, a small chuckle creeping into his speech.

"What do you make of this?" asked Findlin, quickly regaining his composure and carefully looking about him at the strange underwater shaft they now found themselves in.

Stearborn shook his head, still dazed by the sudden turn

of events. "It beats anything I've ever seen. I don't recall ever coming across water that wasn't wet before!"

"I hawe newer seen the likes of it either, my friend, and I'm a waterman by nature and by trade! I wish Lorimen were here so we could ask him. We may hawe a need to know more of its nature before all is said and done."

Owen stepped forward then, with a tiny red stone in his hand, which was throbbing with a dull, glimmering light that grew stronger with every passing moment. "I found this on the floor here. There are others over there. They seem to mark some sort of trail."

"That looks like the stone the young Gortlander is wearing," observed Stearborn gruffly, examining it closely, then looking away at the others Owen had pointed out.

"There is some noise acomin' from down that direction," added Lofen. "It was all aboomin' when I slipped in, and then when I hit the bottom here, it all got quiet like, until I thought I was adrownin' for sure."

"We'd best take a look," confirmed Findlin. "We came here to explore this cawe, so we'd better know all its secrets while we're at it."

"If it's all the same to you gents, I's would just as soon hightail it for the boats," protested Lofen. "There ain't no way to know how to gets back from here, far as I can tell! Look!" He pointed up toward the roof, where a cool, pale sheet of glass-smooth water hung in the ceiling, like an opaque window.

"Now if that don't beat all I was ever aseein'," said McKandles. "How in the name of Balkin's Mare is that ahangin' up there like that?"

Stearborn peered for a long time at the mysterious floating water, then turned back to his friends. "I said this place was old. It's beyond anything I could imagine. Ephinias and Gillerman would most likely be able to tell us something about it."

"And they're nowhere to be found when you really need them," grumbled Owen. "They make a habit of being away when you need them most."

"They do that to try to make us depend less on them," explained Stearborn gently. "They know they can't always be snatching us from the dangers that we face on our journeys."

"I'm worried about the others," said Findlin, his face grave. "If we can't find a way out of here, they'll miss us and be looking for us soon."

"Do you think this empties out somewhere lower down? Maybe we can just walk on until the end. It might have a drain hole at the river."

"I think we should follow the red stones, Stearborn. Look! They lead in the right direction, too!" Owen pointed to a dimly lit tunnel, which pulsed with the pale fire of the strange, round stones.

"There's them bells again," reported Lofen. "I thoughts at first it was just my noggin aringin' from the tumble, but there they is again!"

The companions stood still, hardly breathing, to try to detect what it was that made the noise. There was the faint sound of water burbling and lapping, and the hollow echo of another slight sound from somewhere ahead or behind them.

"That almost sounds like Lorimen," breathed Findlin, shaking his arm and jingling the small bells he wore on a bracelet. "We'll see if we get a reply."

"I hopes it ain't one we doesn't want," grumbled Lofen. "It ain't no kind thought of meeting up with some stargee down this here fish skittle!"

"I hear it now," confirmed Owen. "It seems to be coming from ahead."

Stearborn looked nervously about, lifting his long sword

in and out of its scabbard. "I don't like these cramped quarters! No room to swing a blade!"

"There may be no need for blade swinging, if we're lucky. Those bells hawe the sound of a different nature. It seems I'we heard something like them before, ewen if they're not Lorimen."

"The Elboreal," suggested Owen. "They sometimes have those bells."

"Could that be possible?" asked Stearborn. "This cave is old enough to have seen the elves, there's no doubt of that."

"Old enough to sees the end of this old horse tender, to boot! Whichever ways we goes, it ain't agoin' to be to my likin', unless we is suddenly out of this here slippery spot and safe aground somewheres a good bit from here!" Lofen's eyes were wide with fright, although he clutched his sword and dagger resolutely.

Findlin and Stearborn crept forward, hugging the cave walls closely, peering intently into the dim gloom ahead. The sounds of the water noise continued to grow, until Owen called out a warning from behind. "There's water coming down this channel," he cried, pointing behind him.

"Drownded like rats," wailed Lofen, searching about frantically for an exit.

"The only way out is how we got here," called Findlin. "I don't know the workings of that, so we'll hawe to go on here and hope it empties outside!"

The dull roar of the rushing water could be heard quite plainly now, and the companions bolted forward, fleeing the flood that came on behind them, thundering louder as it neared. They had reached a split in the underground channels, where the old watercourse parted, and stood catching their breath, trying to decide which way to take.

Owen raised a hand and pointed to the flickering light, which looked like a faint rush lamp, and caught the dim fire of the red stones that led away into the closeness of the tunnel on the right-hand way. "There's our course," he said. "It's our only hope now!"

Stearborn nodded his agreement. "I'm not much of a hand at reading this sort of trail, but I'd put my weight on Owen's side that this is our only chance at shooting through."

"There's that light again," cried McKandles. "They hasn't got too big a lead on us now! If we puts our legs to it, we could be acatchin' them up afore long."

The small party started out again at a dogtrot, the sound of the rushing water still behind them, with Owen and Findlin in the lead and Stearborn bringing up the rear.

The old Steward was blowing hard when they pulled up again. "I haven't been afoot in a good while. When you reach my age, you tend to let your mount do most of the work for you." He laughed shortly, wiping his brow with his hand. "I'm glad Chellin Duchin's not here to see this, or I'd be ragged like a baited cock until I'd be forced to thrash his thick hide."

"I'd like to see him, if he knew the way out," said Owen, watching the older man carefully. His gruff demeanor was the same, but a slight look of pain showed in the clear blue eyes, and it was plain to see that he was quickly becoming fatigued.

"Are you feeling well?" asked Findlin, who had noticed Stearborn's quick breath. "You look like you might be pulling a fewer, by the sweat on your brow."

Stearborn grumbled a protest and heaved himself up from where he'd been leaning against the clammy wall of the tunnel. "It'll take more than a little run like this to wind an old Line Steward! I just needed to catch my breath a bit."

Lofen, who had been standing next to Stearborn, blinked his eyes rapidly a few times and took deep breaths, leaning on his friend McKandles. "I don't feel so chipper, neither," he said weakly. "There's a bunch of stars astartin' to spin around in my old noggin!"

Findlin nodded. "It's getting hard to breathe down here! We've got to reach the outside!" He helped McKandles hold Lofen up, and they struggled on a few more steps.

Owen began to feel a hardness in his throat, and found himself gasping for air. "I can't breathe," he began, noticing in his panic that Stearborn had fallen heavily to his knees. Owen sank forward onto his face right behind him and tried to reach out to the older man, but found instead that he was sinking into a pink haze that seemed to grow denser, then lighter, then turned completely black. A bitter taste was in his mouth, and he remembered it for a long time after he could no longer see beyond the dark wall. And then there were the bells again, chiming faintly in the distance, twice in succession, then once more, closer still.

He vaguely dreamed, or dreamed he dreamed, of a journey in a great, clear bubble, floating on the underground river, which now was colored a silver-blue and lit by hundreds of the small red stones. There were others there, although he could not quite recognize them.

Owen remembered Deros then, even in the dream, and he tried to pull himself out of the vision, to swim to the top of the heavy sleep that weighed down his eyes.

They passed through a fall of water, glimmering and shining in crystal brilliance. The bells had grown louder and louder still, and were joined by the other sounds, of harp and reed, and words that lingered just on the fringe of comprehension.

Owen turned in his dream and found himself face to face with Deros, who was dressed in a white cloak, wearing a crown which was ringed with the red stones that had lined the cave floors. She seemed to stare past him, into the wavering haziness that was behind him, and did not answer when he tried to speak to her, but his own words seemed garbled to him. There were others dressed in the same white cloaks, chanting an odd song that hovered on the verge of his understanding. In the midst of the group surrounding Deros was a figure in a black robe, with the hood drawn so that Owen couldn't see the face. He tried to get closer to the figure but found himself unable to get nearer to it.

A series of bumps jolted him half awake then, and he spiraled away toward a light, bright and dazzling, that bore into his consciousness until he found himself blinking in surprise in a high, airy place, full of the sound of bells and voices. When he lifted his head a bit, he saw he was lying on an odd-shaped boat, floating on the crystal-clear water of the underground river. He struggled to raise himself on his elbow, and came face to face with a figure in a white cloak, which was kneeling over the unmoving McKandles.

"Leave him alone," mumbled Owen. His hand sought the long sword Gillerman and Wallach had given him, but to his shock and dismay, there was no familiar feel of the handle, or the reassuring light or song. He called out weakly for Gillerman or Ephinias, then remembered dimly that the two masters were away, and there would be no one to help him.

One of the hooded figures spoke. "No harm will come to those who favor the Order of the Sacred Thistle. You have nothing to fear, if you are not enemies."

"We are enemies to none but those who warrant it! If you are Keepers of the Light, then you will have heard of the Line Stewards. We have others with us, but we all wish no harm to you."

"Question them all," suggested another cloaked figure. "See that they are not those who fly an alien's banner! We have been fooled before."

The figure in the black cloak loomed up behind the

others, and a strange, garbled laugh came from beneath the folds that hid the face. "It is well to be cautious, o Sister of the Sacred Order. You would have done well to have avoided me, yet you did not."

The scene began to swim in a silver mist that rose higher and higher, until it vanished from Owen's sight. He thought he heard McKandles call, but when he reached out to him, there was no one there, and he had the sensation of falling, slowly spinning about into a pitch-black hole that seemed to swallow his very breath.

Owen tried to call out then, but found his tongue thick and useless, and he choked and gasped for breath. After what felt to him a long time, his head stopped spinning and his vision cleared, and he looked around without daring to raise his head.

There was a high, domed roof, a deep slate-blue in color, with silver stars that seemed so real it could have been the heavens outside. At the very center of the dome was a great five-sided star, which held a rune of some sort, and which gleamed faintly in the deep stillness of the room.

Owen struggled to his feet. He noticed with surprise that his long sword was lying on a long table draped with a dark cloth, humming softly in its scabbard. When he pulled it free, the blade was luminous, glowing with a soft white light that echoed the glowing star in the dome at the top of the vaulted ceiling.

"Stearborn? Findlin? Are you here?" His voice felt flat and lifeless, and it seemed as though the huge silence swallowed up his words as soon as they came out of his mouth, but he tried again in a louder voice.

A low sound stirred the perfect stillness of the heavy air then, as light as dust blown on a breath of wind in a sunlit room on a lazy summer afternoon, slowly growing louder until it was a gentle swaying of notes against his ear, lull-ing him into a mild drowsiness. It finally died away, as silently and quickly as the last brief flash of light in a sunset.

"You have come to the hallowed halls of the Sacred Thistle, young one."

Owen blinked, seeing no one at first. Then his eyes fell at last on the form beneath the star, dressed in a robe of the same deep blue as the walls and ceiling of the high room. "Who are you?" he asked, still startled.

"My name is Rewen. I am the Daughter of the Altar."

Owen moved his legs gingerly, testing his weight. His steps were wobbly, but he found he was able to stand, and he approached the figure who stood before a high stone structure.

"You must not near the altar," she said, holding up a hand. "It is not for any but the Order of the Sacred Thistle."

"What have you done with the others?" asked Owen. "Where are my friends?"

"They are safe. They did not have the sword of Skye, so they are held in another place. We could not decide upon you, or where you came upon the sword, so it was agreed that we would question you to find where you have come from, and what brought you to our halls."

"My name is Owen Helwin," replied the youth hastily. "My father is Famhart the Pure, who fought in the Middle Islands. We have been driven from our home by Olgnite, and are going to the coast to gather our strength. I am sailing with the Lady Deros to Eirn Bol, where she hopes to join her father."

The hood of the figure before him fell back then, revealing a young woman not much older than Deros, with long, dark hair and haunting gray eyes that touched Owen deeply. "You have the Lady Deros with you? We did not see her."

"She's aboard our boat, waiting. If we aren't back soon, they'll start searching for us."

"Where are the boats? How did you reach our chambers?"

"From the grotto on the river. We were attacked by raiders from Lachland and escaped with the boats. We came on the great stone bear, and slipped in behind to try to find calm water, and saw the grotto there. It was safe, so we thought to explore the caves, for we may have need of them when we return to The Line to drive out our enemies."

The young woman smiled faintly. "I had forgotten the old cavern on the water. That was left by the Old Ones, when they were the Keepers here."

"Which old ones?" asked Owen, brightening. "Ephinias or Gillerman? Wallach?"

"The grotto was the landing place for the followers of Borim Bruinthor. They held these lands against the winged snakes in the early days."

"Are they still here?"

"No. They have been gone for many turnings. Our Order has been at watch here since. Now even the Elboreal are gone. There are none left but us."

"Can we go for the others now? Deros will be worried."

"I have sent someone to bring the others to us."

"How could you have done that? You haven't left, and no one else has been here."

"They will be here soon enough. You seem to be very slow in your ways. I think no one must have ever taught you full use of your powers. That is strange for one who possesses one of the swords of Skye."

"I know this one can sometimes contact my friends, or warn me of danger. Could you call Gillerman and Wallach?"

"I know of no one by those names. If they are of the

Order, then we shall be able to call them, if need be. Perhaps they do not always have the same names." As Rewen spoke, a small red light flared up on her hand, and Owen saw it came from a ring like the one Ulen Scarlett had taken from the dead Hulin Vipre prince, and his thoughts raced. Cursing himself for his reckless trust in the beautiful young woman, he felt his spirits sink. He had betrayed Deros. Surely this woman was with the Hulin Vipre clans who had vowed to capture her. And now he had been the unwitting traitor who had turned her over to her enemies.

A thin, acid feeling cut through his stomach, and he turned toward the table where his sword lay, hoping in some way to redeem himself, if only in slaying the deceptively beautiful foe who stood before him. He reached the table in two steps, but as he pulled the sword from its scabbard, a faint hissing sound was heard, and once again he floated in a dreamless trance that seemed silent and endless.

Daughter of the Altar

When Owen came back to his senses, he lay quite still for a long time, trying to collect his wits and to find how great the danger was before he committed himself to action. The room was quiet, except for the sound of a tiny thread of running water. At intervals was the sound of small bells that chimed in time to movement. It reminded him of Findlin's bracelet, and he was tempted to open his eyes, but he remembered the red stones and the ring worn by Rewen.

He was about to move suddenly and lunge for his long sword, which he remembered to be upon a table somewhere in the vast room, when the sound of voices came clearly to him, mixed with laughter. The speakers were in high spirits, and came on laughing and talking until they were very near where Owen lay. He seized that moment to leap up from the soft pallet where he had been placed and, wild-eyed, search frantically for his weapon.

"Here! Grab the lad!" bellowed a voice. "He's down with a fever!"

"Cuts him off, Kandles! He's aheadin' for the pool!"

Owen drew up short, stunned. Here were his own comrades, surrounding him now, patting his arm or clapping his back, and all asking at once how he fared. He blinked about in confusion, until his eyes met Stearborn's, and the old commander flashed a brief smile that belied his gruff look. "You've certainly caused enough mischief here! I'm surprised the Lady Rewen hasn't had all our ears cut off after these outbursts!"

"She's a Hulin Vipre," shot Owen under his breath. "I remember Deros telling me of their eyes, and how they could be detected."

"What in the Great Wault of Tarinbal makes you think she's a Wipre?" asked Findlin, who was standing next to Stearborn.

"No one told me! Just look at her!"

"We has put an eyeball to her, and it ain't every day we sees such a sight," reported McKandles. "This here hole may be one of them strokes of luck we has been aneedin' ever since them devils from the Leech came on us!"

"Is Deros safe?" asked Owen. "Did she get away?"

"Where would she go without us? No one has gone anywhere, lad, and the Lady Rewen is with Deros now. You would have thought they were blood sisters, the way they're carrying on."

Owen's heart sank to his boots. "Then we've failed to protect her! It's all up now!"

Stearborn took Owen's arm and led him to the table where his sword lay, a soft hum emitting from its blade, which was again in its scabbard.

"You may take it, lad! We aren't in an enemy camp here. We've found the allies we need to help us on this journey, not someone who will thwart us."

"Of all the times we hawe been up and down this riwer, I never dreamed this was here, or that such an Order still existed in these troubled times. Even stories of the Sacred Thistle are rare now, and I doubt many still liwe who knew of it when it was in full bloom." Findlin's face was sad as he looked about the vast chamber. "This is holy ground to all who follow the Light. I'm a lucky Archael to hawe been giwen this gift."

At that moment, Owen saw the two young women at the entrance to the chamber, dressed in identical white cloaks. "Deros!" he cried. "Are you all right?" He remembered the dream, or what had seemed to him a dream. There was no sign of the black hooded figure, and Owen had not seen a face, but he was sure that it had been Ulen.

Deros bowed to Owen, smiling. "Rewen has been telling me the history of the Sacred Order. I have shown her my necklace. It is the symbol of our line, and goes all the way back to our ancient histories, when the Lady Bright Star was alive."

"My lady," replied Owen, bowing. He turned to Rewen. "Forgive me for thinking you were an enemy. I saw the red stone at your hand, and all I know of that is cursed, borne by a Hulin Vipre prince, then taken by one in our own party."

"Your suspicion was fair, Master Owen. I have told

Deros of the years of treachery, and how the Order was finally brought to this poor state, where we must hide from our enemies, and keep ourselves from sight."

"They were betrayed by Gingus Pashon." Deros came to sit beside Owen in a carved wooden chair before the table. "I had never heard all the story before."

"He was an Elder in the Order when he was a young man," continued Rewen. "It is an old, sad story."

Findlin's eyes lit up, for he was always one for hearing a tale, and he asked if his comrade Lorimen had also been brought from the ship.

"All your companions will be with you in a short while. They have gone to secure your boats, and to make sure no others have found the entrance to the Bear's Grotto."

"Ulen?" Owen's face remained calm as he asked Deros about the horseman, but his hands felt sweaty and his heart hammered in his throat.

"He stayed to make sure the ship wasn't set adrift," replied the girl.

"He may have been trying to save his own hide again," said Owen. "He seems to make a habit of that. I tried to warn Stearborn and Findlin about that when they decided to take him along."

"It's not so bad as you make out," argued Deros, noticing how easily she could anger Owen by defending Ulen.

"It's been bad enough twice before, and you should be the first to say that was so."

"Do they have any stores here?" asked Stearborn. "I'm of a mind I should like something to fill up my hunger with while we're about down here. I can't seem to remember my breakfast!"

"There wasn't no such thing as abreakin' the fast, and you knows it, sir," shot McKandles. "Them sly-foots from Lach was aseein' to that, and I is right alongside of your point, seein's how ain't none of us had no victuals in a spell."

Rewen rang the tiny bells on her bracelet, and a dozen servants appeared as though through the walls themselves, and began to set the table with clean cloths and bowls of water and spiced wine. A trio came in behind Rewen and Deros, bearing huge platters of baked cakes and cheeses wrapped in succulent green leaves, and a variety of fruits.

"Please! Sit and refresh yourselves." The young woman motioned for them all to sit at the feast.

Owen's eyes narrowed as he looked at the food, and his stomach growled, and his mouth watered. The others sat noisily down and began to devour the tempting fare.

"Are you eating, Deros?" he said.

"I couldn't eat right now," she replied. "I have had too much distressing news of my father, and the sad fate that has befallen the Order."

"My Lady Rewen?" asked Owen. "Will you join us?"

"Go on, Master Owen. I shall have something later."

Owen sat on a stool by McKandles and searched the table for something he could pretend to eat. Taking a piece of fruit, he watched as all the others of his party devoured the rich feast. Owen was ravenous, but there still was some faint alarm in the back of his head. No matter how friendly or helpful the beautiful young woman of the Order appeared to be, there was something in those gray eyes that at once attracted Owen and repelled him. There was something that seemed strange in Deros's behavior that troubled him as well. It went beyond baiting him with Ulen, for he had grown to expect that; it was something in the way she seemed never to get far from Rewen's side.

He toyed with another piece of fruit, watching all the while, and leaned over his friend McKandles to break off a hunk of honey bread. "Do you feel all right? Is the food good?"

McKandles answered him with his mouth full, so that the words were garbled, but he was nodding his head vigorously.

"It doesn't taste like it's been poisoned?"

The Gortlander stopped his chewing, his eyes widening.

"I don't trust this woman," Owen went on under his breath. "I can't say what it is, but I don't like it."

His companion hastily ducked his head under the table and spat, his face drained of color. "Why wasn't you after atellin' us afore we crammed oursel's full?"

"It may be nothing."

Ulen Scarlett, Lorimen, and the rest of the exploration party came into the high chamber, talking animatedly among themselves.

"They doesn't look like they has been spelled on," said McKandles out of the corner of his mouth.

"Maybe I've been too quick to judge," admitted Owen. "I wish I could get a better feel of my sword. If only Gillerman were here."

"This here lass don't seems so bad," said Lofen. "She's a pretty one."

"Your stomach is doing the talking now," replied Owen. "Even if the woman had fangs and claws, if she was setting out a spread like this, you'd find something nice to say."

Lofen bristled. "Now lookee here! That ain't no way to be atalkin' to me, just acause you ain't so all fired alongside Ulen Scarlett, with him all soft on the lady. You is just a young'un when it comes to grab and scuffle, and that ain't nothin' to be alookin' at when you sees all that these old blinkers has been aseein' all these past times." Lofen's face had reddened and he slammed his cup on the table for emphasis as he finished.

"I'm sorry, Lofen. I'm just worried, and I shouldn't have let loose on you. Just keep your eyes open, and let me know if anything looks suspicious."

"It's all alookin' fishy to me, ever since we has been aboard of them ships! I ain't seen nothin' that's alookin' rightsides to me since I has left the old Gortland Fair, as was aplayin' up in that snug little village afore we got slabwise to them squashers in Sweet Rock."

"She's acallin' for you, Owen," interrupted McKandles, pointing to the young woman who called herself Rewen.

"Please come and sit with us. We have much to discuss. Deros tells me you are the son of the Elder of The Line, and are next to wear the Cloak."

Owen went to sit at table with the young woman, and sat shyly looking at Deros out of the corner of his eye. He could see nothing different, for she watched him with the same aloof coolness she had since they went aboard the Alogan Mag.

"We shall have plans to make before you leave these halls," said Rewen, calling his attention back to her. "There are many dangers abroad in these times, and our powers have been slowly fading over the turnings, as our followers have been lured away by others."

"What others?" asked Deros. "Why would anyone forsake the true way?"

"There are those who say they have more power to bestow, more riches to give. It does not take much in the way of tempting away an ignorant man. And times came when it seemed that all we stood for was a waste of time, and an act of foolishness."

"These are all who are left from the old days here, Owen," explained Deros. "Rewen is the granddaughter of the woman who was in Trew. The Order has been everywhere, but now falls on these times where they must remain in hiding."

"We had many allies in the early turnings. My grandmother was sent to Trew as a younger woman than I am now. The Order was still strong, and the times were not so troubled." Rewen's eyes clouded, and she looked away.

"What happened that changed your fortunes so much?" asked Owen.

"Gingus Pashon was high in our Order, and a trusted Keeper. His domain was strong, and he was held in great regard in many of the more distant lands. He traveled much, and was looked upon as an emissary from the High Elder, and all respected him."

"Isn't that the Hulin Vipre Emperor?"

"Was the Emperor," corrected Deros. "That was long ago."

"There were always enemies, always those who wished ill to the Order, for it kept the Light too brightly for those who wished to dwell yet in the cloak of darkness that was the realm of the Dark Queen. She had singled Gingus Pashon out as the one weak link in the defense of the Order, and she devised a cunning plan that has touched us all, right down to the moment as we sit speaking here in these hidden chambers. Her plan to reduce the Sacred Thistle has been most effective, but she won't be able to destroy all of us, not as long as there are yet those who believe."

Owen watched the young woman carefully, searching for any sign of subterfuge or lies, but was taken mainly by the gray eyes that never left his as she spoke.

Rewen seemed to gaze into his thoughts, for she smiled then. "You are afraid of me, Owen Helwin. You are right in doubting everyone, for these are disturbing times, and it is hard to tell your enemies."

Owen blushed and looked away quickly. "Please, my lady, I meant no offense. We have been tricked before, and I don't want to be the one who is responsible for our mission failing because I trusted too easily."

"If we had wished you harm, we could have slain you all when you were helpless to save yourselves."

"What was that spell? How did you do that?"

"The Sacred Thistle still has thorns," laughed Rewen. "That sleep was brought on by old secrets well kept."

"Why did you do that?"

"For the same reason you question me, Owen. We have been betrayed time and again by those who have pledged their hearts to us."

"What changed your mind?"

"The sword of Skye you wore. They are only given to those of great honor. When I found the sword, I knew we were in the presence of one who might help us."

"And she knows of the ring of Tien Cal," went on Deros. "It was taken from the Order when Gingus Pashon betrayed us. He was sought out and wooed by a beautiful infidel who succeeded in winning him from the Light. Her name was Astrain, and she still lives today. He gave her the sacred Rhion Stone as a wedding gift. They have great powers. They can speak to others, much as you use the sword of Skye."

Owen's face clouded. "Is there another of those stones in the hands of the Hulin Vipre?"

"There must be," replied Rewen. "I have seen much of the stone's voice, and I have heard many things that are not the doings of the Order. It is the spies and reports of those Rhion Stones that are held by our enemies. They may know we can hear and see, but they don't fear us any longer, since we have been reduced to hiding and staying away from all the others yet on Atlanton."

"Then I was right when I told Stearborn we should take that ring from Ulen."

Rewen made a sign for Owen to hold his voice down. "You must say nothing more of these stones," she said quietly, placing her lips near his ear. "We have plans for the ring the horseman wears."

Deros held out her left hand to Owen, and he saw another of the blood-red stones in a ring there. The face was cloudy, but a fire burned below that, much like a stream that ran with mud. "We have our own way now of keeping track of our enemies. I would never have known about this if we hadn't come here. Rewen has given me all the pieces to the puzzle, and now we may be able to help my father."

"If we can reach him undetected," said Owen.

"We shall have the help of the Sacred Thistle. That was the help we needed before now. Mere arms and men were all I sought, but all the help I could have gotten that way would not have aided my father as much as what I know now."

Rewen rang the tiny bells on her bracelet again, and the room was suddenly filled with white cloaked figures, circling around the altar that stood in the center of the vast chamber. There were other sounds then, a thin reed pipe playing, as if from some great distance, and the faint, familiar smell of mown hay. The water came alive, and the noise it made seemed to speak to Owen, as if the water's voice came from a single being, which wished to tell him of dark silver secrets that it kept far below the sun and stars, and beyond the curious eye of the world above.

"We shall arm you with all the powers we hold at our command," said Rewen, motioning for two of her followers to approach, bearing between them an ancient wooden chest, carved with such cleverness there were no clasps or hinges showing, and adorned with a dozen or more small scenes that were beyond Owen's comprehension.

Findlin pointed to one of the carvings in a gleeful tone and grabbed Lorimen's arm to show him his discovery. "Look, citizen! It's one of the old Archael wessels! See the sails? It warms the old heart to see how they carried their shoulders in a breeze."

"Why would they have those carwed on this box?" asked Lorimen.

Rewen smiled at the two old seamen, and pointed to the other intricately carved scenes. "We have been there in your fair lands, good Archaels. The Order was within your borders, even though you might not have known of us."

Findlin and Lorimen shook their heads.

"They've not made themselves known here, either," admitted Stearborn. "I have always prided myself on knowing all that was to be known about the lay of the land, and here I find a stranger's camp on the very River Line that has been here for longer than I've drawn breath!"

Rewen opened the elaborate chest, smiling. "You are not a dull man, good captain. There have been few who knew of us."

"Who else knew?" asked Owen.

"None you would be familiar with. The Elboreal, and the old Keepers were our allies, but they have crossed the Boundaries, or gone to the Havens, so there are only a handful now."

"There is one among our other party who came from Trew," said Deros. "She was saved from a dragon spell by the elves. Would she have knowledge of the Order?"

"She would be able to hear us," acknowledged Rewen. "If she were nearby, she would hear our call."

"Elita? I wonder how far along their trail they are," asked Owen. "I hope they haven't run into the Lachlanders we met this morning."

"No difference if they did," growled Stearborn. "The Stewards are yet strong enough to handle that lot. The Lachs aren't the Olgnite, nor the Vipre, and their numbers couldn't be telling enough to threaten our party."

"Here are some gifts you may make use of," offered Rewen. "Your journey will be perilous enough with the winter coming on. We can't control the wind and sea, but these things may help you along your way where there are lesser enemies involved." She pulled from the chest a beautiful brocaded vest, stitched with silver and gold thread that danced and shimmered in the soft light of the chamber.

The young woman of the Sacred Thistle handed the garment to Deros. "Put it on."

Deros removed the white cloak and drew on the vest, standing back to show it off to the others.

The companions gasped aloud, for Deros had vanished from sight.

"If you wish it, you can change your form, or take on the features of someone else," said Rewen.

Another change came then, and the air in the chamber smelled of early morning dew, and the sweet grass that grew beside a still lake, and there before them was a grazing fawn, its large brown eyes opened wide to them.

"Deros? Is that you?" asked Owen in a dazed voice.

With another breath, the familiar face of his young friend had reappeared. "This is wonderful," she said.

"It must be used wisely," cautioned Rewen. "If it falls into the wrong hands, there could be a great deal of misfortune. And you can't use it for evil ends."

"I's could get mysel' a good stable with that there rag," observed McKandles. "Ain't no wild brute alive that could gets away from me then, 'cause there ain't no way they could be aseein' old Kandles acomin' up on them all crafty like! We's would be in fair good shape then, Lofen."

"Do you have any soldier's toys in that box?" asked Stearborn. "We'll be in short service, with just the two boats. Anything that could give us an edge would be put to good use."

"You have already seen what weapons we have," replied Rewen. "The spell we put you to sleep with can be called up by this. It works if you are near whomever you want to work it on. It lasts for a day." She held out a small white stone, ringed with brilliant blue markings, which Deros took.

Rewen then opened another small chest inside the larger one, and drew out a delicate golden ring, set with one of the fiery red stones, which matched the one she wore on her own hand. "You must guard this with your life," she said gravely. "Your companion who has the other stone must not know of this one, or the one you wear, Deros. It will help you in times of danger, but not in a way of arms or men. Knowledge is its secret, and that calls for your own courage and faith." She placed the second ring in Deros's hand, kissing her on the cheek as she did so. "The blessings of the Sacred Thistle go with you, little sister. You must decide who will wear the other ring. May you fare well, and restore our Order to its old place."

Deros was still looking at the rings and vest, and could find no words of thanks.

Rewen spoke again. "Before you return to your ships, there is one more matter."

Rewen's Promise

A bearded man bowed and entered the cavern, a slight smile drawn thin across his angular face.

"This is Coglan," said Rewen. "He shall travel with me, for we have to go with you to Eirn Bol. Our next quest is hidden there, deep in Cairn Weal."

The Archaelian Findlin stepped forward then, with his awkward seaman's gait. "You might ask an old salt to see who shall go and who won't. Our wessels are hard loaded now, and waggle enough as it is. Not to be disrespectful, my lady, but these seas we're going to face will require all the free board we can spare, if we're to find ourselves a safe hawen in Fionten before the Werges."

Rewen smiled and turned to Coglan. "We shall sail with you, but we will make our own way. Show them."

Coglan made a sign for the others to follow him, and set off toward the brightness that formed a halo of light about the end of the tunnel.

As they walked, Owen caught up with Deros. "I was surprised to see you in the cavern," he stammered, feeling the old, familiar awkwardness creeping back upon him.

"Rewen had things to show me," replied Deros in a cool manner. "The Order of the Sacred Thistle has its secrets, and must be protected."

Owen's anger burned through his shyness. "You have no need to hide from me, my lady. This is Owen, your friend!"

She warmed somewhat then, and touched his arm as she apologized. "I didn't mean it like that."

Stearborn, who was walking next in line behind his young companion, made a chuckling noise in his throat, which sounded like birds talking in the dark. "You're the one who has put up the most fuss over a certain party being alongside of us. I would think you'd be the first to piece out why there should be some secrecy involved here."

Feeling stupid and slow, Owen thought of Ulen, and the ring he wore.

"This here ain't no taterskate, Kandles, and I isn't arter no more time asloshin' around in no fish pond. I says we oughts to scout back a ways, and get us on back to the boats. Leastways, we could keep a blinker on good Master Ulen, and find out what's he's about."

Owen looked over his shoulder at the two Gortland men, and broke into a smile. "That might not be such a bad idea. It would ease my mind a bit."

"We'll be at the boats soon enough," said Deros. "You must see the things that Rewen has to show you."

"Does she have anything that will protect a wessel in a good gale of wind?" asked Findlin. "All the time we waste down here just giwes the sea more time to find ways to torment us."

McKandles rolled his eyes and protested. "We don't needs no more of the insides of this here dirt's belly. I is for agoin' now and agettin' on with the business of them dadblamed boats. The sooner we is agettin' on with this, the quicker old Lofen and I will be aputtin' some daylight atween us and all this water."

Rewen had gone ahead. Coglan stood by her side, watching. As they neared, he pointed toward a small archway that was blocked by a door of solid stone. "We turn here to find our vessel. It has been waiting for more than a few lifetimes."

"When we came here in the olden days, these were the wings that carried us to all the lands beyond." Rewen spoke:

"In the Throat of the Wren, I call to you, O Eilendor,
    The boatmen of the Thistle,
        My coat of arms and shield
        Since the last Swans
            Came to the Spring of Col."

Then the great stone that lay across the entrance came to life and started to slowly roll into a cut in the wall, revealing what lay beyond. A faint silvery light shimmered softly.

A sound, very low and dim at first, rose from the very floor of the cavern, and slowly built in strength, until it became a distinct song that was pleasant to hear and that lifted their hearts.

"It's almost like one of Emerald's old ballads," said Owen, wishing that the minstrel were there.

"It is an old ballad, Master Owen," said Rewen, "as old as the Thistle, and as old as the quest we protect. This song was sung by my mother, and her mother, and her mother before her. We were but a thin ghost of thought on these lower meadows when Gingus Pashon fell in love with Astrain. She was so beautiful, it never seemed to anyone she could be evil."

"Sometimes it is the most beautiful thing of all which is the death of us," muttered Findlin.

"Power be to them that has the sense to see that," muttered McKandles. "I was awaitin' for more than my share of time for one of the fillies to be amakin' up her mind, and then she up and run off with a hostler from down near the Leech. My old gaffer was atellin' me all the time she wasn't no good. I got a whiff of a tale later that she had stabbed him through the ticker and stole all his horses and gear."

"Come on. Let's look to a brighter side to it," protested Jeremy, feeling the strange tugs at his heart every time he looked at Rewen. He blushed as he caught the lady's eye, and his breath hung in his throat when she smiled at him.

"Indeed, we must look to the brighter side of it, Master Thistlewood. Your name has a mystic ring to it. I would not doubt but that you might have had kinsmen who belonged to the Order."

Jeremy looked perplexed. "How did you come to know

my family name?" he asked, turning to Stearborn. "Have you been casting it about?"

"It is no small mystery," explained Rewen. "Part of the Sight of the Rhion Stone is the ability to see to the heart of whomever it is near."

"You mean them shiny rocks is like having a spy awork-in' for you?" asked McKandles. "Them would be handy things to have when it come to certain kinds a dealin's with some folks I is aknowin'."

Beyond the archway, an ehco of the song began again, repeated in a voice very like Rewen's.

"What is that?" asked Owen.

"Our vessel. It is what we have come to show you. Please come with us." Rewen led the way through the low passage. Owen and the others had to duck to avoid bumping their heads.

"Who built this place?" mumbled Lorimen. "Were they so ill-fed and weak they were unable to cut a proper door?"

The young woman laughed. "These stones were worked by the Dralich Ean long before humans walked these Lower Meadows. My Order was an ally of all those peoples who filled Atlanton before the time of the great floods."

More of the soft music filled the confined space of the tunnel, and grew louder. Rewen answered, and the sound took on another dimension, weaving colors of golds and blues into a moving streamer that wound about the companions, beckoning them on into the deeper part of the earth. The river sounds were louder now, and the splash and roar of the water was blended into the strange music. At the last note of Rewen's voice, a hazy outline began to form before their eyes, and a long stone quay came into focus, as finely pointed and finished as the work of any great mason, and there, floating lightly on the smooth, shiny surface of the river, was a boat of clear, shimmering air, floating silently at its mooring.

"What is it?" stammered Owen.

"The Thistle Cloud," replied Rewen, stepping forward to touch the shimmering, transparent vessel. "It was another of the secrets given to us when we came to protect the Alberion Novas."

Coglan lightly stepped aboard the sleek craft, and the others watched in amazement as he moved about, for they were plainly able to see him walking about on a transparent deck. "If the need arises," he said, "we can cover our tracks easily enough." He spoke a short verse, and the craft vanished, along with the young man.

"Now where has he been agettin' to?" blurted Lofen. "Is this here more of that flamfoozle we was alookin' at down in that fishbowl?"

Rewen, who had been standing by Stearborn, laughed and spoke a verse that brought the sleek craft back into sight. "It is our protection. It is a way we have traveled safely from one place to another when we didn't want our presence known."

"Is there some way we could do that to our own wessels, my lady?" asked Lorimen. "It wouldn't stand us in any better stead with a gale of wind, but it would go a whistler's distance where it came to dealing with hostiles."

"We will come to that," said Rewen, going aboard the craft to stand by Coglan. "First we must make preparations for departure from here."

"Are you leaving The Line?" asked Owen, suddenly upset that the beautiful young woman would be taking the Order away.

"No one ever really leaves, good Master Helwin. What has been will always be. But we are leaving, to return to our ancient homelands. There will be others to take our place here." She paused, turning to Deros. "I think you understand now, my sister."

Deros had tears in her eyes, and tried to smile, but couldn't. Her voice was too shaky to speak, so she simply nodded.

"I don't understand," cried Owen. "Is there something I should know? Are you in some danger, Deros? Have you news of your father?"

"Her father is in no more danger than he has been for these past turnings. The time has come for a changing of the guard. She has been brought to me by a fate as surely as the sunrise. Over and again it is written that the Order shall keep its own, and that there will always be a renewal, even in the darkest times."

"You mean Deros is to take over your vigil here?" Owen's mind was clouded with conflicting storms of thought, ranging first one way then another. He was glad to learn that the headstrong young woman would be bound by duty to The Line. Yet there was another part of him that recoiled at that, for he had already refused the Elder's cloak from his father.

"Deros will return here once we have met our enemies on Eirn Bol. The Hulin Vipre wait upon no one, and even now they are posed at the island's edge, waiting to strike a death blow."

"Have you other reports we haven't heard, my lady?" asked Owen.

"The Rhion Stone hears and sees much from its brothers. There is a plot afoot in the dark fastness of Blor Alhal. The Hulin will not wait much longer before they make an all-out attack to take Cairn Weal."

Deros stood beside Rewen, silently weeping. Owen reached out a hand to comfort the distraught girl, but stopped himself.

"We'll soon have better news firsthand," growled Stearborn. "If we have any luck at all with those floating tubs, I wager we'll be in fine shape to find an end to all this, lass. Either that or old Stearborn's bones will catch in the throat of an enemy and plague the lands with his ghost."

"Let's pray it doesn't come to that, good captain. There will be time enough for the shedding of blood, yet we want to make sure it is the blood of our enemies, and not ours!" said Deros.

"Now, that's spoken like a Steward," replied the old warrior. "You must have gone to school in the same quarter as this old war horse!"

"I hope there's someone here who has gone to school in the watching of weather," broke in Findlin. "Otherwise we are all going to be fish food before the Werges have their last play with us. We can stand down here jabbering from now till doomsday, but we aren't getting any closer to finding our way out and slipping our moorings!"

Deros had regained her composure and took Findlin's arm. "We must go on. Our good Archael is right. If we are to see my homeland, we must sail now."

"You could come with me, Deros," offered Rewen, "on board the Thistle Cloud."

"I must go with my companions," replied the girl. "They have stood by me in times of great danger, and I can't desert them now."

"Then they can all come."

Findlin and Lorimen exchanged glances. "There's no room aboard that wessel for all the hands we hawe! She'd sink to her gunwales if all this mob boarded her."

"You'd be surprised to learn all this craft can do, good mariner. There are things that even you, with all your life spent on the sea, don't know."

"What about Ulen?" Owen asked. "Will we take him aboard with us, even knowing he carries one of the spy rings?"

"We'll have to find a way to get it from him," suggested Jeremy.

"No. We leave the ring where it is," said Rewen. "They already know in Blor Alhal that someone other than its master is wearing it. If we change it now, they will suspect that it has been found out. It would only put them on their guard."

"I don't know how much more on their guard they could get," grumbled Stearborn. "If they had the strength to send forces all the way to The Line, then I hate to think what they would be like nearer to home."

"They have always been a power to reckon with," Deros said. "After Gingus Pashon turned against the Order, they grew stronger and seemed to revel in the destruction of anyone who still followed the Light."

"The Dark One does her work well, my sister. There is no trick left unworked, and no deed left undone where she is concerned." Rewen stared into the distance. "She has left her mark on everyone below the Boundaries, in one way or another."

"Won't it arouse more suspicions if we aren't aboard the Hulin boats? We might use them to some advantage, since we are to be sailing into their own waters," Owen suggested.

"If we had the time, I would say yes to your proposal. As it stands, we shall not be a moment too soon in reaching Eirn Bol," Rewen replied. "But now we must make all speed. There is a call from White Bird we must answer before we leave for Eirn Bol."

"Good," said Owen. "I shall have a chance to say goodbye to my mother and father. They will be surprised to see that we have this craft, and that we won't have to rely on the Hulin boats at all."

"We can't show ourselves there, Master Helwin. Our best chance of arriving unannounced in Eirn Bol is to not let anyone know we are on the way there. The Hulin Vipre have their spies all along the coast, and they would certainly report the sighting of one of the ancient vessels of the Sacred Thistle."

Owen said nothing, but looked evenly at the two young women. "Then we shall sail without their knowing. Would it be possible to leave word with them that we are already upon the way? They will be waiting for our arrival down the River Line. If we don't show up aboard the Hulin boats, they'll worry that we've been lost."

Rewen smiled sadly. "We shall leave them word. It will be a long passage, and they may not have news of you again for some time."

"Them was my very words, you mark me," shot McKandles. "I knew we was agoin' into a cat squabble the minute I laid my blinkers on this here mess with the fish pond, and water that wasn't no wetter'n bird spit! If I was ahavin' my way about it, I's would be agettin' shed of this here whole kaboddle just as quick as my old pins could be acarryin' me!"

"Them is my own thoughts, Kandles! If we wasn't all crosswise with our thinkin', we's would be ahoofin' it off now back down toward the Reed Plains, alookin' for a good mare and a plot to puts up a corral on." Lofen shuffled his feet nervously.

"There may be no need for such drastic measures as that, my good fellow," said Stearborn. "We'll see when it comes to it what must be done. Now what we need is a quick head count, and to take stock of stores and arms we will need to bring from the Hulin boats."

Rewen shook her head. "You won't need anything from the enemy vessels. Everything needed is aboard the Thistle Cloud."

Stearborn started to protest but was stopped before he uttered a word.

"You are used to your soldiers thinking, good captain. A certain number of men requires a certain number of supplies and arms. The Thistle Cloud was created by those with a different way of looking at things, and has spent many lifetimes providing for those that use her, both in security, and in provisions."

"I bow to your wisdom, madam," apologized the old Steward. "You will have to forgive my bull head. I only know what has always been needed to keep soldiers in kit and food, and I haven't dealt any too often with folks of your kind."

"You shall have all you need. Come aboard. I'll show you what the Thistle Cloud was built to do." Rewen stepped lightly up the invisible gangplank, finally stopping beside Coglan. "Someone give me their waterskin."

Jeremy nudged Hamlin out of the way and hurriedly went to stand beside the young woman. He looked doubtful as he trod carefully up the gangway to the boat. "This is strange," he said. "I couldn't see it before I got on it, but now it looks just like a boat as solid as the Alogan Mag!"

Rewen took the waterskin from him. "You see? I place this half-empty upon the deck, and behold!" She held a full skin aloft, still wet as though it had been held underwater.

"Try this, my lady," suggested Stearborn, tossing up an empty quiver to Jeremy. "If it can do with that what it did with the water, my doubts will be put to rest."

The quiver no sooner touched the deck of the Thistle Cloud than it was filled with a dozen white arrows, tipped with brilliant blue and yellow feathers. "These are finer than even our Line shafts," reported Jeremy, taking one out to examine it.

Stearborn turned to the others. "Well, what are we waiting for? Let's get this puppet show aboard that craft."

Findlin and Lofen were still reluctant to go, and held back, standing with Enlid at their side.

"Come," urged Deros teasingly. "Do you doubt the Lady Rewen's skill?"

"No, I don't," said Findlin, "but I hawe a long memory that stretches all the way back to before I was old enough for a spoon of my own, and it wasn't ewer told to me about seafaring women. There are just some things that a man should do."

Rewen laughed. "Then you two shall be mates under Coglan. He shall command the Thistle Cloud, and that should put your fears to rest."

Findlin blushed, looking down at his feet. "No offense, my lady. I don't know what came ower me. Old habits die hard."

Lofen, still hanging back from the water's edge, spoke in a plaintive tone. "You's can all go aclimbin' aboard of that there piece of air, but I is awantin' to have a shade more boat aneath me than that there little bit of nothin'!"

"You can see it from aboard," assured Jeremy. "Come up."

"I ain't agoin' until Kandles goes," insisted Lofen. "It were all his fault we is in this mess."

"You isn't agoin' to blame old Kandles for this bout of mullhash, you bloated old goat! You is the one what fell into the fish drink."

The two were preparing to argue further, when a noise in the tunnel behind them took their attention, and there in the archway stood a frowning Ulen Scarlett, looking from one to the other, and finally settling his gaze on Deros and the Lady Rewen. Owen could not be sure, but he thought he saw a fleeting touch of fear cross the young horseman's face, but it was quickly replaced by a forced smile as Ulen stepped forward to meet the Daughter of the Altar.

The Quays of White Bird

There were large flights of birds overhead, large and as snowy white as drops of snow against the pale blue afternoon, as the silent boat of the Order of the Sacred Thistle emerged from the river beneath the mountain. Owen's eyes were not accustomed to the brilliance of the midday sunlight, and he had to squint against it, raising his hand to shade his eyes as he looked at the surrounding countryside. It was a part of The Line he had not seen before, and he turned to Stearborn, who stood beside him at the rail.

"Do you know this country? Was there a patrol out here?"

Stearborn shook his head. "In all my years there was never trouble here."

"It seems odd that the Lady Rewen and her Order have been here all this time. Maybe they kept it safe."

"That would explain it. If I had been an enemy of The Line, and had water craft, I might have used this country for landings."

"I guess no one could, so long as Rewen was here."

"And the bears before her. That's what she said. The old Keepers used that grotto before her Order came."

"I wonder if any of this means the Elboreal might be about? It's hard to think of going off on a dangerous journey without Ephinias or Gillerman, and it's strange not to have Gitel and Seravan."

"It seems odd to me to be without my squadron," conceded Stearborn, "or knowing that the other squadrons are about."

Owen studied the high, white clouds that blew away toward the sea like tattered banners. "I wish I could see my father in White Bird. He might have something to say of all this. And I might be able to get Emerald to come along."

"Aye, the minstrel! You would be hard pressed to lure him away from his new bride!"

"If he knew how important it was, he'd go. There's even more at stake here than Deros's homeland."

"More by a long bow shot," agreed Stearborn. "The hand of the Dark One is all over it, and I don't mean to leave my doors open to that way of thought too long."

Deros joined them at the rail and watched as the shore slid rapidly by. The Thistle Cloud lunged ahead into the turbulent water faster than the sails above their heads could carry her. "It's amazing that we make such good way."

"The current," mumbled Owen, although he knew that was not the only reason.

Findlin and Lorimen came next, and they shook their heads and rolled their eyes.

"You would be counting knots on the seamen's log for a long while before you'd find what was driving these wessels," said Lorimen. "I know a thing or two of the sea, and been blown about by more gales than I care to tally in my old noggin, but there's none of either of them has to do with why we seem to be flying on our way to White Bird, with the bone in her teeth like she has now." He paused, looking at Rewen, who stood talking to Coglan. "There are some things a seaman would better leawe alone than to discover."

"I don't know why you wouldn't want to know," protested Owen. "How could you not want to find out everything you could?"

"It's not that he wouldn't want to know," explained Findlin. "There are things you hawe to hawe a discipline for before you can handle them. We hawen't had enough time aboard this wessel to know how to skipper her, or how she handles in a breeze."

"It looks to me as though there isn't anything for us to do but stow ourselves aboard until we are needed," added Stearborn.

"That may be sooner than we think. Look!" Deros pointed toward the shoreline, where a lone rider appeared, obviously trying to find a place to ford the river.

"He can't see us. I wonder who it could be?" asked Owen.

"Not one of the renegades who chased us back upriver. This fellow may be out of White Bird." Stearborn squinted into the afternoon glare, trying to make out the dress or arms of the man. "I wonder why he's trying to find a way across here? There's plenty of slack water back a way."

"He's stopped there! He's looking at something on the ground," said Owen.

"It looks like a body," replied Deros, standing next to him.

"Hawe Rewen run in closer," ordered Lorimen, forgetting his words of a moment before.

"Old Stearborn's nose is beginning to pick up an old familiar scent, and it doesn't make me glad of it. There's something here I don't like. Look at the ravens!" He pointed to the wheeling black shadows in the sky, and another flock of the grim birds hovered about on the ground at the river's edge.

Rewen had Coglan steer the Thistle Cloud closer to the shoreline, which was knee-deep in reeds and tall grass that ran down to the water. The rider had dismounted and chased away the birds so he could examine the object on the soft ground. The reeds had been beaten down in all directions, as though men and horses had ridden back and forth through the grass and reeds. A heavy stench reached them then, as the wind from behind them died down.

"There's been some butchery here," growled Stearborn.

"Look! It's one of the refugees from Sweet Rock!" said Owen. "Look at the shields there on the ground!"

Stearborn grasped the rail, his face gaunt. "That's a Steward shield. I have to get off! I must find what's happened here."

"Rewen said we couldn't," reminded Deros, trying to speak gently to the old warrior, for he didn't look in a mood to be argued with.

"This may have a bearing on the rest of our trip. If this group didn't reach White Brid, there may be a chance the others didn't either. We have to know."

Owen's heart stopped, and an icy fist knotted in his stomach as Stearborn spoke. "Do you think all our people were attacked on the road?"

"I don't know what to think, Owen, but I want to find out." He turned to the young woman of the Order. "My lady, I must ask you to land me here. It's an old man's job to trail along after disaster, and this is one I must find out about."

"I can't let the boat be seen," said Rewen. "I will land you ahead here, out of sight of the horseman. The Thistle Cloud has a shallower draft than you would think, and we'll come close to shore."

"I'll go with you," said Owen simply. A gnawing dread had numbed him, and he knew from past experience it was better to be busy than sitting and waiting for something to happen.

Stearborn studied the lad for a moment, his eyes guarded.

"It's not necessary for you to go," he said at last. "I can as easily take Jeremy, or Hamlin and Judge."

Owen shook his head. "I have to go."

"Come ahead, then. Madam, if you'll come in close enough around this bend, the pup and I can wade ashore from there. Keep a sharp eye, the rest of you. We'll have an advantage in our pocket by not being seen, but don't let anyone else come on us."

"There's more in the woods behind there," said Rewen, gazing at the tree line that came down to where the marshy flatlands began at the river.

"How can you tell that?" asked Stearborn. "I can't make anything out there."

"I see their outlines through the trees," she replied. "It is an old gift."

"Are they friendly?" asked Findlin.

"They aren't moving. They seem to be watching our lone rider here."

"Then they must be more of the raiders," concluded Stearborn. "We'd best bring the man with us, whoever he is."

Ulen Scarlett, having come up from below, watched from the companionway, his eyes full of contempt. "The Lady Rewen said we couldn't risk letting anyone know of our passage, and now you ask to be put ashore to pick up a straggler! I would cast my vote to leave him to his fate. If the others suspect we're here, it'll all be up."

"No one asked your opinion, Gortlander," snapped Stearborn.

"My opinion is given freely when it's needed," replied Ulen. "We can do the poor devils there no good!"

"There's one alive," said Owen coldly. "If nothing else, we can get him away safely."

"He's one, and we're many! Our whole mission is in jeopardy here, all for the sake of a single man! Deros must reach her homeland. Nothing is worth keeping her from it!"

Deros looked at Rewen a moment before speaking. "I don't know what to think. There's one in danger we can help, yet my heart speaks against offering aid. I hear two voices at odds with each other."

"We shall put our good captain of arms off, sister. He can find out what he needs know, and bring back the man. There will be no one the wiser."

"If they see us from the trees, they'll know something is afoot on the river," argued Ulen. "If we have to stop at all, let us do it by night. That will give us cover enough."

"It will be a good moon tonight," replied Stearborn. "If the wood is full of their scouts, they will pick us up just as easily as in broad daylight. I say we go now, and be done with it."

McKandles and Lofen had been watching from the rails as the lone man went from body to body, kneeling to examine each carefully and making the sign of the Sacred Tree over each. "Some of them blighters up in the wood line there is amovin' around now."

"I see them," answered Stearborn, checking his weapons and preparing to go over the side of the Thistle Cloud. Owen was poised beside him, looking away in the direction of the trees. A slight movement caught his eye farther down toward the riverbank, and he had to look twice at the spot to detect what he thought he had seen. It came again, this time no more than a small bush trembling slightly as a crouched, small figure moved swiftly through the undergrowth.

Before he could alert Stearborn, the darting shadow was gone, simply vanished into thin air. "I think I saw something else there. It may have just been some of the ravens, but it was bigger."

"There's another tilt to this pot," agreed the old Steward.

"I'd lay my sword arm to the fact that this isn't the regular millrun works! Come on, Owen! Let's look to it." He heaved himself over the gunwale of the Thistle Cloud, and splashed quietly into the river, which came up above his chest. He turned and half waded, half swam for the grassy banks, and was almost ashore by the time Owen went over the side.

Tales of the Red Mountain

The water was cold as Owen slipped into it. A hundred thoughts ran through his mind, but he tried to think only of keeping his footing and holding tightly to the sword from Skye, which sent a jolt of white-hot energy through him as he neared the reeds at the water's edge. The strong stench of the rotting corpses stung his lungs. The feasting ravens cawed from the woods. Birds of ill-luck, he thought; black in color, just like the burial ministers who tended the dead in the settlements.

Stearborn had risen out of the reeds almost next to the horseman, and the startled man leapt back from him as if he had been struck by lightning.

"Hold, friend! Stay your hand. I am Stearborn, of The Line. What squadron do you hail from, brother?"

The man shook his head, his eyes rolled back in his head, and he kept muttering something unintelligible over and over, trying to draw the sword slung over his back, although his hands seemed not to work right.

"What's he saying?" asked Owen. "Is it the common tongue?"

"The poor devil's been shaken from his moorings," growled Stearborn, looking away toward the trees. "I don't like the lay of this play, my buck. This blighter is armed and dressed as one of The Line, but it seems to me that he's not really one of our own."

"He might have come with one of the settlements we picked up when the spidermen attacked Sweet Rock," suggested Owen, holding his hand out to the man, showing him that he was unarmed, and a friend.

A single horn note came from the slope, and was answered by another from the right.

"Ahoy, shore!" cried a voice from the Thistle Cloud, coming quite plainly, although the speaker could not be seen. It was Findlin, calling out in a bold note, his voice resonant and full, vibrating in the moist river air.

"We have a blighter here that doesn't understand us," shouted Stearborn. "Can you see anything of the others ashore here?"

"The lady Rewen says to get back! They are circling around you even now."

"Ugggh," muttered the stricken man.

"Do you think he's really one of the enemy?"

"I think he may have come loose of his sockets, poor beggar! Too much of this sort of thing will do it. Let's have a quick look to see what's what here." The old Steward began a quick lope through the sprawling corpses, looking briefly at each. "They have Steward arms, and are dressed out of a Line Squadron, but I don't recognize any of them. And these others are a bafflement to me, as well." He stopped short and knelt beside one of the slain men, rolling him over to look for any identifiable marks that might give a clue as to his country.

"Look at this, Stearborn! This fellow has a tattoo! Didn't

Findlin say something to us about tattoos when we first met them? They asked us if we had them."

"You mean those pictures on their skin? I think they did."

"We'll find out more if we can get one of them ashore. They might know this lot."

"I don't know if you can get them into the water. For all their blustering about being seamen, neither one of them likes the feel of being in water without a boat. That current is pretty strong near the shore."

"Let's see if the fellow there has tattoos. We might take him with us for the Archaels to look at."

"If we could get him to understand what we're up to. He's got that wild look I've seen often enough after a battle. I wouldn't want to get him stirred up while he's like that."

Owen was looking at the man as they talked. He had crept on his hands and knees toward where his horse was standing, making noises that frightened the animal, and which finally caused it to bolt.

"Rewen might be able to get him aboard with her powers. That might be the best."

"It would do. We need to make our move now, if we're going to. The blighters out there are creeping in on us." Stearborn didn't look toward the advancing ring of men, but he indicated their position with a twist of his head, and by motioning with his eyes. "I can't quite figure these fellows. They don't seem intent on bush-ganging us, yet they hang about out there."

Stearborn crept to the shoreline and called out quietly, "Are you there?"

"Aye, we're standing by," replied Lorimen shortly. "If you don't make a go of it now, we're liable to be caught up here trying to get you away from your new friends."

"Do you remember the tattoos?" asked Owen, trying to hold his voice to a whisper.

"The tattoos?" Findlin's voice was tight. "The lad is speaking of the skin pictures at a time like this?"

"Some of these men are covered with them."

"Daelers," shot Lorimen. "Sounds a lot like Daelmen to me. As I stand on this deck, it does!"

Findlin's voice came clearly then, speaking in a language that neither Stearborn nor Owen could understand. The man on the ground lifted his gaze toward the invisible voice and made some reply, which Findlin answered. Beyond them, the others who were circling the two companions halted, and one of them rode forward cautiously, his bow laid across his saddlehorn.

"What are they saying, Findlin? Are they friendly?" asked Owen, clutching the sword of Skye tightly, yet afraid to draw it for fear of frightening the men into attacking.

"They are from The Dael. Odd lot, but friendly enough. Says they were set on by raiders."

"Ask them where they got the Steward gear," said Stearborn, frowning.

"They can't find who's doing the talking," laughed Lorimen. "They think you two must be some sort of high priests, making the air speak like this."

"They'll think we're more than priests if I find out they've harmed a hair of a Steward to get this gear," growled Stearborn.

Findlin spoke again in the strange tongue, and the leader of the Daelmen made a short reply, which seemed to take the Archael a moment or two to translate. When he spoke, his voice was heavy. "This man is Rioche, and he is the last of the line of Bralen, who was their king at the time of the flying snakes. They are marching from their home near the Red Mountain. I hawe heard of it, but it is far inland, and none of the Archaels to my knowledge hawe ewer gone so far upriver. There is a story that says there is wast treasure somewhere in a cawe on the mountain, and that it was put there by a dragon, one of the flying worms! A party of these men wearing the arms and clothes you see came into The Dael some turnings back, chasing a band of raiders."

"That would have been the Birch Squadron, under Ulesis Howen! No one heard of him or his squadron again! Speak out! Did these devils here have anything to do with that foul business! Speak, man!" Stearborn's features turned a terrible crimson, and his hand hovered near his sword.

Rioche dismounted and fell to one knee before the old commander, speaking rapidly in his own tongue while Findlin continued to translate.

"He does not want to anger the Seer, he says. He only tells the truth to the man who can control the air. No one of The Dael laid a hand to any of the strangers, and offered them food and shelter. They left after a day and asked that their spare gear be kept safe for them, for they wanted to be able to ride swift and light. They told Rioche they would be back in two days. They never returned. He says they saw fires on the Red Mountain that night, and heard strange horns calling. Some said it was the Dark One, calling back the flying snakes. He thought it might hawe been signals from the raiders, who were lying in ambush there. None of the men ewer came back to claim their goods, and ower time, his own men began to use the arms, for they were well forged."

"Did no one go in search of the others to see what happened?"

Findlin's voice droned on again in the alien tongue, and replied after Rioche's answer. "They tracked the others as best they could. The only thing he could see that happened to them was that the Colwages Domel must have come back to his old haunts."

"What in the name of the Sacred Fire is that?" asked Stearborn.

"The spawn of the great firesnake. The sorrow of all that's decent and good in these wide meadows, and a curse on all men."

Owen rolled the words over on his tongue. "The Colwages Domel. Is that Colvages Domel, Findlin?"

"That's what I said," replied the Archael shortly. "The Colwages Domel."

Rioche looked up, his face drawn and pinched, and spoke pleadingly to Stearborn, who shook his head slowly, unable to understand a word.

"What's he spieling on about?" asked the old warrior. "Tell him he has nothing to fear from me, if what he has said is the truth."

"What do you want to do with the men ashore?" called Lorimen. "Shall I tell them to ride on?"

"Tell them there is some safety to be found in White Bird. As far as we know, they can find haven there." Stearborn quickly wrote a few lines on a scrap of parchment and gave them to Rioche. "Tell him to give that to any Steward, unless he wants to find himself looking at the sword of one who wonders who he killed for his gear." Then he turned his back on Rioche and bade Owen join him in wading into the river. "Keep calling out to us, good Findlin! We can't see you."

"You are coming straight for us. Keep your way on, and you'll plow right into us amidships!"

Owen had turned to glance over his shoulder at the incredulous men left ashore in Rioche's party, who all now had fallen to their knees and watched the progress of the strange priests. He turned back just in time to knock hard against the hull of the Thistle Cloud.

"I've found her," he reported. "This will give our friends ashore a jolt."

"It will do them good," snorted the old commander. "Drive them a little closer to whatever they believe is running their little show. If they're infidels, it will give them pause for a good noodling."

A History of the
Flying Snakes

Ulen Scarlett stood next to Deros at the rail of the Thistle Cloud as Owen dried himself off as best he could. She watched the startled men on shore babbling among themselves and pointing to the empty river, where but a moment before the two strange men had vanished into thin air. Stearborn was talking earnestly with Findlin and Lorimen.

"Where is the land these men come from? Do they dwell near Fionten?" asked Owen, pulling his soaking cloak and tunic off, and laying them to dry on the deck. He, too, was gazing over the rail of the boat. The same small movement he had seen before appeared again in some low bushes a few yards to the right of the riders, and Owen concentrated on the movement this time, trying to detect what it was. Something was nibbling at the back of his mind, just out of memory, when the figure emerged briefly into plain sight and gave a little wave before it disappeared again.

"Twig!" cried Owen. "The Lame Parson's friend! There on shore!"

Findlin and Lorimen were at the rail in a flash, searching the shoreline. "Where did you see him? Are you sure?"

"As plain as day! He was just there. I thought I had seen him before."

"That means the Lame Parson is not far away," mused Findlin. "It is a strange omen to come upon Daelmen and the Parson all in one day."

"Endlin!" ordered Lorimen. "Hop to, lad! Fetch my old chart book. I'll hawe to see when we last had this sort of day to log." The Archael turned to Rewen, bowing. "Begging your pardon, my lady, but I wonder if you know this small fellow?"

"You mean the ruffian Twig? He also goes by the name of Tyro, and Tirhan, although he is the same scoundrel he always was."

"You know Twig?" asked Owen. "Has he been to your cave before?"

"He has come often, and been welcome," replied the young woman. "There are certain visitors who were always looked for in the grotto. He was one of them."

"Then you must know the Lame Parson as well," said Findlin.

"By other names," confirmed Rewen. "He has been in the Lower Meadows longer than the Order. He is the one who showed us the secret grotto. He gave us the cave, and helped us protect ourselves when all were against us, and when Gingus Pashon was determined to slay all who followed the Order."

"We have only heard some of your story, my lady," said Stearborn quietly. "I wonder how much more you will tell us now? It would ease an old man's heart to hear it."

Rewen laughed. "If that's all it takes to make your burdens easier, Steward, you would hear my story without delay. It has been written and rewritten time and again by different characters over the turnings. It would do me good to sit and recite it from the beginning to now."

"I look forward to it, my lady."

"It would do us all good to hear it, but I fear time won't stand still for us to hear all the wonderful words that would come from your lowely mouth." Findlin bowed and pointed again toward the shore, where Rioche and his group were wading their horses into the water and thrashing about with their swords, trying to find what might have happened to the two strange men who had disappeared there. "They are a curious lot, ewen terrified, it seems, and want to find our good lads."

"I'll give them something to think over," said Stearborn, laughing, and he bellowed out in a great voice, "Begone, you Daelmen! Leave the river!"

"They won't understand you," reminded Owen.

"Findlin! Tell them for me!"

"Aye, good Steward, with pleasure." He turned his back on the old warrior and went to the rail, where he cried out in a voice as awesome as Stearborn, and translated the message to the frightened Daelmen.

"There. Now they'll hawe something to tell their wee bairns ower a fire. It will be a good yarn to spin, about how they came on two water spirits."

"Water spirits or not, we need to have a look farther on here to see where those other blighters who came on us have gotten to. They must have some reinforcements if they were attacking a group as large as what the Daelmen had." Stearborn had unbuttoned his wet tunic and stamped his waterlogged boots on the deck of the Thistle Cloud.

"We is agoin' to be stuck on this here floater for a good spell, I's bound, Kandles! I just hopes we is agettin' to White Bird afore too long, though, so we's can hightail it off on some good solid dirt just once more afore I plugs my snout with them burial flowers and ends up worm soup!"

"You ain't agoin' to ever plant a hoof off this barge, and you knows it, Lofen! We is plumb stuck now, and we ain't never agoin' to ride no more, nor set a boot to stirrup, nor look at no high grass awavin' over the Reed Plains! We has made our fatal mistake in ever atryin' to get some fancy boots and saddles and aridin' with this here Gortland Fair, with Mr. Fancy Lad hisself." McKandles turned and bowed low to Ulen Scarlett, who stood stock-still at the rail, his face drained of color as his old underling addressed him.

"You'll live to regret this, you leech-heart! I haven't had my final say about where you'll end, and you can wager that when we are ashore again, and we have mounts beneath us, you will think long and hard about this breach of the sworn oath you gave when first you rode with the Fair. My memory is long, and no matter how far we travel, I'll remind you of this!"

"It ain't agoin' to do you no good athreatenin' us now, Ulen Scarlett. I has had a pipeful of all your rantin' and ravin' all them years with the Fair, when you wasn't ever no kinder to any of us than you was to that there Tarrier, peace rest his poor wild spirit! This here floater of the lady has done gone and unglued my tongue, I swears, but it is sweet music for me to be ahearin' it."

"Stow it, mates," urged Findlin, sensing a storm brewing between the old master and his servants. "You can bolster up your points when we reach the coast. There's nothing sours any quicker than a quarrel on board of a wessel!"

"Whether we is aboard of this here floater, or astandin' with our own two pins on solid dirt, ain't no matter! We has been agoin' slabwise of our own health and good interests ever since we was fool enough to be asignin' on with this Master Scarlett and his Gortland Fair."

"Do you think you've been so ill-used that you never got

anything back from your service? You were fed and clothed, which was more than I could say for you when you showed up! Speak up, you dung shoveler! In all your time with the Fair, do you dare to look me in the face and say you got no wages or board?"

"We isn't agoin' to be sayin' one way or t'other! You is your own worst enemy, Ulen Scarlett, and Lofen and I is aspeakin' our piece now, so's all these good folks aboard of this here floater can stands up for us once we is back on good black dirt. Lady Deros and Lady Rewen both says we should haves our says."

Ulen turned sharply, looking at Deros. She returned his gaze evenly, nodding. "I spoke with McKandles and Lofen at some length. They have told me of their time with the Fair, and how they were treated. I simply gave them my idea of what would be a just agreement."

"Just agreement!" Ulen snarled, his lips curled back into a cruel smile. "What sort of just agreement can you have with two illiterate brutes from the Reed Plains, who come to you half-starved and begging for work? They got more than they deserved, and a chance to make something of themselves in the bargain!"

"If you is acallin' agettin' up afore dawn every morning, and haulin' and feedin' and groomin', all for no more than a bowl of gruel and some feed for our nags a bargain, then we had a bargain! Nobody never took no notice of Lofen or McKandles, 'cept to holler that there wasn't no water in the trough! We has been alongsides you for a fair number of turnings now, and you ain't never once said so much as thankee! It never made no bother, till I talked to the Lady Rewen and the Lady Deros. You can't keep an old Reedlander skint shy of his reason for overlong no more. Not when they is in company with the likes of these kind folks!"

Ulen held his hands behind him, clenching and unclenching his fists. He felt the ring burning hotly on his finger, and clutched it even more strongly. A strange power emanated from it, stirring up a deep hatred against his companions. "That's all the worse for you simple fools," he sneered. "My Lady Deros and the Lady Rewen are just the ones to fill your heads with all these grand ideas, but I wonder how you will fare when you are without their protection?" Ulen bowed low to Deros. "My undying thanks for stirring up my men against me, my lady. They had never found fault with my treatment of them before."

"Awast there, my buck! You be aboard this wessel as a guest of the commander," blurted Enlid, pausing nervously to look at Rewen. "I mean the Lady Rewen is officially charged with the souls aboard her ship, since we are in the same boat, in a manner of speaking, and must get on with one another until we land."

"You shall be a good Cairnbar," said Lorimen. "But there are times when you need more force than a suggestion. Threaten eweryone here with a trip off the short end of a gangplank and you might get some compliance!" The stout Archaelian had raised himself onto his toes as he spoke, and his face was flushed with a menacing scowl.

"There will be no need for your threats," said Ulen. "I am no blind fool. I know you are all against me, and have been ever since Helwin began poisoning your minds. I have known how the matter stands since I first set foot in Sweet Rock, and saw the way the folk there treated those who came from outside The Line. I make no threats, nor plot against you, yet I am treated as a man who plans your overthrow! That wears ill with me, I can tell you. It isn't fair." He looked hard at Deros. "If you tell these louts of fair play, then you will at least do me the courtesy of offering me the same!"

Owen was on the verge of replying, when Rewen cut him off. "No one is in a mood to banter with you, Master Ulen. Our journey is a long and dangerous one, and there is no room aboard the Thistle Cloud for ill-will among the crew. It would be best to leave these questions aside, for they have no bearing on our destination. It is never good to think of two things while facing danger."

"It is time now to turn to our next task. There is a small cove ahead where we shall rendezvous with good Tirhan and see what news he has of his master."

"Another stop?" muttered Ulen. "We seem to have a regular ferry here."

Owen and Stearborn both wanted to reply, but remembering Rewen's comments, they were silent.

Coglan had steered the Thistle Cloud in close to the bank of the river, where the water was quieter, and those on deck could see the crystal-clear shallows teeming with fish. Near the bend of the river, where the channel took another turn back toward the heavier woods that lined that part of the country, Twig rested on a boulder and waved to them.

"How is it he knows our whereabouts?" asked Findlin. "No one else can see this wessel, can they?"

"None but those with the Sight. Tirhan can see us easily enough. So can his master." Rewen smiled at some thought she did not share, and waved in return.

Ulen's ring had begun to burn intensely, and a slow, throbbing pulse began to run from the ring into his hand, and up to his shoulder, making him move uneasily. A slow, recurring thought began hammering in his mind, dull and leaden, pulling him under some heavy spell that lulled him into sleep or a trancelike state. A faint, greenish glow shone at the edge of his vision, and he saw indistinct forms, of men in cloaks, from the corner of his eye. A frightening, searching presence sought to enter his thoughts. He fought against the steel weight of the presence, until at last, in a fit of panic, he tore the ring from his finger and thrust it into the leather pouch in his cloak. As soon as it was off his hand, his sight cleared, and he noticed Deros watching him strangely. She turned away when he returned her gaze.

"Do you find me so intriguing?" he asked, trying to clear the frightening presence from his mind.

"I thought you might be ill," returned Deros shortly. "You looked so strange a moment ago."

"Ships and water are not my favorite things. Sometimes they disagree with me."

Owen broke into the conversation, ignoring Stearborn's stern look. "You could get off at White Bird. I'm sure the Lady Rewen would stop long enough for that."

Ulen smiled wickedly. "I simply said ships and water are not my favorite things. I didn't say I wished to be free of them."

Twig had scuttled off the rock, and was waiting near the river.

His clothing was tattered and torn, and he didn't wait for help but scrambled aboard by going hand over hand up the side of the ship, and tumbled cleverly onto the deck at the feet of Rewen and Deros.

"You ruffian! Look at you," scolded Rewen, reaching down to gently touch the small, legless man. "What brings you to such places as this?"

"To look for you, my lady," replied Twig, doffing his cap. "My good friend has been scouring high and low for the dwellers in the mountain."

"Is he with you?" asked Findlin.

"No, no, my good master is looking for snakes! He has no time for visits on the river now. There are dark skies, and black clouds away to the east. Makes Twig afraid, when he remembers the bad days from the other time."

Rewen's face drained of color, and she knelt beside the small figure. "What are you saying, good Tirhan? What snakes do you speak of?"

His youthful face aged, and his clear eyes darkened.

"Days of old, my lady, when the skies were full of fire and ash. Twig sat below the mountain then, and watched the horrible beasts come to burn and kill. They would have hurt Twig, if they could. He was smart, Twig was. He came to you to hide."

The young woman held his hand, and turned to Deros. "He is speaking of the Freolyde Valg, the flying snakes. They have been gone from the face of these Lower Meadows for many lifetimes now."

"Gone, but coming back, my lady! Twig has seen them in their nests, high up in the Malignes."

"When have you been into the Malignes, my man?" asked Stearborn, squatting beside Twig. "Were you there with the Parson?"

The small figure somersaulted backward, landing on his feet beside Owen. "Twig knows many secrets of this captain! I saw you in the Fords of Silver once! You had slain many men."

Stearborn looked startled. "Where were you, my good fellow? Have you been spying on the Line Stewards?"

"Twig sees everything. No one gets away from my eye. I know many things, but only tell some. Secrets are what Twig loves best."

"I hope he hasn't been telling anyone else these little secrets of his," added Jeremy. "Times are not the best for us lately. With all the enemies we have, the less said about our whereabouts, the better."

"Twig is no snitch! Twig likes his friends from The Line. They save Twig from the big snow, and help him find a nest to hide for the winter!"

"That's good, my friend. The Line Stewards are the brothers of all who follow the Light. They helped you, and you can help them."

"He helps more than you think," said Rewen, rising and looking away downriver, where the forest began to give way to a coastal plain, with lush, tall grass that reached higher than a mounted man's head. "If his master is trying to learn if the Freolyde Valg are back, then there are more things on this journey to fear than the weather. The fire-worms left scars across the lands that are not yet healed, even after all this time."

"My mother and father told stories of them," said Owen. "I thought they were destroyed."

"Twig says the sky is black, and the ash has fallen again on many settlements not so far from here. The good folk of Fionten helped Twig, and he will warn them about the firesnake that is coming." The small figure did a little dance on his hands, and ended by sitting on the railing beside Rewen.

"Are you sure, good Tirhan? There have been no reports or sightings for so long. They were said to all be gone, or slain." Rewen looked to Coglan, who was standing at the helm of the Thistle Cloud. "Have you heard stories of the firesnakes in your travels?"

"None, my lady," reported Coglan. "But they have always been known to be the most secretive of all beasts. No one would know until it was too late. That was the way of it before."

"Twig knows. Twig sees in the wind's eye, and listens to the earth's breath. Twig hears the groans in the darkest part of the stone's heart. They all tell Twig there are new firesnakes. They have been nesting in the Malignes, far from any who would slay them."

"This is no good tiding," growled Stearborn. "First we have the squashers come loose from Leech, then the rumors of these brutes again! It does not sit well on my breakfast."

"It will sit less well if it prowes to be true," said Lorimen. "We would hawe the latest news at White Bird if we could put in there without being seen."

"Surely we could do that much?" asked Findlin, speaking to the young woman who commanded the Thistle Cloud. Her face was drawn, and she seemed to be thinking of other things, then smiled wanly at the Archael. "My plans may have gone awry, good sir. I had no thought for such dangers as the Freolyde Valg when we came from my haven. It was to be nothing but a straight journey to Eirn Bol, to deliver Deros safely there, and to put my ship and powers at the command of her father."

"Does this change your plans, my lady?" asked Deros.

"Not in intent, but I fear it adds another problem that we shall have to solve sooner or later. If the fireworms are upon us again, then it means that the circle is come full, and Quineth Rel is once more in full strength."

"Quineth Rel? What is that?" asked Jeremy.

"The Dark One. She was driven into a snare in the Middle Islands, and was silent for a while. There is no way to drive her from Atlanton, for it is hers, but by the same stroke, the Light is not allowed to pass away, either."

"We's heard a yarn or two on that there Black Mare," said McKandles, his eyes wide in fear. "This ain't no place I wants to be asashayin' to, if we is atrottin' off to be anglin' for a ride on the ilk of her likes!"

"Kandles is dead right! This ain't no doin's that I is awantin' to be clapped into." Lofen sat down heavily beside the railing, looking up hopefully at Rewen. "There ain't no need to be agoin' on where there's agoin' to be all this flapdoodle, is there? We was only puttin' up with this here floater so's we could reach the coast. White Bird is astartin' to sound awfully good to old Lofen Tackman."

"We'd all be wiser if we put in to White Bird," sneered Ulen. "That way we could sign on a new crew with something where a backbone should be. We might as well, for all the worth this crew will be, if a blow is struck. I'll be the first to sign up a strong brace of lads who won't be put off by stories of flying snakes."

"You'd be better served if you were tempted to leave the flying snakes alone, my young buck," said Stearborn flatly. "If you had any idea of what they were, or what they could do, you'd change your tune at a quick pace."

"There have been stories of them since I was a colt at my father's saddlehorn," laughed Ulen rudely. "They were stories that didn't frighten me then, or now."

"It would be wiser to wait until you know what the Freolyde Valg are," suggested Rewen. "Even your boldness would be nothing against one of the fireworms."

"We shall find that out, should the time ever come when one of the beasts actually comes upon us. That cripple can't make his living with his legs anymore, so it's proper that he should make it by using his mind to dream up these poppyrot tales to amuse us with."

Owen was prepared to speak, but Stearborn held him back. Coglan stepped forward and knelt so that Twig could mount his back. "Come up, Master Tirhan! Let us steer this vessel back out into the river, and leave these louts to argue among themselves. You can regale me with your stories, and give me your latest poem!"

Twig laughed a light, clear laugh, but his eyes caught Ulen's glance and held it. "Twig has a new poem. No new stories. A man who goes about on a tall animal should be taller than Twig, but he's not! No kindness for his small friend. Twig feels a great breath trying to find the horseman! It comes from far away, and burns Twig."

Ulen's eyes flashed, and he darted a look of sheer hatred at the disfigured man. "You will sing a lot longer if you keep your thoughts to yourself!"

"He means no harm, Ulen," snapped Deros. "Leave him alone. You have been rude to him, and now your threats make me wonder at what goes on in your mind."

The horseman turned to the girl, bowing. "I beg your pardon. I forgot that you have appointed yourself guardian of the downtrodden. First it was those wretches from the Reed Plains, and now you take up the quest with this poor legless toad. He is in fine company."

"What's gotten into you?" shot Owen. "I am used to your rude remarks to me, but you have no cause to attack this man. He is the friend of the Lame Parson, and it won't sit well to have you insult him."

"I don't see anyone else here. If the fool takes offense at my banter, then that is his own fault, not mine." Ulen looked down at his ringless hand, wondering how the crippled Twig could read his thoughts. That frightened him and made him determine to stay away from the strange character who talked nonsense and looked through his soul with pale blue eyes.

"We hawe something else here," reported Findlin. "Look to your steering, lad! There's a current there, and I don't see how you'll manage without oars."

"We do not need oarsmen, for we have our own way of dealing with these currents." Rewen moved her hand above her head, and within a heartbeat the Thistle Cloud had regained her headway and moved clear of the powerful current that ran to the shore. Downriver the stream grew broader, and the forest was thicker and closer to the edge of the water.

The Whirlpool

The Thistle Cloud sailed swiftly toward White Bird. Ulen Scarlett went below in a foul humor, accusing the others of plotting against him. He came on deck periodically to look around, and twice Twig made faces at him when the horseman's back was turned, but there was no further exchange between the two.

Just as Owen was thinking he could sit quietly on deck and enjoy the voyage, Rewen called to Shearborn, "Look, there in the thicket! Do you see the fire?"

Owen looked where she pointed and saw green fires burning brightly in the strong afternoon light.

"Soldiers' campfires?" asked Stearborn.

"Not troops of this realm. I would need a piece of the charcoal to find out who built the fires."

"We'll put in, then. Hamlin! Jeremy! Up lads. We have a bit of snooping to do."

"We will see if there is a place we can creep in. I am not pleased with Tirhan's stories of the new firesnakes. It does not sit well that the young horseman has fallen so foul with us, either. The ring is taking its toll on him now. I feel the eyes Twig spoke of. It is the mind of Blor Alhal searching for its brother."

"What do you mean?" asked Stearborn.

"The mind in Blor Alhal sees through the Rhion Stone that Ulen wears. It belonged to the slain Hulin Vipre prince." She pointed to the green flames. "These are another reminder of those who bear us no good will."

"The lads will find out soon enough what they are. Jeremy and Hamlin are best when it comes to scouting. I've never seen a pair more blessed with noses than the two of them!"

At the next turn of the river, there were shallows, and Coglan steered the boat in close enough for the two Stewards to go over the side and wade ashore, with instructions to simply find out where the fires were and who was there, and to return. McKandles and Lofen followed them, for they both insisted they needed to touch good solid earth.

A short while later Owen spotted the two Gortlanders thrashing back through the wood, eyes wild, plowing straight through the thick underbrush. He leapt over the side to stand in the shoulder-depth water to guide the two horsemen back to the Thistle Cloud.

They spluttered and babbled in their own brogue. Owen could not understand at first what they were saying, but once on board, they calmed enough to tell their tale.

"Pigs!" hissed McKandles, clinging to the rail. "They was changed into pigs right afore us! Wasn't no warnin', no whistlin', no nothin'! I ain't never seen the likes of that nowheres!"

"Are you sure?" asked Owen, incredulous.

"We was just about up to where them fires was, when Jeremy up and shouts at someone who was arunnin' away, and Hamlin is apoundin' away after him so quicks old Lofen and I was like to have had our skins scared plumb off!"

"They was wimmin," Lofen panted. "I thoughts first it was the Lady Derös and her friend, but then there wasn't no sense to that. Old Kandles even was acallin' out to her, but there wasn't no answer."

"Never said a word," confirmed McKandles. "Then we

saw them two Stewards astandin' there like they was agoin' to reach out and grab 'em, and, kaplonk, there was a bitter lot of smoke and noise. Then the next thing I sees is them pigs astandin' there where them Stewards had been afore."

"And the wimmin was alaughin' to beat all get-out! That's when I pulled in my cinch. Old Kandles was apoundin' alongside, so we was ahightailin' it back here to get help."

Rewen had been listening to the improbable story. "You were wise to seek help, good horsemen. The two you speak of are not ones you would want to meet alone. I fear even now we must act quickly, or we shall have lost our two good Stewards."

"By the Gore of Tralain, I'll have something to say about this," roared Stearborn, preparing to go over the side of the Thistle Cloud in pursuit of the ones responsible for the act against his young comrades.

"Hold, good captain," warned Rewen. "These are not enemies you can confront with your sword and shield! They do not do battle in ways you would understand, or could protect yourself against."

"By Windameir, they will learn to fear a sword stroke!" he swore, unsheathing his great long sword, which had been the end of many enemies of The Line.

Rewen held up a hand, and Stearborn felt as though he had run against a solid wall. He stumbled backward, fighting to regain his balance, and fell painfully against Owen, who reached out and steadied the old Steward.

"You must go lightly, captain! The two who have your friends would welcome another hotheaded victim. We must hold our tempers and let me think of what will work against them."

"Do you know who has Jeremy and Hamlin?" asked Owen.

"I think so," replied the young woman. "Wherever the Order exists, there are also the followers of the Dark One. Astrain was one of them, and long ago she lured the Hulin Vipre king into the service of her mistress. I have thought there would be some of her servants awaiting my return from the Keepers' cave, and now I am sure."

Ulen Scarlett stood glaring about, and finally held out a hand contemptuously. "Any fool can see what has happened. It would take nothing to get them back."

"What would you suggest, good horseman?" asked Rewen, looking at him carefully. She saw that he had the ring on again, and that his eyes seemed to have a hollow cast that gave his face a blank expression.

"Pick up the two pigs Lofen and McKandles saw, and be done with the rest. Surely you would be able to call them back from whatever witch workings they're under!"

"I have the Law to follow as well as anyone else," replied Rewen. "It is not mine to do or undo. There are some things that even the most powerful workings cannot interfere with."

"Then you tell us now that you don't have the strength that we shall need to reach Eirn Bol? Don't disappoint our good crew by saying you aren't as powerful as we thought. That might disillusion some of us."

"We shall reach Eirn Bol, my good horseman, with or without the ancient skills of the Seekers. If you are so interested in these workings, I would suggest you begin to learn enough about them so that you don't fall prey to dabbling where an innocent should never tread." Ulen's eyes were red-rimmed and seemed to burn into Deros when he turned to look at her.

At that moment, the small man spoke. "Twig hears the wind from the old castle. It blows hard now, and brings cold to his heart. Poor Twig has seen the time when there was no sun to warm the cruel king, and everyone hated the light."

"What's that cripple babbling about?" muttered Ulen. "We would be better off if we left him here. Let those harpies who have changed the two Stewards into pigs have another plaything to make them happy!"

Twig ignored Ulen and danced, twisting his broken and bent body about adroitly. "There were times when Twig could swim from shore to shore in blood in the old days! No fun for Twig! No time for songs, or watching the sea swallow the big yellow fire!"

"When did you swim in blood, good Twig?" asked Findlin, humoring the little man. "Were you with the Parson?"

"Twig was with his friend then. Always with his friend. Sometimes he wore the great cloak of the Bruinthor, and sometimes he walked with a crutch like Twig. He has been many faces."

"Why do you listen to his babble?" snorted Ulen. "Put the legless beggar back ashore, and let's be gone! If we can catch the pigs, well and good! If they are gone and there is no chance to redeem them by your powers, my lady, then we should leave them to their fates."

Owen's face was flushed, and he gripped the sword from Skye with so much force, his knuckles showed white. "Would you be of the same mind if it was you captured ashore, Scarlett? Would we hear this hard line of talk then?"

"You wear your skin too thin," scoffed Ulen. "These times call for more spine than you've shown since I've crossed trails with you in Sweet Rock."

Owen had stepped forward, his features drained in anger, but Stearborn and Lorimen held him back with firm hands.

"This is not the way to begin this," hissed the Archael.

"Something else is loose here, but I don't know what to call it. Hold up, lad! It's a passing thing, and we need not set our storm jibs yet! Not till it's blowing a gale and the yards are coming down on our heads! That's the time to mowe!"

"Babbling old fools aren't going to get us to Eirn Bol," snapped Ulen. "Are we to go on, my lady? Or do we hang about here, risking the rest of us with this foolhardy plan of landing again?"

Rewen turned to Coglan and motioned for him to reach into a quiet spot near the shore, where the Thistle Cloud might ride to a light anchor while Stearborn and the others searched for signs of the two young Stewards.

"Twig feels the cold wind," muttered Twig, pulling his tattered cloak over his head. "The cold eye is moving again. Poor Twig must hide."

From the shore there were eerie flashes of green lights, and the fires that had first caught the attention of the companions flared up again, some of them very near where their boat prepared to anchor. Coglan shook his head and pointed out one particular patch of wood that ran down close to the riverbank. "I don't think it wise to put us within reach of the bank there, my lady. This doesn't have the look of anything kind to our cause."

The young woman nodded and had him take the Thistle Cloud farther on, until they reached a slight bend in the river, where one side had silted up over the passing of time, and formed a small natural harbor behind the sandbar that stretched halfway across the flowing water.

"This would be a good spot for a settlement," said Owen, looking about, despite his anxiety for Jeremy and Hamlin. The river was very broad, and there was a dense forest of ash and oak that ran to the water's edge on one bank. On the other bank a wide sweep of broad, flat land was covered with berry bushes that still bore fruit, even though it was well past harvest time.

"When we return, I shall tell Famhart of this place," announced Stearborn, then corrected himself. "I mean, when we return, I'll suggest you have this place settled, little brother."

"It's all right, Stearborn. I haven't taken on the Cloak of Elder yet. We shall tell my father. It would be a lovely place for a new Sweet Rock."

"This puts me in mind of Fionten," said Lorimen, gazing wistfully at the beautiful scene. As the Thistle Cloud glided silently in toward shore, a buck and doe stepped clear of the tree line on the far shore and waded a short distance into the river for a drink.

"Deer ford," suggested Stearborn. "A good omen."

"Except that we've lost Jeremy and Hamlin. Maybe this means that whoever has them doesn't control this side of the river."

"There are only a few who could be responsible for this," answered Rewen. Astrain is elsewhere, or we would have heard more of her by now. She has two sisters, Dolcia and Moria, and they are the ones I suspect are at work here."

"Are them folks bad?" asked Lofen, grimacing. "I don't have no need to be amessin' with more of them as has old Lofen a bad turn in mind!"

Rewen smiled faintly, a trace of sadness touching her eyes. "They are not evil, but they have ill will toward any who follow Windameir. When Gingus Pashon fell in love with their sister, and was banished from the Council of Light, she and her two younger siblings were cast down, too. Now their bitterness rules them, and they bring pain and suffering to all they can touch, in revenge. It becomes a habit, after a time. You forget what wrong you had been done, and it simply becomes the act that begins the act."

"Living too long with the sword," added Stearborn. "In time, if you're lucky, you see where it has taken you, and maybe you can stop. But there's always the chance that the end never comes, and in the end, it is the sword which spells your own fate."

"Twig sees! Look! See the poor pigs! They run from the two who bind them, but poor piggies can't be free!" The legless man swung himself effortlessly up onto the railing, and stood balancing there on his hands, looking at the others upside down.

At the same time, they saw the two pink animals scrambling along the bank of the river, squealing in terror, and right behind them came two large hounds, solid black, with massive heads and large white fangs.

Deros pointed to the animals on the shore, tugging at Rewen's cloak.

"It's Dolcia and Moria," she confirmed. "They take on any form they want when they are at their games. They sense I am near. They will not run the risk of getting too near the Thistle Cloud. They can feel we are near without seeing us. They are very old, and have learned much of the Dark One's ways. Astrain was an excellent teacher."

"Bring me my bow," growled Stearborn, clutching the railing. "I'll show them they have something to fear from a simple soldier."

Judge jumped up to fetch the old Steward his bow, but Rewen held him back. "Hold your hand, captain! We have a chance now to take your friends. Tirhan, sing me a song of the stones."

"Twig remembers all songs, my lady," replied the cripple. "Twig hears what they sang in the old halls before the firesnakes came. Rocks and stones and mountains. They know many of Twig's friends."

"What's he talking about?" asked Enlid. "He speaks as though he's old enough to know things like that."

"He's old enough to know the lore of most beings who were ever here," replied Rewen. "He taught me once to speak to the spirits of the stone, but I have forgotten now."

"Twig knows. Twig will sing the old song for his friend." He paused, turned another cartwheel on the deck, and raised his clear, thin voice in song. The words were garbled and hard to understand. Then he lowered his tone until they could barely hear rumbling noises in his throat.

"What's he saying?" asked Findlin. "Is it the old tongue?"

"Older still. Those are the thoughts of the rocks ashore there, and they have told him of the short-lived ones who trod on them, and break their backs with the dark magic."

Twig's youthful face took on a mask of hatred as he mouthed the words of the stones, and listened to their inner agony. He broke into a cold sweat and cartwheeled back onto the railing beside Stearborn. "Twig can't listen more. They made Twig's mind full of their bitterness."

"Then don't listen to them, Tirhan. You must send back your kindness, and tell them there are friends here now who will help them."

"It is cruel to them," protested Twig. "They sleep now. It will only bring back more pain from the old order."

"Tell them," insisted Rewen. "We must get Jeremy and Hamlin back from Dolcia and Moria. We need the stone's help. They must hold the two sisters for us."

"It would only take two bow shots," argued Stearborn.

"They are not slain by shafts made by man," said Rewen. "Slaying the forms they hold would not harm them."

The huge black dogs suddenly stopped and stood panting, their white fangs snapping at air as they turned this way and that, as though trying to find an elusive scent. The frightened pigs ran squealing into the cover of the underbrush.

"They know we are here," whispered Rewen. "They have felt us."

"A fool couldn't miss this shot," begged Stearborn. "Look at them!"

"They would use the shafts to track us," warned Rewen, putting out a hand to stop the old warrior. "If they have something that you have touched, they use it to guide their witchery."

The crippled man had lowered himself from the railing onto the deck of the Thistle Cloud, and brought his broken body to rest at Rewen's feet. "Twig will call the stone's name, but it is sad. They have hummed the old laments for so long, it will be unkind to wake them."

"What are you talking about? What stones?" asked Findlin.

Rewen nodded toward the shore. "He can hear what the rocks and stones say. I don't know where he learned, but then I forget he has been here since before most of us came into these Lower Meadows."

"Do you mean to say he can understand dirt and such?" asked Lorimen. "What an odd gift."

"Not earth," replied Twig. "Stones still have their heart. Earth is like water; too many pieces, no center."

"The old legends speak of an army of stones when the Lower Meadows first came into existence. They guarded the realms, and were used to keep the peace."

"You means to says a bunch of rock like I was apickin' up and pitchin' as a strapper was a live thing just like you and me?" McKandles's eyes were wide, and he ran his tongue nervously over his lips.

"Before the first War of the Dragon, there were many things you wouldn't recognize, good hostler. The mountains of my homeland were known for their sweet voices. At night, you could hear the sound of them singing for a day in every direction."

"Then why isn't we acallin' them back to lay a hand to them two hell hounds there! Or lets the good Steward put a shaft in them beasts. That would set us a good way down the road toward afindin' our way out of this mess."

"Tell the stones, Twig. We'll wait for them to answer us. If you don't rouse them, you know how long they can go without knowing we are here."

"My lady can hear them now. Listen! Twig still had his own two pins when he first heard this tune."

"I don't hears nothin'," said Lofen. "Is them rocks asingin'?"

"They are answering," replied Rewen. "Dolcia and Moria hear them, too. They know they are in danger."

Deros had been watching closely as the two great beasts paced back and forth along the water's edge, turning their noses to the wind and casting about in all directions. "They are getting nervous," she said.

Rewen went to the rail and stood next to Deros. "They know who it is now. We must be quick, my sister. Gather your strength."

"Damn my eyes, they're just sitting there begging for a shaft through the throat," growled Stearborn, his bow clutched tightly in his hand, with an arrow notched and ready to shoot.

Ulen Scarlett had moved away from the railing, and now stood beside Coglan, who was awaiting orders at the great tiller. "We would be better served to make a run on to the coast, don't you think, brother? No sense in staying to lose all our hides to these witches." He looked sideways at the man to see his reaction, but Coglan ignored him, watching Rewen for her orders. Ulen's eye fell on the ring the man wore.

"I see you wear the red stone, too," he ventured. "They have strange powers, I hear."

Coglan replied without looking at Ulen. "It is a mark of

service for my Order. There are many rites, and much lore to learn before they can be mastered. They can be dangerous for those who are ignorant of their strength."

"Their strength can be matched by other than those who belong to the Order," shot back Ulen sarcastically. "It is not only the high and mighty who are able to master these things."

The two pigs came out of the brush farther down the river and stopped, looking about in panic. The great dogs saw the pigs and loped off after them, bounding away with a swiftness that startled the onlookers.

"Are the stones ready?" asked Rewen, kneeling beside Twig and touching the small man's shoulder.

"They have time to sing," chanted Twig, rocking back and forth in an odd rhythm. "They hear the black eyes who would crack their backs and make them sand. They do not like black eyes who harm them."

"Will they help? They must hold the black eyes, Tirhan. Tell them that."

Twig rocked another few beats, then opened his piercing blue eyes wide and looked long at Rewen. "Will you give them the sweetness?" he asked, his face bright and as young as a child's.

Rewen matched his gaze, and nodded solemnly. "If it is what they wish."

"All wish the sweetness," chanted Twig. "Even poor Twig, who has no pins, could dance again."

"You can't leave us yet, Tirhan. Your friend has a need of you yet."

"Twig hears. Twig knows the tune you sing. His friend can't feel his way through the trees without Master Twig aboard. No, no, Twig won't go, but the old tunes wear thin for the ground-eggs. They want the sweetness."

"Then they shall have it. But they must take the black eyes with them. Sing them that."

"Twig hears the black eyes. They are angry with Twig. They are coming to pull him into the dark holes where the wind howls!"

"Tell the stones to hold them," ordered Rewen. "They must not escape now!"

Rewen turned to Stearborn. "We must hold them here long enough for the ground-eggs to do their work. Shoot, good captain! And pray your arrow finds its mark!"

A faint twang came from the bows of both Stearborn and Judge, and the shafts hissed straight to their marks, striking the two great beasts ashore through the throat. The animals leapt high in the air before collapsing into two shapeless heaps, which began to smolder and melt into a small whirlpool of green fire and ash that rose upward into the afternoon sky, blocking the sun. A cold wind sprang up. Twig shivered in his thin cloak and cried out in agony as two great black talons reached out to grasp his heart, but Rewen reached down and touched his head, her bare arm pulsing with a white-hot light that flowed into the cripple, making his torn body jerk and twitch.

"You must find the two pigs," she shouted. "Quickly, or we shall lose them along with the rest! The sisters won't be held long by this."

Owen leapt over the rail of the ship, followed by Ulen Scarlett.

"What's this? The great horseman getting his feet wet over someone he hardly knows? I thought you recommended we leave them here."

Ulen smiled a crafty, disarming smile. "If worst comes to worst, and we can't get your two lads back into their right form, we might always use them for pork, in case the voyage takes a wrong turn!"

Owen had no time to reply, for at that moment, the pigs came into view again, squealing their way down to the water's edge and frantically trying to paddle their fat, round bodies out to where their friend stood waiting for them by the unseen side of the Thistle Cloud.

Ashore, the whirlpool of smoke and splintered stone grew higher into the afternoon air, and a smell of fried flesh and bone hung heavily over the place where the two great beasts had fallen to the Steward arrows. Stearborn felt a flash of pain in his shooting arm, and for a moment it was as though a lightning bolt had shaken him. His mind reeled and staggered at the vision of a great, dark maw filled with deadly, gleaming fangs, slowly coming his way through a fine green mist that had blocked the sunlight and filled his heart with dread.

The Chain of Orlan

Rewen and Deros knelt beside the old Steward captain. His eyes were rolled back in his head though he still held his bow tightly. Somewhere inside a looming, green mist, he fought savagely against the shadow beast that lunged for his throat and tried to suck the life from his lungs. A thin red cloud of his own breath held back the attack, but he felt his strength slipping. He recalled a time long before, in the high hills of the Upper Malignes, when he had been wounded by the shaft from the Malig warrior. It had pierced him through the throat, just as his arrow had caught the black devil on shore, and in his mind he was there again, his hand grasping the arrow as he prepared to pluck it free.

"I would have died," he gasped aloud, his voice making the strange sound it had made as the air leaked through the wound. "I would have died."

Rewen reached out and touched the vivid white weal of the old injury under his beard, and spoke a soft flurry of words. A faint strain of reed pipe music hovered about Stearborn then, and his eyes focused on the worried faces gathered around him. He grumbled something to Judge, then tried to pull himself upright. From the shore, a cold wind stirred up dust and what appeared to be ashes from the place where the black hounds had been, and an eerie screeching noise could be heard, almost like a heavy iron grate being dragged across stone.

Twig had covered his ears, and lay in a heap at Rewen's feet. "The sweetness," he begged. "They have done as you wished. Twig can't stand their cries!"

The young Daughter of the Altar rose and lifted her hand toward the shore. A faint, high song filled the air and drowned out the harsh sound, making the fading afternoon light seem brilliant and dazzling to the eye. The Thistle Cloud began slowly slipping away into the flow of the river, with Owen crouched at the side of the two terrified pigs, who grunted and squealed in wild-eyed fear. Ulen had reluctantly helped him bring the two aboard, and now sat watching sullenly.

"Now we have the crew complete," he sneered. "A regular animal keeper's scow! We might have picked up a milk cow to go along with the rest, if we'd only thought."

No one paid any attention to the surly young horseman, for all were watching the shore, where the bitter wind whipped the hard ashes and dust into the air with the grating noise that grew louder, finally becoming a roar that deafened all those who heard. Rewen raised her hand again and gave another command, which was swallowed by the howling of the wind and rocked the Thistle Cloud about the river like a cork caught up in a flood.

"Stand by for grounding!" shouted Findlin, knocked from his feet by the icy blast, and holding on to the railing by one hand. "We're being blown onto the beach! By the Lights of Namia, stand to, lads!"

Coglan wrestled with the tiller of the ship, and with a superhuman strength, he managed to regain control of the vessel, and she righted herself and made headway into the main stream of the river. "We've got steerage way," he reported to Rewen. "I don't know how long we can keep it, but if you can hold them off a little longer, we'll be around the point there, and out of harm's way, my lady!"

Rewen called another word, this time accompanied with a flash of light that blinded the companions and crackled about the air with a blistering heat that singed their skins and left Stearborn's leather tunic smoldering dangerously. Owen's sword had become red-hot to his touch, and emitted a high, thin hum, and broke into a brilliant white burst of radiant color when he slipped it from its sheath.

"We're here, my lady," shouted Owen. "The sword is here to help you!"

A greenish-gray lump formed on the shore, where the two sisters had been held by the stones. A slow-moving mass began to flow away from the intolerable light of the sword from Skye and the powers of the Lady Rewen. There was one last flaring green mist that boiled out over the water toward the invisible ship, but it was caught and held by the light from the sword and slowly blew back ashore, where it then was drawn into the very earth, leaving the late afternoon sunlight pale and weak after its passage.

"Are they dead?" asked Judge, who stood stunned at the rail, watching.

"Not dead," replied Rewen. "They have been forced to

abandon their shields. It will take them some time before they gather their powers again."

"Twig sees the piggies! Piggies are hurt!"

At the cripple's feet, the two terrified pink animals writhed and squealed about the deck in throes of pain and agony, biting and kicking at Owen and Judge when they tried to hold them to examine them for wounds.

"What is it?" cried Owen. "Are they dying?"

Rewen motioned for Deros to help her, and the two of them reached out to try to quiet the frantic animals. "They are burning with the last of the binding that Dolcia and Moria put on them! We must not let them slip away from us. I have seen this before. Your friends run a grave danger of being lost, if they lose sight of the way back."

"How do you mean?" asked Owen. "Can't they see us?"

"They see only the walls of the prison the sisters placed them in."

"Twig sees where the piggies are! It is the hole where the black eyes live!"

"Can't you do something to help them? Surely you can show them the way back." Findlin's brow was knit into a troubled frown. "Is there anything any of us can do?"

"Owen has the sword from Skye. It might help if he touched them with that," suggested Rewen. "Between all of us, we may be able to reach them."

Lorimen called their attention back to the shore they had just left. "Look at that! They've splintered the shore there! The riverbed is changing out of its banks!"

The companions on the deck of the Thistle Cloud looked behind them and saw where the Archael was pointing. Where there had been a rocky bank, there was now a rushing swirl of white water that filled the air with a misty white plume of spray. The whirlwind and green forms were gone, and all that remained was the new streambed of the river.

"Twig heard the sweetness," he crooned. "They sing sweetly now, good-bye, good-bye."

"Is he still talking to the rocks?" asked Ulen. "Maybe he can speak to the water as well, and ask that we be given all speed to the coast."

"We will have all speed," replied Coglan. "The River Line becomes a rapids not much farther on here. I shall need your help to steer, Archaels. Her helm is already hard to move against the current."

"Stand to, Findlin! We'll see to it this wessel has all the hands she needs to steer us safely on."

"This is the part of the riwer we always awoided," confirmed Findlin. "It was always too much for our ships, and we could newer get up the channel that leads to this branch of The Line."

As Owen and Judge struggled to hold the two frantic animals, Rewen began a soft song over them, and motioned for Deros to kneel beside her and do the same. She pulled a long coiled golden chain from her neck and placed it lightly over the heads of the pigs, which seemed to calm them.

"What is that, my lady?" asked Owen.

"The Chain of Orlan. It has been in the Order since the first. I have seen it undo the bindings of these sisters before. My mother used it to free the workings of Astrain, when we still dwelled in Trew."

Rewen touched the animals again with the chain, and spoke another lilting pattern of words. A faint tremor passed through the pigs, and the smallest change began to occur around the ears first, then spread slowly to the eyes and snout.

Owen watched in amazement as the animals half changed back into their human form, but remained repulsive to look upon, with their pink snouts broken by partial mustaches, and lucid, knowing eyes hidden behind the sloping brow of their pigs' heads. A faintly recognizable voice escaped one of the animals, which reached Owen's ears.

"You're going to be all right, old fellow," reassured the lad. "Rewen has seen to that! Just don't get stuck there! You look horrible!"

Another slight change transformed the animal's hind legs into a resemblance of legs, and the half-man tried to get up and walk, stumbling and falling in the process.

"The sisters' spells are stronger now," said Rewen. "They did not have this holding power in other times!"

As she spoke, a slight shudder shook the ship from bow to stern. "This is the work of the sisters! I thought we got away from them at too little a cost." She stood and made her way to Coglan's side. "We must call on all our craft's powers now, or we shall be lost before we clear the River Line!"

"This current has grown stronger, even on this side of the river, and it looks as though the banks have changed again," Coglan told her. "You'd better help me keep what way we can, Archaels! There is white water there ahead, and I don't see a way around it."

"Can we find a safe place to anchor?" asked Lorimen. "If we can get out of the tug of this eddy, we might be able to make our way back upstream."

Coglan shook his head, hanging on tightly to the helm of the Thistle Cloud. "Nowhere to go now but straight through."

The current strengthened, and the roar became deafening. A fine white mist covered the river where the worst of the rapids began, making the blue of the sky a stark line above it. Coglan and Findlin struggled to keep the helm of the Thistle Cloud centered, while the others clung to the masts and rails, holding on for their lives.

"Isn't there anything more to do?" asked Deros, still beside Rewen.

"We can call on Windameir's mercy," she answered. "And hope the Thistle Cloud has not grown weak in all the turnings of disuse."

The boat bumped and pounded heavily, and lurched away beneath their feet as it began the first of the rapids, but she held her shoulder down and kept her footing well through the terrifying stretch of water that roiled and boiled, and drenched all aboard.

Deros was thrown roughly against Owen, and they both fell onto the deck, tumbling about for a moment before regaining their balance.

"Are you all right?" he asked, helping her to her feet. He noticed a slight bruise on her arm, and reached out to touch it, but she pulled away from him.

"I'm fine. We shall have to keep a better eye than this for upsets. I guess there are no easy ways of dealing with the likes of the two sisters back there."

"Where did you get the bruise? I didn't do that when we fell just then."

"I must have bumped against something earlier," she replied, avoiding his eyes. "There is always something on board of ships that seems to be in the way when you're trying to get around."

Another rough stretch of water jolted them all again. Coglan was torn loose from his tiller, and had to scramble back across the deck to recapture the wildly swinging helm, which he was able to do with the help of Lorimen and Findlin.

"We've got trouble on the shore again," warned Stearborn with a harsh shout. "Look to it, lads! All along the east shore!"

Owen looked over the top of the railing, and there on the stony riverbank was a sight to chill him even quicker than the icy water of the River Line. Spread out in a long file, and gathered in milling knots, were hundreds of strange-looking creatures, half-men who walked about on two legs, yet had the bodies of large snakes. Their skins shone a burnished green in the sunlight and their tongues darted rapidly in and out, and they appeared agitated and worked into a great frenzy.

"Sarlin!" hissed Twig, making an odd noise in his throat. "They smell Twig and his friends."

"What in Windameir's Bread are those?" gasped Stearborn, loosening his weapons. "I never heard tell of a lot like that loose in The Line."

"They have been brought by Dolcia and Moria," replied Rewen. "They are servants of the Black Hood."

"Is they agoin' to come on us?" asked Lofen, looking about wildly. "I hates snakes!"

"They sense we're here," said Rewen. "They can smell live things. It may be a help that we are coming this way in daylight. The sun hurts their eyes."

"We're coming too near the rocks," reported Coglan. "I can't hold her to the middle of the channel!"

Lorimen and Findlin struggled with the tiller, trying to help the helmsman hold their course, but the Thistle Cloud had slipped dangerously near the outcroppings of the east side of the river, and ran perilously close to smashing herself upon the jagged rocks there.

"They'll be on us in a flash if they hear us hit," growled Stearborn. "What poor timing this old Steward has! This breaks all the rules of taking an enemy by surprise."

"More like jumping into their laps," replied Findlin. "But they may find we hawe a surprise or two left up our sleewes!" He turned to Lorimen and Coglan. "Heawe, lads! We can squeak this old bucket by here, ewen if I hawe to showe her off those stones with my bare feet!"

The Sarlin along the shore had become more agitated,

and their thin black tongues flickered about wildly, sensing another presence that promised victims close at hand. More of the snake-men had appeared farther along the shoreline, and a dull, heavy drumming had broken out among them.

McKandles had pulled his sword and stabbing dagger, and clutched the weapons to him, his jaw clenched. "We's in the stew for sure, if this here floater don't keep on afloatin'," he managed. "I never thoughts I's would be asayin' I was keen on no boat ride, but I hopes this one is agoin' on a bit farther now!"

"They ain't even ablinkin'," added Lofen. "Them things don't shut their eyes none!"

"I'll see if they bleed," growled Stearborn, as he and Judge let fly shafts. "They may be the devil to look at, but I'll lay to the idea they can be pricked by a Steward arrow easy enough."

Two of the Sarlin let out a screeching cry of pain and crumpled into a heap, which set the others into a frantic hissing noise, and the drumming intensified to a point where those aboard the Thistle Cloud could barely hear themselves speak. Coglan had recovered the helm somewhat, and now steered a course farther out into the river, and it began to look as though they would make it past the rocks.

"They're coming into the water!" warned Enlid. "Stand by to repel boarders! Look alive, there! They can see us!"

A dozen or more of the snake-men had slid into the strong current and swam powerfully toward them, gliding across the surface like serpents, slithering through the white spray in seemingly effortless motion. Enlid and the others stood ready at the starboard side of the Thistle Cloud with their weapons at the ready. Almost in a heartbeat, two of the intruders were over the side of the vessel and struggling hand to hand with the Archael.

Owen was bound in an iron grasp from behind, and he

smelled a faint odor of rot, which turned out to be the breath of one of the snake-men, hissing over his shoulder. Deros let out a yell of surprise and slashed at the attacker with the knife that Stearborn had given her. The Sarlin recoiled in pain, releasing Owen long enough for him to draw the sword from Skye. Its blade flashed a brilliant white in the afternoon sun, and a terrible slow dirge began to emanate from it, until it pulsed and throbbed with the dull beat of the drumming from the shore. The enemy intruder who had attacked Owen fell backward over the side of the Thistle Cloud, his head cleaved in two by a sword stroke from Stearborn, but there appeared three others to take his place.

"Where's that blackguard Ulen?" snapped Judge. "I wonder at times who he is really for!"

Deros pointed to the companionway. "He went below before all this happened."

"Roust him up! I want to keep him out where I can see him." All the forgotten anger boiled up in Owen's heart. "Now these things can see the Thistle Cloud, and I wonder how that is?"

"There is no need to send for me, good Helwin," called the horseman, suddenly standing beside him. "There may be a lot said against my good name, but you can't blacken it by calling any who go by the name of Scarlett a coward!" His hand held his sword, and Owen saw the blazing Rhion Stone turn the horseman's face an unhealthy shade of crimson. He had no time to examine the man any further, for they were washed over by a wave of attackers who came over the side of the Thistle Cloud and were among them in the merest blink of an eye.

Owen hacked the head of one of the snake-men off in a single, clean blow, and Lorimen, standing behind him, opened a gaping hole in another with his double-headed battle-ax. They lost sight of Ulen in the frenzy of action, but quickly spotted him, carried to the deck by two of the Sarlin, who were trying to place a blade into his throat, although he was struggling violently with his assailants. He got the ring on his left hand into the face of one of the snake-men, and a high, thin gargling escaped its throat, and it fell back, blinded by the fierce red light that came from the stone. The other attacker fell back, hacking at Ulen feebly, and it seemed to be stunned. Enlid, fighting nearby, finished the beast with a sword stroke, and rushed on to help Findlin and Lorimen, who had made their stand by the helm of the Thistle Cloud.

Rewen was beside Owen then, her face flushed. "His ring has somehow betrayed us! The Sarlin can see us. The Thistle Cloud is no longer protected!"

"How can that be?" cried Owen, looking about wildly and seeing the throngs of snake-men making straight for the surging boat.

"The Rhion Stone the horseman wears has found the voice that speaks to the heart of the boat. It has ordered the Thistle Cloud to show herself!"

"Undo it! Can't you undo it?"

"It will take some time. In the meanwhile, the Sarlin already know we are here. Moria and Dolcia have been overcome and trapped for the moment by our bindings, but they called up these henchmen to try to finish their work for them!"

"How long will you need?"

"Long enough to recall the color from all the wood and canvas. That can be short or long, depending on the weather," replied Rewen.

"Duck!" shouted Judge, striking as he spoke, and one of the snake-men fell dead from his blow, directly at Rewen's feet.

There was a slight lull in the fighting, and Owen noticed

that Ulen was gone once more. "Has anyone seen Scarlett?" he called.

"He was off down the companionway just before this," panted Findlin, trying to get his breath. "I lost sight of him after that."

"I've got to get to him," said Owen. "If I can't get that ring off him, the boat will stay visible to all our enemies. Rewen says it is his stone that's done this!"

"The ring? How could that be?" asked the Archael.

Before Owen could answer, Lorimen cried, "They're coming up from the riwer on the anchor tackle."

Voyagers
All

Death on the River

A dozen more of the Sarlin swept over the rail of the Thistle Cloud, bearing down on the outnumbered defenders who stood resolutely on the deck. Owen had worked his way to be beside Deros, and Stearborn stood with his back to theirs, so they would leave no opening for the snakemen to strike. The boat shook through her very keel as the current took her over more rocks that were spread all along the eastern shore of the River Line, and Owen heard Rewen's voice calm and clear above the rest of the din created by the noise of the water and the sounds of the pitched battle being fought on deck. "Coglan! Twig! To me!"

Owen thought the young Daughter of the Altar had sounded a final rally call, and he was trying to fight his way to her when the blur of struggling bodies on the afterdeck of the Thistle Cloud seemed suddenly transformed into a giant form with reddish fur wading through the clumps of Sarlin as a man might splash through shallow water. There were hideous screams from the snake-men, and a low, rumbling noise. "I'm coming," he cried, to hearten Rewen. "Hold on!" He held the sword high, and it caught and reflected the sunlight into a dazzling white ray on the furious battle that was being waged.

As he neared the spot on the deck where Rewen stood, he was shocked to see a huge animal beside her. There was no Coglan or Twig, but the deck ran red with the blood of the snake-men, and their bodies were heaped knee-deep next to the young woman. Owen came face to face with the fierce muzzle and flashing claws of a great red bear, who stood a full two hands higher than his own head, and stared deeply into the animal's fearsome blood-red eyes that promised death and destruction to all who came near. Owen fell backward over a fallen Sarlin, trying to hold the sword of Skye out before him to ward off the terrible animal which lumbered toward him. There was something in the fierce countenance that made his blood run cold.

"Stearborn! Judge! To me! Help!" The shadow of the huge animal slowly covered him, and he looked upward into the cavernous maw, rowed with long white fangs that dripped the blood of the slain Sarlin. It occurred to him that he was about to die, but the thought came to him then of Seravan and Gitel, and the way the two horses had talked of their other animal friends.

And there were the stories of the Lame Parson, and the tales his mother and father told of the Middle Islands.

"All hail, Bruinthor," he called, finding his voice choked with fear. He tried it again, this time with more success.

"All hail, little brother," replied the huge animal politely. "Come up! We have more work this day than to lie about the deck watching the others do our fighting for us!"

The voice was vaguely familiar to Owen, but he was too startled to try to piece the mystery together. Rewen joined them then, and put her arms around the great bear's neck. "You do remember all your old training," she said. "It would please our friend to see how well you have acquitted yourself in this business."

"He would have my hide to think I did otherwise, my lady," replied the bear. "After all the effort he put into my teaching, it is well for me that I have shown myself fit to have been his student."

Twig appeared from beneath a stack of Sarlin bodies, and did a back flip to end up on the railing next to the bear. "Twig has seen the slithery ones before! They tried to make Twig sleep with their venom. They are friends to no one but the black eyes!"

"No one but you is seeking the black eyes, you villain! If you have word of more of them, tell us now. Do you see more ahead of us?" asked Rewen. "Your eyes are far-reaching. Can you see White Bird?"

"I can see to the end of Twig's nose, and he sees many of these dead things that hiss. They are nasty things. Spoil the river for Twig."

"Something of more use would be to tell us where Ulen is," snapped Owen. "If that ring he wears is what betrayed us, then we need to find him and remove that danger!"

"The Rhion Stones are difficult to control," answered Rewen. "To one who is not used to their powers, they can gain control of thoughts and will. They sometimes may take over and bend the mind of those who wield them. I think that is what has happened to your young horseman."

"He was already prone to listen to any voice that might have given him a way to more power!"

"You have a hot temper, my young buck," put in Stearborn. "Especially where the horseman is concerned. Yet there is some truth to the idea of his being touched by a greed for power."

As Owen turned to see if Ulen had come on deck, he

saw the bear was gone. "Where is he? He was right there a moment ago!"

Rewen laughed. "You have much to learn of our good Coglan. He is right here, where he has been all along."

The young man at the helm bowed low to Owen. "It sometimes comes as a shock to people when they realize they don't always see the true nature of things." His voice was the same as the bear's, and Owen remembered then why it had sounded so familiar.

"My mother and father told me of the Old Ones who were with them in the Middle Islands. I just thought you had all gone over."

"Not all of us," replied Coglan. "There have always been some of us left below the Boundaries. I have been at my studies here since the great battle you spoke of took place in the Maloran Isles. It is true a lot of the old masters returned Home, but they left a number of us to help."

Lorimen and Findlin, covered with gore from the fierce fighting, came up.

"How goes the helm, lad?" asked Findlin. "Are we standing well enough off the rocks to pass?" Neither of the Archaels had seen the bear, and were in ignorance of Coglan's true nature.

"I could still use another hand to help me steady her," replied Coglan, smiling. "With any luck, we should be clear of these rapids beyond the next turn of the river there. From then on, it is smoother, and we shall have a chance to shelter awhile, and clean the Thistle Cloud."

"I'm for that," mumbled Lorimen. "I'm up to my shanks in these slimy things. I don't want to know where they've come from, or anything more about them. I'm grateful we never ran afoul of them before this, and I shudder to think how many times we've come right up The Line, just as though we had our good wits about us."

"Look!" cried McKandles. "This here floater ain't alone!"

Turning to gaze back over his shoulder, Owen's heart skipped a beat as he took in the scene. Another boat, with deep red sails, was bearing down upon them.

"Do them things knows how to steer one of these here floaters?" asked Lofen.

Rewen stood by Coglan at the helm of the Thistle Cloud, peering back to study the pursuing craft. "They don't have vessels like that."

"It looks familiar," added Coglan. "There's something to the cut of the jib that puts me in mind of someone."

As the river became calmer, they sailed down a long channel that emptied into a vast lake. "This is nothing that I recall seeing on a chart," said Findlin. "As long as we hawe been coming up The Line to perform the rites, I newer recall any report that there was a lake this size anywhere between the coast and the Grimpen Mire!"

"You never sailed this part of the river," replied Rewen. "If you had, you would have noticed this place before. It is called the Great Bend Broads. We are very near the coast now."

"Twig smells the tall trees where the Old Ones are. They are near us now."

"What? Old Ones? Where are they, Twig?" asked Owen, his mind jumping to thoughts of Gillerman and Ephinias, or the two horses.

"Close by. They are sailing."

"You mean the boat behind us?" asked Findlin.

"That's where I recognize her from," said Coglan. "All those boats off that part of the Delos Sound carry those odd jibs. We'll heave to soon, and have ourselves a gam. I'd like to find out what brought them up this way, and what news they have of the Sarlin."

"Are we still visible to them?" asked Judge, standing at

the rail. The two half-transposed pigs were at his feet, struggling as if they wanted to be out of their skins.

Stearborn knelt beside one and held out a hand to calm him. "Is there nothing you can do to aid these two?" he asked, looking up hopefully at Rewen.

"They are free of the worst. When they began to take on their human forms, it was the passing of the gate to the binding."

Small, half-human sounds were coming from the throat of one of the tormented ones. As the old Steward listened, he made out Jeremy's voice, high and odd sounding, but there was sense to it, and he leaned closer.

"He says the two women were witches!"

"Then they are coming back safely. They can remember what happened. Sometimes those workings might take days to recover from."

Owen knelt beside the two. "I think I can make out Hamlin," he confirmed.

Stearborn laughed. "Those two were always known to go to any degree to avoid a duty. Chellin Duchin would have their backsides up between their shoulders if he were here now and caught them lollygagging like this."

The animals began another transformation, and took on distinct human characteristics as the companions watched. The broad faces were flatter now, and their noses began to reappear. Where the hooves had been, there appeared definite hands and feet, and the short, stout pig middles began to extend, until they had their old shapes.

"Piggies are going," crooned Twig. "Good-bye, piggies. They escaped the black eyes."

"What happened?" asked Hamlin. "We were just ready to catch those two witches."

"It seems that caught you first," said Rewen. "You were

lucky they did not keep you longer, or we would have had a harder time bringing you back."

"I can still smell that smell," shuddered Jeremy. "The place was dark as the inside of Chellin's heart, and there were others there. They called out to us for help when they knew we were there."

"Twig knows that place! Twig has smelled that awful blackness!"

"I didn't think anything was wrong until I looked at Jeremy," went on his friend. "You could have knocked me over with a feather when I saw what had happened to him."

"It's over now," comforted Rewen. "There may be memories of it, but it won't linger too strongly, unless you are around the sisters again."

"The sisters?" asked Hamlin.

"Dolcia and Moria. They were the two who put you into the bindings."

"I only got a quick look before it happened," said Jeremy. "They were so beautiful."

Coglan was calling for the sails to be trimmed, and he prepared to heave to, so the ship following could catch up to the Thistle Cloud. Owen and the others left the two recovering Stewards and went to help. The craft behind began to make better way, and slowly drew nearer. Findlin and Lorimen stood by the rail.

"She has a good stand of canwas," observed Lorimen. "Her bow is cut a little steep, but she has nice lines."

"Looks like some of the shipwrights from farther around than Glen Osriel. They like that sprit out forward."

"Do you know them?" asked Deros, joining the others to watch the boat's progress.

"Might know of them," returned Findlin. "We cross wakes with a lot of folks at one time or another."

"You mentioned the Old Ones, Twig. Do you mean there are Old Ones on that boat?"

Twig laughed his high, clear laugh, and rang the small bells on his bracelet. "Old Ones dance to no tune. Rhymers like Twig see their music, but they only come when the moon is cracked and the times are hard."

"The times couldn't get any harder," growled Stearborn. "We've seen the death of Sweet Rock, and a dozen ways of getting gutted since."

"Twig knows the hard road to the Old Ones. His friend tells Twig all the time of the caves, and the red rugs. A game it is to Twig."

Ulen Scarlett had emerged from below, and now stood defiantly in the companionway, glaring at the gathered companions.

"So the good horseman has come up for tea," said Judge. "We shall be pleased to have you."

"You may be pleased to have me, but I will wonder if that feeling will be mutual," returned Ulen, stepping out on deck. "I have heard all the harsh words that have been spoken about me."

"Is there truth to them?" asked Owen. "Do we have need to hold you, or have you a good explanation of what happened to bring the Thistle Cloud to the vision of the snakemen?"

"I have no explanations for them, or anyone else. If this bucket suddenly showed solid to an enemy, then I have no more idea of the reason than the rest of you. I certainly did nothing that would have endangered any of us. I can't say the same for others among us, who risked the ship and all our lives by putting in among that nest of witches. Think a bit more on that, Helwin. Who has put us at most risk this day?"

Owen looked at the defiant young horseman's hand, and noticed that the ring was gone.

"Ahoy, ahoy," came the cry from the other ship as it moved closer to the Thistle Cloud, her red sails being lowered as the two vessels slowed. "We are the Marin Galone, sixty sunrises out of Pan Dorsla, on the Delos Sound."

"Thistle Cloud," called Coglan. "Most lately of The Line. Outbound for White Bird and the South Roaring Sea."

"We've got some other tars aboard of this wessel, too, lately of Fionten. My good comrade Lorimen, and the new Carinbar are with me. May you always fetch your home waters!"

"Greetings, Fionten. We have news of your home that is of grave consequence. I hope you bear no grudge for the bringer of such tidings, but you must come to know of it sooner or late."

"Who be you?" asked Lorimen. "What news is of such grawe nature that it must find us on strange waters, and be deliwered by those unknown?"

"My carryby is Lanril Tarben. To our sorrow we must tell you the entire settlement of Fionten is burned to the foundations, and the fleet is scattered all over the Straits of Horinfal. There are many survivors, but they have had to flee. We have been scouting for safe quarters for ourselves, for the same fate has befallen many ports along the Delos Sound."

The Archaels whitened as they heard the news.

"How long back is this?" asked Findlin, putting his arm around the young Enlid.

"We've been beyond Fionten for this past mark, friend, so our news is thirty sunrises old as we speak."

"That might be a lifetime," mumbled Lorimen. "We hawe lost our two good wessels, and a dozen or more good

Archaels on this trip, and now we find we hawe no home port to make for at the end! These are hard times for an old salt that has put many a log-knot of sailing behind his transom."

"He said there were survivors," reminded Deros. "You have that small comfort. There may be many of you left. It is the same news I fear of my homeland."

"Do you have news as to the nature of the trouble?" asked Coglan. He lashed the helm of the Thistle Cloud, and came to stand by the rail next to the rest of the crew.

"The scourge of every decent living thing. It wouldn't take long to find who would be at the bottom of this, friend, unless you had never heard of a sea dragon, or the name Railan Dramm."

"Who might that be?" continued Coglan. "I am familiar with the Freolyde Valg, but the name is strange to me."

"Railan Dramm," muttered Findlin. "He has been with us for a long turning or two! No one expected this, though."

"He has courted the Red King and his Conductors in Blor Alhal," said Lanril. "He has a pact with those devils in Blor Alhal, and they have called back some of the firesnakes. They have made new invasions all along the ports of the Delos Sound, and are said to be as far ranging as down through the Horinfal Straits."

"They have been all the way here," called Deros. "The Hulin Vipre have followed after me, for they think they will force my father to give up Cairn Weal if they take me captive. The settlements of The Line have been fired by the Olgnites and Hulin Vipre, so we are set out to return to Eirn Bol, to take Alban Ram what help we can to contain this plague."

"You will need more help than you have there, my lady! Railan Dramm has the firesnake, and two hundred ships or more, and that tally doesn't count the ones who serve the Black Hood."

"Two hundred ships! There wasn't a soul who could list that many wessels to their name when we left to bring Enlid for the rituals! How could that be?"

Lanril raised an arm and pointed eastward. "They began to gather in the shelter of Gurlen Bol. That has long been a safe haven for those who live beyond the terms of sailing for decent seamen. That's where they got their promises from the Black Hood, as well. No one on the Silent Sea is safe anymore. We have been seeking the survivors, to bring together a force to retake the sound and all the rest of that stretch of water."

"I told you the Hulin Vipre were dangerous," said Deros. "I knew they would not be content with just Eirn Bol. They always had their plans for the rest of the lands beyond, once they had what they wanted from my father."

"And what might that be?" asked Lanril. "Does he have a fleet to be used?"

"More than fleets or men, good sir. He has been the steward of the Alberion Novas all these past turnings, and is so still, I pray. If the Black Hood had their secret knowledge, there would be no place left to turn, and we would all be doomed."

The ships drifted closer, and those aboard both vessels stood by with boat hooks to fend off. The captain of the Marin Galone looked perplexed, and shook his head. "I don't know the meaning of your words, my lady, although I have been well aware all my life that Alban Ram of Cairn Weal has been a defender of the rights of all men who sail the Silent Sea. That alone makes him important."

"More important than you might believe," replied Rewen. "We are on our way there to bolster his defense, and to gather all who would give us aid."

"Then you can count us among your number," vowed Lanril. He turned to the men on the deck of the sleek vessel. "Do I hear it, lads? What say you to sailing with the Thistle Cloud?"

A shout of approval rang out from the sailors on the Marin Galone, and they raised their voices as one in a pledge.

"Then we shall have a beginning," cried Lanril. "We are but two, but it is the seed of a fleet."

"We have a need for further talk, good captain," said Coglan. "I purpose to put in at the first favorable anchorage. How say you?"

"Aye, cap'n, we shall keep a weather eye for a porting. We never thought to cross wakes with anyone on this slip of a river, and especially after we had gone up to the white water back a bit. I want to hear how you got up or down it! That will be a seaman's tale worth hearing!"

"You would be more surprised than that, my good fellow, if you knew the whole of the story. But you will have our yarns, and more, and we shall lay out what we can do to go on to White Bird."

"They were in danger there, too," answered Lanril. "But reinforcements came from other settlements. It was rumored that there were Elders who had been to the Middle Islands among the new arrivals."

Owen's heart leapt to his throat at the news, and he felt a great wave of relief wash over him, for the strangers aboard the Marin Galone had confirmed the fact that his father and mother had reached White Bird and were there awaiting them. Without realizing it, he clasped Deros's hand and squeezed it tightly. The girl was surprised, but made no effort to pull away, and looked quietly out over the great, broad lake that spread on until it reached the waiting waters of the sea.

In Blor Alhal

A dark splinter of shadow hung over the long table, flickering about like a phantom snake. Three figures dressed in black were seated along the benches, poring over a great chart that lay spread before them. Dim reflections gleamed from the brasswork at their collars and on their cloaks, and they talked in low voices as they studied the map, moving their fingers here and there, or jabbing at a place to make a point. Two of the men were older, with long white beards and wrinkled brows and deep-set gray eyes, who seemed to be arguing with the third, a much younger man with a dark beard clipped closely to his chin, and eyes that were a cross of blue and gray. He had a slight limp as he paced away from the table, heatedly arguing over something one of the older men had said.

"You have no proof that my brother is dead! I refuse to believe that he has been lost, for we still have the Eye."

"We have done the ritual, and spoken to it from the Norith Tal, but it will not explain the riddle we taught it. I say it is on the hand of a stranger!" persisted one of the older men.

"Salun Am is right, Baryloran. Tien Cal is lost. I dread that news as much as you, but it is true! All the answers we have from the Eye are dull and vague, and there is a feeling that it is weak. When Tien Cal replied to us, there was never the mists, or the vagueness."

"Then he may be held captive. That would explain it! They may hold him captive, and he has no chance to reply to you for fear they will find him out!"

"That would answer," said the older man quietly. "I am an old man, and my family name goes back to a time when we were one, Baryloran. To think that Tien Cal is lost stings me to the quick, yet I know what we must do. We cannot assume that your brother is still upon his quest for the snippet from Eirn Bol. She has escaped him, and he is lost. We have to face that fact sooner or later."

"Jatal Ra speaks for all of us on the Mardin Council. We must leave behind our heartfelt loss of your brother, and press on with the finding of the girl. Eirn Bol is ripe, as it has never been before. The old doddard in Cairn Weal is weakening daily, and all that remains for us to do to achieve our lost heritage is to bring the girl before him. Then the Alberion Novas will at last be held by their rightful owners. Long live Gingus Pashon, may his memory burn forever!"

Baryloran's brow darkened, and he turned suddenly and marched to stand at one of the diamond-shaped windows that ringed the room. Outside it was dark, although a scattering of stars shone through a ragged cover of clouds, blown about by a strengthening wind that came up off the cove at the bottom of the cliff. The waves lapped the small stony beach, and wore white plumes farther out, and the small skiffs that lay tied to the stone quays bobbed at their tethers like brightly colored toys.

"We shall have our time to strike! My father is ill and cannot command you, but I say as his second that we wait for more word from Tien Cal!"

"Lacon Rie would not advise us, Baryloran. We have been with your father for many turnings, and even he never dared to go against our counsel." Salun Am grew angry, and his face turned crimson beneath his beard.

"I am not my father. I argue with you, sir, because of my love for my brother. He will come through."

"A Conductor is not used to having schoolboys contradict him," snapped Jatal Ra. "We know more of the world and its doings than you, and need to remind you of your place, Baryloran. It is not your duty yet to make judgments and decisions for your father." He paused a moment, then went on. "There is no more time, Baryloran. If the weather keeps on as it is, we shall lose a perfect opportunity to send our longboats to seize the Southern Ride! If we secure that stretch for our landings, Alban Ram won't be able to stop us! He's a doddering old fool now, and ill like your father. They have held sway over Hulingaad and Eirn Bol for countless years, and it is time for another season to come to pass!" Jatal Ra was flushed and perspiring as he finished speaking.

"You are unwise to think I won't carry your words to my father," replied Baryloran quietly. "He is old, and I think dying, but he is yet the Emperor." Baryloran had paced back from the window of the fortress, and went to look at the great chart laid upon the stone table. "I have known for some time you were no friend to my family. It is as well we have it out in the open."

Salun Am hastened to lighten the damage. "He is only worried about losing the chance to land on Eirn Bol. If we miss the tides and wind, we won't have another chance with such fair conditions until next year. We need to move now, or lose our advantage."

Baryloran shook his head stubbornly. "We will wait. There will be word from Tien Cal soon, I know."

Jatal Ra looked to his companion, making a signal with his eyes. "Then we should at least send out a watch force, my young counselor!" He dipped his pen to ink, and made a small cross on the shoreline along the coastline called the Southern Ride. "Here is where we would do the most good. If there is to be any news, we should be able to get it from there."

Salun Am nodded. "A good plan. If we are not to have useful information from the Eye, then it is as well to find our sources elsewhere."

The young man studied his father's two Ministers for a moment, then seemed to come to a decision. "I shall see to it that a scouting force is assembled this very day. We are sending a new fleet against Eirn Bol in a day or so. I shall have a part of that group deployed in the place you marked." Baryloran looked again at the map, then started for the door. "I must take my leave now for my father's tea." He bowed stiffly and limped from the room.

As the young man left, his two companions leaned over the table with their heads close together, talking earnestly, once they were sure they would not be overheard.

"It is the end of Lacon Rie. Poor devil. Such a shame that a fine specimen like him would be taken by a case of the Richlige Plague!" Jatal Ra laughed a short, cruel laugh. "It is handy that someone in Blor Alhal knew something of that dread killer." He laughed again, then grew more serious. "But we may have to hurry our plan before the old fool is dead, if Baryloran keeps on with his meddling."

"And if Tien Cal is not dead, as we suppose?" asked Salun Am. "We will find ourselves at a garrote post if we are mistaken."

"You know yourself the Eye won't answer the riddle." Jatal Ra pushed himself away from the table and rose slowly. "It may be time for us to go on with our work. Perhaps Gingus Pashon will smile on his own tonight."

Salun Am whispered urgently to his companion. "You need not have given the whelp so much to think on! He knows where we stand on the matter now!"

"He has known all along, idiot. Anyone could see that

waiting on the doddering old fool in the throne room is but asking for defeat. And his young brother, the hotspur tapped for the next mantle wearer, is nothing more than rotten flesh and bones somewhere down in the empty barrens of the west."

"That may be, but it is not the best of counsel to give away too much of our plans. Since we have been at work upon the Book of Warl, we are best advised to keep Lacon Rie hopeful of our good support for as long as he lives. It will cost us nothing to play at both hands here."

"Then that is what we shall attempt, my good companion. Diplomacy! We have long been known as tactful diplomats here in Hulingaad." Jatal Ra smiled a dark smile, which made his features appear grotesque. "Then if we find that Tien Cal returns on the tide tomorrow with the accursed wench from Eirn Bol, and our Emperor survives still another day, we are no worse than we were. But if not, then we know of the binding that will call the Varolyde from their slumber. Then it will be all over for the petty fools who oppose us, both here and abroad."

Salun Am was pale as he spoke, and he twisted his hands into his cloak. "It has been many turnings since those beasts have been free. Are you sure the Warl Writings will control them?"

"You saw the drawings of the Doom Fields, and read the runes. It is written that anyone who holds the Words of Warl will hold the beasts in hand like a man might drive a horse."

"I hope that's so," said his friend, with small beads of sweat across his forehead. "I hope that's so. If it proves to be otherwise, then we will be at risk to the frightful anger of the dragon, along with everyone else. How will they know we were not the ones who tricked them into the Fire

Pit? I have read that they are unpredictable, and savage, even to one another."

Jatal Ra looked evenly at his companion. "You must brace yourself, my faintheart. There is no place on the Council of Mardin for a Conductor who wilts at the thought of what it will take to reach Cairn Weal, and to take the treasure there."

"I am concerned that we remain alive to find that treasure, brother. Dead men have no glory." Salun Am's eyes narrowed to slits as he looked at his companion, and his hands made a faint gesture in the air. "It is of no use to us to reach Cairn Weal if we have not the strength to hold it. The Lost Fire is a powerful thing, and once we have them called back, we'd best be in a place that we can control them. The Book of Warl has been neither opened nor used in a long time, and we have no way of knowing if it will work at all for any but Lacon Rie."

"Trust that all shall be well. We need but a third to recite the chants.

"I believe Frishon El could be brought over to our side if we went slowly."

"We might test him a bit. He is in the Lower City this night. It would only take us a short time to find him." Salun Am's eyes had grown bright in his dark face. "There will be others there, as well."

Jatal Ra smiled in slow comprehension. "The Arbon Players? And how well we have loved them, eh, old friend! That wench who casts bones and reads the wind will be there among them."

"I hear they have just come from settlements down along the Folspire. There are spies who ply the waters between there and the northern side of Eirn Bol. We may have news that will be more pleasing to us than what we have heard here tonight. Baryloran is a young fool. I would hate to think of what we would become should he replace his father as Emperor."

Jatal Ra smiled a wicked smile, and walked to the high, thin window that overlooked the Rolate Wing of the fastness of Hulingaad. "There are stars again," he said. "It begins to blow from the north. That is a good omen."

As he spoke, the air in the tower chamber became charged, and a face appeared in the mist cloud that had formed before the two men, wavering and fading from time to time, but becoming stronger and more focused as Jatal Ra held out the hand with the Rhion Stone upon his third finger. "Speak, my lovely! Tell us what you have to say, and what you are seeing."

The misty grayness began to part, and the two stood still and began to watch as a great, gaunt shape began to form before them, causing Salun Am to fall back in horror. "It is the Paluge! They are becoming too strong to be held! I thought you had not completed the recitations of the Book of Warl. You said you were not through!"

"Shut up, you fool," commanded Jatal Ra. "If we are to take Cairn Weal, and we have no king's wench to open the door, then we shall have to rely on something that can reduce it to ashes for us. They have thwarted us for the last time. No one can resist the Paluge!"

"Neither can we, if they turn on us," countered his companion. "I don't trust them. Why should they spare us?"

Salun Am saw for the first time there was something different about his old companion that night. The ring's fire reflected in his eyes, and in another moment, he forgot that and was face to face with a vast, dark mind that searched for him and found his heart and held it like a small, helpless bird in a cruel claw that poised to crush it. Salun Am whined and fell to his knees on the cold stones of the tower of Norith Tal.

The Heart of Stone

The crude torches along the wall smoked and flared, casting a poor light on the shiny flagstones of the floor, and a draft found its way through a small chink in the massive structure, whipping the flames about like fiery puppets.

"There is someone else in here with us," said Jatal Ra, speaking close to his companion's ear. "We may surprise them at their work. Let us send the Nod."

Salun Am could not disguise his pleasure. "Yes. Yes."

A small shard of light erupted from Jatal Ra's hand, and from beneath his cloak there crept a small lump of black charcoal. "Here, my little friend! Take the breath of Jatal Ra, and sweep this hall clean of intruders!"

There was a moment of silence. Then the very faintest sound began, low and beguiling, a hiss that might have come from the lips of a dying man, or the warning signal given by a deadly asp prepared to strike. The formless lump writhed and turned about the floor at the feet of the two Hulin Ministers, and slowly began to grow in size, until it was almost as tall as a small boy, and thick enough at the shoulders and neck to be a fully grown adult. Dull eyes shone through sunken sockets, and where a mouth and nose might have been, there was a gaping red hole, which made an ominous hissing noise.

"Search them out, my purge! Bring them the gift of your

embrace!" Jatal Ra smiled a crooked smile, watching his deadly apprentice form more solidly.

"Go!" ordered Jatal Ra. "Fetch me his breath!"

Whirling forward, the wraith glided toward the inner chambers of the Norith Tal, hissing and rumbling like a stalking beast.

From somewhere ahead, a sharp cry went up, and the sound of running feet was clearly heard, ringing distinctly on the flagstones.

"Hurry! They will escape us!"

Another second passed, and the noise of a closing passage caused the two men to groan in disappointment.

"Gone! The swine escaped us. Call our friend back. I don't want to have him loose down here too long. He has grown harder to control, and I don't want to lose him before we could put his talents to good use." Salun Am looked uneasily at the dark form that scoured the room before them as a dog might, sniffling here and there for the scent of its escaped victim.

Jatal Ra motioned in the air with his hand, and spoke three harsh words that rasped and rattled his tongue, and which felt like small blows to the ears. The wraith fell motionless, then started to retreat from its master. "Come here, you wretched shadow! Come to your master!"

The form fell back farther, making threatening noises.

"Use the bone," urged Salun Am, growing more distressed as he watched. "Don't wait any longer. If it gets away from us, we shall have the devil to pay!"

"We need to keep the power of the Relic intact. I don't want to use it yet."

"Lacon Rie is just above us here! He'll feel it down here if we let it out much longer!"

"Lacon Rie is ripe for planting," sneered Jatal Ra. "It will make no difference if he suspects or not. The time is ripe for our new order to proclaim itself."

"Then get that thing back! We don't want to risk our plans by revealing ourselves too soon."

Jatal Ra motioned with his hand again, jabbing a finger with one of the Rhion Stones toward the retreating shade. This time, the shadowy figure began a hesitating motion toward them, growing smaller in size as it came, until it was once more the lump of blackish charcoal that lay at his slippered foot. The Minister reached down and plucked up the dark object. "There may not be another time as tidy as it was here. I don't know who our spy was, but if he is employed by Baryloran, then our work must go forward even more quickly." Jatal Ra shook his head. "If only we had been a moment sooner!"

"We don't have time enough now," protested Salun Am. "We should leave here now, and try again tomorrow night."

"Hush! Listen! See the stone! It's speaking again!" He held his ring up, and they watched together as the fiery forms flowed and ebbed across time and space, forming vague shadows and ghostly forms without substance, and an odd, moaning sound came forth, distorted at first, but more clearly as they cleared their minds and tried to pick up what the soft voices were saying.

At first, a face that was unfamiliar to either of the men was seen clearly for the briefest moment, the eyes of the stranger staring straight into their own, as if he was looking directly into the Rhion Stone. He was handsome enough, and young, and Salun Am thought it might be one of Tien Cal's men. Next a great storm at sea flooded their minds, and the howling shriek of the wind hurt their ears.

"Where can it be? It is at sea, but bound for where?" Jatal Ra was trying to focus upon the wearer of the Eye, to probe the mind of whoever was there. There were brief visions of a vessel struggling in a storm, lashed by high waves that washed over the deck, and a wind that shrieked its fury like a lost demon.

A pale face appeared close against the Eye, and Jatal Ra cried out as though he had been struck. "It's the slut from Eirn Bol!"

"Then it could be Tien Cal aboard that vessel," said Salun Am. "It could be as Baryloran said."

Jatal Ra shook his head, his brows furrowed in confusion. "It's the wench, I vow, but I can't make odds from ends of this. The Eye wavers."

"Were they trying to warn us the girl is on her way here?" asked Salun Am.

"Or on her way somewhere," concluded his companion. "There is no doubt that she is aboard ship, but we don't know where, or in whose hands."

"Can you call the Eye back to you?"

"It wavers too much for me to command it. That's why I think there is someone else who wears it. Tien Cal was under its power, and I had no trouble then." I shall have one of the Paluge called up from the Pit. He can find out for us what has gone on."

Salun Am's hands shook as he listened to his companion, but he dared not disagree, for he did not want to feel the terrible crushing of his heart again, nor stare into the dead eyes of the Protector. However terrible were the Paluge, they were nothing to the anger of the Dark One, so he held his peace.

"Come and help me." Jatal Ra went to the center of the room and stood near the stone table that had been placed there when the fastness had been constructed. He removed the pile of books and papers there, and moved the charts back into their place in a wooden cabinet beside the window, and turned to his friend. He knelt and slipped a large key into a lock that seemed to be built into the very stone itself, and drew open a block of the wall, revealing a musty-smelling chamber behind.

Salun Am bent down beside his companion, and together they pulled out a large, leather-bound volume that was almost too large for the small opening. A smell of burnt flesh and sulfur filled the room, and another noise, a deeper rumble than the roaring of the sea, seemed to shake the foundations of the building to the very ground.

"Lacon Rie will know," hissed Salun Am. "He was in charge of the Varolyde! He knows about this!"

"He was too weak to complete his mission," snapped Jatal Ra. "He called the Paluge back before they could complete their work."

"They were attacking everything," protested his friend. "You remember the stories. Once the beasts had gotten a taste for blood and treasure, there was no controlling them!"

"He was not up to the task! We have the Protector's aid. She wants that blemish of a man on Eirn Bol erased. We shall please her in this, and you and I shall sit in power there. Think of it! The Alberion Novas! Ours for the using!"

A faint tug of terror pulled Salun Am's heart, but he let his thoughts linger on what it would be like to have access to the unbelievable powers that were locked into the ancient scrolls that had eluded the Hulin Vipre for as long as he could remember. It was an old tale, and he had only heard the version that labeled Alban Ram the traitor who had selfishly broken the Council of Mardin into factions and retreated to Eirn Bol with the scrolls.

"It won't take long," urged Jatal Ra, laying the huge tome down upon the stone table and opening it to a well-marked place. He chuckled under his breath. "Lacon Rie may have most of the guard and all his army to rely upon, but they are nothing to the Paluge. If we are only able to awaken one of them, it is better than having five thousand foot or horse."

"And twice as dangerous," reminded Salun Am. "Make

sure you have the beast's destruction in your hand before you spell his coming."

"It is all here," said Jatal Ra smoothly. "They have put everything here."

"That didn't help before. It took the infernal workings of the outsiders of the Circle to lure them back to the Fire Pit. It would have been our end if they hadn't stepped in."

"Lacon Rie lost his nerve," insisted his companion. "We were on the brink of victory when he asked those meddlers for help. Look where it got us! They constantly spied and plotted against us, and treated us as though we were the transgressors! Well, the time for vengeance has come, and we shall show them all how well we have learned our lessons!" Jatal Ra's eyes were wide in anger, and he brought his fist down hard onto the open book. "We have the power before us that will strike our enemies before they have time to know we are moving against them!"

Another sound reached them then, after the sound of Jatal Ra's voice had died away to a whisper. It was subtle, and hard to distinguish from the rising wind outside. A flaring torch near the door that led into the tower stairs pulled their attention there, and for a moment both men stared, hardly believing their eyes. The bent figure was swathed in heavy robes, and had difficulty in walking, but despite the faltering step, they had no trouble recognizing Lacon Rie.

Jatal Ra recovered his composure first. "Sire," he cried, hurrying along the cold stone floor to offer his hand to the Emperor. "You should be in bed."

Lacon Rie pushed the hand away. His voice, although old and ill, was strong enough in its anger, and his white head was held high. For a moment, he was the old Emperor, full of youth and promise, and with a holy war to wage against his oldest enemy, Eirn Bol, whose king had scattered the Mardin Council and stolen away the Alberion

Novas. "You have gone against me for the last time! I have heard your plans, and listened to your schemes long enough to know that you are ready to move against me. Baryloran has told me all I need know, and if I doubted him, all that remained a mystery to me was revealed tonight. You will not call back the Paluge, Jatal Ra! I forbid it, and if you disobey me, I shall have you confined to the Glagnbar until your eyes rot!" He had to stop to catch his breath then, his eyes flashing. Salun Am began to speak, but Jatal Ra cut him short.

"You have thwarted your people long enough, my Emperor. They have waited until they have died away, and you have become a toothless old dog that no longer has a bite. You could have finished the matter with the Paluge, but you chose not to out of fear! Your heart was not strong enough to take the risk, and you called in your cowardice for help from outsiders, who have bullied and treated us like common criminals since. Look where that has gotten us!"

Lacon Rie pulled a small bell from his cloak and prepared to ring for help, but Jatal Ra was on him like a cat before the signal could be sent.

At the Crossroads

In the pale fire of the autumn sunlight, the distant arc of the sea stretched out across the horizon, flowing from one end of the visible world to the end of sight. Owen stood transfixed, gazing out into the sunset, breathing in the salt air, and listening to the distant sound of the Sea of South Roaring thundering in onto the shores. It was a moment of great gravity for Owen, who had never before seen that boundless body of water, and who felt a dozen feelings pulsing through him, leaving him very near tears. Deros was at the railing, her thoughts focused on a land farther away than mere miles could count. Beside them, bobbing at its anchor, was the Marin Galone. Deros watched for a time, then turned to Rewen to speak.

"Will we stop over at White Bird?"

"If the settlement is unharmed, it will be necessary. If it takes some time to renew the Thistle Cloud's workings, then it would be senseless to try to bypass the busiest of all the ports on this coast. And we shall have more time to acquaint ourselves with Lanril and the Marin Galone."

Ulen sulked about the afterdeck, waiting until Coglan had gone to meet with Lanril, then came to stand next to the two women. "If you are thinking of becoming allied with this man, you might at least ask him where he's from. How are we to know to believe him? He says he is Lanril, and that they fight the Hulin Vipre, but what's to keep him from being a spy and taking us all captive? He may have more ships waiting on the coast!"

Rewen nodded. "Those things might be, Master Ulen, but we shall have to take him on his word for now."

"And why was he up the river? How did he come to be behind us, and all of a sudden appear?"

"I think the answer may be that the firesnake is no longer a story, but is in fact a truth, as horrible as that might be to think of. No matter what the case, we shall have to sail on, whether there are enemies there or not, for we must reach Eirn Bol. With some time, and a little help, we shall have the Thistle Cloud protected again. I don't want to think of the Freolyde Valg surprising us at sea. If the ship were caught without her shield, it would be death for us all." Rewen looked straight into the young horseman's eyes, and he felt a wild urge to tear his eyes away from hers. Something inside him was threatened, and recoiled from the clear eyes of the young woman as though she were a deadly enemy.

Owen came to join them. He caught the furtive look the horseman wore, and stepped forward to speak to Rewen. "I see you have been left in good company. And have we any further clues as to why the Thistle Cloud was suddenly visible to the Sarlin?"

"You had best watch your insolent mouth, Helwin. My motives are no more in doubt than yours. What would have happened if we had not had luck on our side back with the two sisters? Or with the snake-men? I won't have my name sullied by the likes of you. If you think you are man enough then come ahead! We'll settle it with dirks before this voyage goes any farther." He plucked a dagger from his belt as he spoke, and crouched in a fighting stance.

Rewen raised her hand and spoke a quick word. Ulen felt the knife turn red-hot, and he dropped it automatically, clasping his singed palm.

"You have women fight your battles, Helwin! Are you not man enough to face me without your witches?" His face drew back into an ugly leer, and there seemed to be something wrong with his eyes, although Owen could not tell what. There had been a slow change that had come over the horseman from the Gortland Fair since he had found the ring on the dead Hulin Vipre prince, although now it was more pronounced than ever. Even Lofen and McKandles, who had ridden with him for turnings, could not seem to make sense of what had happened to the man. Angrily he stepped forward.

Rewen stopped the two from grappling again with a flash of blue-white fire that flared from her hands as she spoke, blinding them momentarily. "Now I may have some peace. Deros, come ashore with me, and help me gather some of the things I need to renew the workings that have kept the Thistle Cloud from the sight of those who have no need to see her."

Deros was looking at the two warring young men, who stood stock-still, gazing away into nothingness. "What have you done to them?"

"It's a simple spell from my old days in Trew. It is harmless, and simply holds them bound for a moment or two. When they come out of it, they will be groggy for a bit, but none the worse for wear. I hate to use my power in such a way, but any more of this squabbling would shred my nerves. There is enough to think on without these two constantly baiting each other."

"I've never seen Owen this way. He's almost like a stranger."

Rewen smiled and held out a hand to her young friend. "Can't you see that you've put stars in their eyes? This endless posing is for your benefit."

Deros blushed, looking away. "I don't know what to think. I wish they would stop."

"I don't think they will do that. They will become worse and worse, until something happens to send them one way or another."

Deros thought quickly of her feelings for the two young men, and grew confused at the tumult that raged there in her heart. To change the subject she asked after Jeremy and Hamlin.

"They are below," replied Rewen. "The last of the spell's unworking is sometimes the most painful, and it leaves its victims in a stupor for a while. It would seem to them they have been on a week's march without rest."

"Did you ever study the spells that Astrain used?" asked Deros, a sudden curiosity arising in her. "You seem to understand them."

"All of the basics are the same," answered her friend. "There is no difference in any of the workings at all, except the use you put them to. Astrain once held a seat on the Council of Windameir, and was as welcome there as any of the others. Gingus Pashon was a friend of all the Elders, and was known to have been a close companion of the Bruinthors."

Deros looked confused at the information, and shook her head sadly. "What happened? How could someone go so wrong?"

Rewen paused at the railing, ready to climb into one of the waiting skiffs. A crewman from the Marin Galone stood waiting at the sweep, ready to take them ashore. "You know, I'm not so sure they did go wrong. There was a time when I was ready to accept any quick explanation of something that ran that deep, but I have had time to contemplate the problem more, and I think I have come to accept the fact that sometimes there are things we are asked to do that are beyond explanations. Without the revolt of the Dark One, and Astrain, and even Gingus Pashon, we wouldn't be living these lives on Atlanton."

"It would be a lot less hurtful," suggested Deros, thinking of the battles that had raged across Eirn Bol since she had been a little girl, and all the pain and anguish she had witnessed since.

Rewen smiled, dropping lightly into the skiff. "We will see what we can do to help keep the odds even. Moria and Dolcia will be renewed again, once they have managed to escape the stones' heart. That will keep them for a while, but it is not meant that they should vanish from these lower planes."

Twig sprang from nowhere and cartwheeled about the deck, finally landing beside the two young women in the skiff. "Twig hears the songs the stones sing! They can't keep the sisters too long, for they have the sweetness now, and will find their way home."

"Here you are! I thought you had gone ashore with the others." Rewen's eyes showed the tenderness she felt for the small man.

"Twig won't go there! He hears the old voices drowned beneath us, and they tell too many stories that make Twig's blood run cold."

"Even here?" asked Deros. "What do you hear, Twig? Are they bad voices?"

"Old voices, my lady. Twig hears a bat's wing on the wind, but it is not a bat! The voices cry out for vengeance, and call in terror. "Twig's eyes had rolled back in his head, and he rocked back and forth on his powerful shoulders and forearms.

The seaman from the Marin Galone had pushed his skiff off the side of the Thistle Cloud and began to steadily stroke the small craft ashore. Rewen sat in silence for a time, then leaned forward to whisper in Twig's ear. "Do the voices speak of the fireworms, my little singer? Are they hearing those wing beats again?"

"There is a dreadful hand that is trying to come for poor

Twig's heart! It is black as the Dark One's breath, and there are some here it seeks! Twig sees the Eye, too!"

"What's he talking about?" asked Deros. "Does he know something?"

"Twig knows things that would make no sense to us. I don't think even Twig understands all he knows. What he is speaking of here may have something to do with the Great Bend Broads. This was once above water, and a thriving settlement, even into the times when we first went into Trew."

"They would never listen to Twig and his friends when they came to tell them of the black eyes," chanted Twig. "Now they sleep with water as their blankets, and mud for their burial stones."

"This whole settlement was burned by the Freolyde Valg," explained Rewen. "We heard the terrible uproar, and came to assist the citizens here, but it was too late. Out of kindness, one of the Old Ones covered the ruins with this gulf, which is peaceful, as you see it now."

With a bump, the skiff ground ashore, and Rewen beckoned Deros to follow her. They left Twig with the crewman and set out at a fast walk toward a low hill, grown over with thick bushes covered in bright blue berries. To the south, the main force of the two ships sprawled comfortably in the sand, or moved about, talking among themselves. Deros recognized Stearborn and Coglan, and the three Archaelians, all in a knot about Lanril Tarben.

"What do you think of the new captain?" asked Deros.

"He is what he says he is. Coglan is one of quick judgments, and they are usually true to form. I place no doubt upon the man, in spite of what the young horseman says."

"If you know Ulen is dangerous, why do you continue to leave him alone? Wouldn't it be better if you simply kept him prisoner, or took the ring from him?"

"That was part of my real purpose for coming here, little

sister. There is nothing ashore here I need to repair the harm done to the Thistle Cloud. I saw these sweet late berries. They are the favorites of our good Tirhan. His mood will lighten once he sees what we have brought him."

"But how can you do anything to keep Ulen from harming us further by coming here? Wouldn't it be better to leave him under the spell he's in now?"

"If that remained, the Eye in Blor Alhal would know of it, and it could force an immediate move on the part of the Hulin Vipre. I have listened to the talk of the Rhion Stones, and I have found out there is a plot afoot in the very palace of Lacon Rie to overthrow him, and to move in force on Eirn Bol. Somehow the Collectors there have managed to free some of the firesnakes from their prisons, and call upon them to spearhead the invasions of the Black Hood."

"You know this as truth?" asked Deros, stopping to look at the beautiful young woman.

"It is true. I brought you here to tell you the news. It is no longer safe to discuss our plans while the bold Master Scarlett is about, for he has fallen to the Eye."

"Then Owen has been right all along." Deros gazed toward the Thistle Cloud, where she could still barely make out the outlines of the two young men Rewen had left immobilized there.

"We must play this as I have set it up. If I let Owen take the ring, our chances will be halved. One of the points I have discussed with Coglan is that if the Eye thinks we are being controlled by the ring Ulen wears, they will not mark the Thistle Cloud for destruction by the firesnake. That would allow us to reach Eirn Bol safely."

"But if you are able to renew the words on the Thistle Cloud, how would anyone be able to see us?"

"The low dragons are half blind, little sister. Tirhan had

it right when he called them bats. They have ears that are sharper than their eyesight. And they are able to smell living flesh from high above. Even when I am finished with the Thistle Cloud, there would still be great danger for us to be afloat upon open water in the presence of one of them. Better to have all the cover we can muster, from whatever quarter."

"I fear for my father," confided Deros. "We have no such protection at Cairn Weal. Lanril has said they have burned Fionten, and other ports. If the Black Hood has gained an ally in the firesnake, then all may be lost before we reach Eirn Bol."

Rewen had reached the first of the berry bushes, and plucked a handful, which she handed to Deros. "You forgot your father is the steward of the Alberion Novas. They have specific bellreams to be read to protect his subjects from the dragon, as well as any of the other vile creatures the Collectors may call to send in an attack."

Deros shuddered. "Are there other things they can call? I thought a dragon would be the worst."

"The low dragons are the remnants of a higher order that once ruled below the Boundaries. They still control the Upper Gates. There are other beasts that have been left below here that the Dark One has created to help her in her revolt."

"We have seen some of her work in the Ellerhorn Fen. It was awful to see."

"She takes a soul like that of any of us, and slowly twists it until there is only darkness there. There are many kinds of terror she uses, but they are all frightening."

"Twig said he knew a name that would keep a firesnake away. Do you know it?"

"Tirhan was with the Elders who sent the low dragons back into their prisons. It is possible he may recall some of those words. I know no names, but there are other protections." She held out her hand to Deros, and moved the Rhion Stone slightly. "We have this."

"But Ulen has the other ring. How could that help us?"

"All the Rhion Stones are a single entity. They were found together in the very beginning, and given to all those who sat on the Council of Windameir. When Gingus Pashon left, he took his ring, which we now see a part of. He was clever enough to know he would never get another, so he had the Dark One cut it for him. With two rings of their own, they would have a way of spying on the Council, and to further their own designs."

"You mean the ring has been tampered with?"

"You see how large the ring I wear is. Ulen's is but part of its size."

"Won't they know there is another Rhion Stone here? If you can hear them speak, can't they do the same?" Deros was staring at the calm, still face of the red stone, and suddenly felt very afraid.

"There is a possibility of that, although the stone Ulen wears is much less powerful now, since it has been cut. And there is a protection that is within my ring, which is the fact that the Council of Windameir still wears their stones, and they are all tied to mine. It would be very difficult for the Eye in Blor Alhal to break through that combined strength. What they hear or see of us is much diminished, although we do want them to hear and see certain things."

"So we are bait in a trap? Won't Ulen simply tell them the truth, if he is under their control?"

"Ulen doesn't know the truth. He will tell them what he knows, but that will be what we want him to tell them."

"Do Stearborn and the others know this?"

"They are learning it now, from Coglan. We are only two days' sail from White Bird. If the weather holds, we shall be there soon."

Deros gazed across the long sand beach toward where the others were gathered, still talking. Coglan had removed his cloak and tunic, and sat bare-chested in the late afternoon sun, which was still very strong. A few of the others of the group had stripped to loincloths and gone in for a swim. Twig sat in the skiff, small and silent, watching the wavelets roll onto the shore. The breeze had shifted from a gentle southerly blow, swinging around more to the east, and Coglan was suddenly on his feet, looking at the sky. She could not hear his voice, but she saw that he motioned to the others to get back to the boats, and made his way toward where she and Rewen stood on the low hill, nibbling at the late season berries. He cupped his hands, and Deros was barely able to make out his voice.

"We must get back! The wind is shifting! There may be a blow coming!"

Findlin and Lorimen were encouraging everyone to hurry, and there was concern in Coglan's voice. Deros looked to the sky, but saw only high, thin clouds. As they sat in the skiff on their way out to the Thistle Cloud, Deros handed Twig a handful of the berries she had gathered in her cloak and watched his eyes light up. They were almost to the anchored vessels, when clouds darkened the eastern horizon and a faint promise of winter rode down the wind, even though the sun still shone. Deros shuddered, but she could not tell if it was from a chill in the air, or some deeper feeling within.

Twig gazed anxiously over the gunwale of the skiff, peering down into the depths of the water. "They tell Twig many stories now. He can hear the bat wing on the wind!" He turned to Deros and Rewen, his mouth covered in the blue juice of the berries. "Twig wants to be away from here."

As they climbed the rope ladder to the Thistle Cloud's deck, Coglan already had the crew raising the sails and hoisting the anchor. As it came up from the clear, shallow water, Twig gave a muffled cry, and hid his head. The others turned just in time to see bleached white bones fall from the anchor and splash back to their hidden resting grounds.

"A bad omen," muttered Findlin. "It's not wise to anchor a wessel where the dead lie waiting to be disturbed."

"The salt sea is full of the bones of sailors, and you travel on its back all your life," said Coglan, trying to cheer them up. "The poor devil was just coming aboard to warn us."

"We're warned," said Lorimen. "And now it would be a grand thing to hawe a head start on this piece of weather down below the horizon there."

As the others stowed gear and secured the deck, Deros noticed that Owen and Ulen had recovered themselves, and were no longer on deck. She went below to try to find them.

The Conductors of

Quineth Rel

In the gray depths of the stone beneath Blor Alhal, there dwelled the sightless one who lay silently in the dark night of that eternal, frozen mind of Quineth Rel, the Dark One. She had eluded the Light, and the attempts of the Circle to banish her from the Lower Meadows, for she knew the Law, and knew that she was one of the constants that kept the balance on those planes. Chaos would follow if they tried to run the Lower Boundaries without her, and she knew that. That she tried occasionally to take those Lower planes for herself was understood, and no one dared oppose her, until she was once more threatening the existence of all.

Salun Am and Jatal Ra had served her long and well in the island realms of the Hulin Vipre, and it was these two servants who carried forward her work there, which would release her from her prison and set her free upon Atlanton once more. The cursed Keepers had tricked her into exile, and skulked away, thinking she was through and could be kept from fulfilling her destiny in the Lower Meadows. The trail that had been blazed by the stalwart Gingus Pashon in the old days had lifted her heart, and the temptress Astrain was yet loose, so it was the dawning of a new round of victories for the Dark One, and many opportunities were ripe for the plucking.

Softly, so softly Jatal Ra could barely discern the sound from a noise in his own head, Quineth Rel called from the deep stones beneath Blor Alhal. A slow, blurred coloring of green haze crept over his vision, and he had to stop for a moment to regain his balance. Lacon Rie, the aging Emperor, was struck speechless, and grasped at his heart.

"What is it?" asked Salun Am.

"Silence! It is Quineth Rel! Repeat your sayings!"

The other man fell to his knees, holding his hands tightly clasped to his head, and began to mumble a pattern of sounds over and over.

"I hear you, O Favored One. Speak to your servant and Conductor, Jatal Ra."

A bitter wind whipped through the stone hall where the three men had been arguing, scattering parchment and pens, and howling through the corners with a noise that sounded like souls in agony. From that sound came the voice of Quineth Rel, frozen and hard. Her two ministers' hearts quailed at the icy hand that gripped them, and as the green mists faded away into the flickering lamps that lighted the dim room, they both prostrated themselves upon the cold stone floor, repeating the name of their mistress.

After a time, Jatal Ra came to himself. "We have much to do."

"How will we carry out her orders?" questioned Salun Am. "It is impossible to kill him here! That would seal our own deaths!"

"We won't need to kill him," replied his companion. "We shall let those closer to him do the work for us." A cruel smile split the man's lips.

"You mean someone of his court? They would know we would be at the bottom of any plot."

"Not if they don't know it is us. We have friends in Blor Alhal who are ready for a change. The war against Eirn Bol has gone on and on, and no one profits, except Lacon Rie! The rank and file of the Black Hood find themselves food for worms. There is not a family in this realm who has not had a death because of Lacon Rie."

"It is not his fault that Cairn Weal has not fallen," protested Salun Am. "I do not favor the man, and will be glad of his death, but I have to give him his due." He looked at the pitiful sight of the ailing Emperor, who had fallen helplessly against the stone table, trying to support himself.

Jatal Ra dangled the small bell temptingly toward him. "I'll give him his due," growled Jatal Ra. "We have been very close before. We were very close last night in Norith Tal. If we can raise the Paluge, we can have our way soon enough. Lacon Rie is not strong enough to resist us now that his son is away, and likely lost! Tien Cal would have thwarted us, but Baryloran is not the man his brother is. We will use him for our own devices."

The old man's eyes flared helplessly, and he made pathetic motions of trying to draw out a dagger he had at his belt. Jatal Ra let him struggle awhile longer, then easily took the weapon from the palsied grip.

"Go easily there! The young whelp has been staying late with that mad seer of his father's. Mortus Blan has enjoyed the protection of his king for all these years, but he knows his time is running out. There is word he has been teaching Baryloran those old parchments."

"They are fools fit for one another," said Jatal Ra. "They can read those worthless hides for all their power. Nothing has come out of the parchments since the death of the priest and all his acolytes. They were out for their own interest, along with the Seventh Shield."

"They took their toll on the rest of us," reminded Salun Am. "It does not take much of a memory to recall the debacle at the Sealith Landings."

"That was before we had control of our powers," snapped the other man, wrapping his cloak about him angrily. "They would never dare to confront us now." He was fondling the dagger, looking carefully at the markings that decorated its handle. "How like the arms of the Purple Cloak this looks! It might be one of the Emperor's own guards could be in league with some dastardly spies, and has murdered him in his sleep."

Salun Am shook his head. "They would never accept that. It rings too thin."

"Then we might have found his grace here in the great Norith Tal, struggling with the recall of the Lost Fire, and he was overcome in his weakness. It would be a grand gesture, sacrificing himself that way in trying to help his beleaguered subjects to reach their destiny in overwhelming Eirn Bol."

The Emperor's eyes were stricken with repulsion and horror, and he struggled with his failing limbs to reach out and strangle Jatal Ra. "You fiend," he gasped. "I have let you live too long!" His old, withered hand touched the throat of Jatal Ra's cloak, then fell away, as the old man bent double, gasping for breath.

"This might serve," agreed Salun Am. "But I would not like to leave the book out for any to see. What if they took it?"

"Who would dare touch it?" asked his companion. "They would most likely call his Ministers to deal with it. After all, who but the Conductors would know what to do with such a thing?"

"That might answer," mused Salun Am. "It is a fragile thing. He is old, but he is still the Emperor. There will be questions. What if they find out we have tried to poison him with the plague?"

"Accccch," hissed the old man, tortured beyond endurance, his eyes bulging from his head and the veins standing out across his brow. His color had deepened to a fiery scarlet, and he slowly sank to his knees on the cold stone floor of Norith Tal.

"Look! See how well he answers our call! Dying upon cue, like the good fellow he is!" Jatal Ra bent down to torment the helpless old man, who lay gasping for breath, his face already beginning to turn blue.

The wind outside had risen again, and shook and rattled the loose stones of the tower like a dog shaking a rat. Lacon Rie was dragging himself slowly along the floor, the breath rasping painfully past his tortured lungs, with his Minister walking mockingly beside him, holding out the small bell.

"We shall find it better for us if we are seen far from here tonight," suggested Salun Am. "This might be a good time to seek out the wench who reads the bones with the Arbon Players."

"You surprise me," laughed Jatal Ra. "Just when I think you have lost your mettle, you come upon the most astute plans." He leaned down to the old man, whose face was a deformed mask of rage and fear. "With your leave, your grace." He laughed, then opened his hand to reveal the small, blackish lump. "I shall throw the Nod a bone while we wait," he said. "No logic to letting a chance like this slip by. We have no room for error now."

Salun Am backed slowly away, watching in horrified fascination as the strange creature took shape again, and heard the desperate cry of the helpless old Emperor cut short as the deadly wraith sucked all the life from the withered lungs, and left the pale corpse still shivering on the cold stones of the Norith Tal.

Going by ways that were unseen by any others in the great fastness of Blor Alhal, the two Conductors of Quineth Rel made their way through the labyrinthine passages that ran through the keep, until they finally emerged into the main square, lit by flaring rush lamps protected by eaves of the buildings and the circled wagons of the Arbon Players. Even before they entered the low hut near the stables, the two murderers heard a drunken voice call out for the woman to read the bones again.

Broached

The wind had come up steadily all the rest of the afternoon, until by dusk the waves in the protected gulf were running in short, choppy swells, making the Thistle Cloud pound and shake as she drove through them. The Marin

Galone was close aport as the two ships reached toward the open sea. Twig sat glumly on a coil of rope at Coglan's feet, staring back over his shoulder at the shore they'd left, and reciting bits of songs in a language no one but the helmsman could understand. Spray blew over the railing of the boat as she buried her shoulder into the rising waves, and collected on the small crippled man, giving him the appearance of an old, bent form gone completely gray. The creaking and twisting of the timbers grew louder, and the wind in the sails howled and threatened to blow away the foresail until Coglan ordered the sails reefed, and shouted out orders to take in all canvas save a small mainsail.

Rewen came onto the afterdeck, looking about her at the growing storm. "Will we be able to make open water before dark?" she asked, shouting to be heard over the racket of the wind and sails.

Coglan shook his head. "At this rate, we'll be ashore off Great Bend Point before the night's out!"

Twig still sat hunched beside the helmsman, and now turned his ancient yet childlike face up to Rewen. "Twig hears the rocks calling! They are hungry for the bones of this ship."

"They will be hungry for a long while, my good scoundrel. The Thistle Cloud was not meant to be the meal of any reef or rock on this seacoast."

"They cry for us," went on Twig. "They are waiting now. It will be dark soon, and there is nothing to keep us from their white jaws."

"We can try reaching into the old harbor at the entrance to the gulf," Lorimen suggested. "There is a safe hole there from a blow from this quarter. It's that or sail out to the South Roaring, but we could run for a week before the storm, and we can't afford the time."

The wind piped up stronger, and a low line of rain

squalls skittered close down to the horizon, making the dark skyline even darker. Spume was everywhere now, and the decks were awash. To port, the Marin Galone valiantly tried to keep pace with the Thistle Cloud. Lanril Tarben came to the starboard rail, and was shouting to Coglan, but the wind carried his voice away, and only the sea roar could be heard. At last, he signaled his crew forward, and the ship bore away from the wind, and began a run back toward the narrower channel where the River Line emptied into the Gulf of Great Bend.

The captain of the Marin Galone raised a hand to salute them, then the ship was bearing away down on a broad reach, trying to keep her footing in the sloppy seas.

"Where will they try for?" shouted Findlin, shielding his eyes against the driving spray.

"I guess they feel their chances will be better in the river mouth," returned Coglan. "There they can run her aground without too much damage and ride the storm out."

"Maybe that's what tack we should take," said Lorimen. "Better to play safe than lose the wessel. The old port isn't much of a target to shoot for in this blow."

"The Thistle Cloud won't let us down, good Archael! She was fastened by the hands of the Elboreal, and given special consideration by the Council when she was launched. There are tricks to her even I haven't had time to find out about."

"The only trick I am interested in her doing is fetching the old port in one piece. If she does that, she has the undying dewotion of this old salt. I'll newer say more, but ship ower on her for her next woyage." Lorimen bowed to the helmsman, and pulled his hat down firmly over his eyes to keep out the flying spray.

Deros, below decks, had found Owen curled into a bunk. Jeremy and Hamlin were in the two berths next to him, looking white around the mouth and trying desperately to hold on to their heaving stomachs. There was no sign left of the animals they had been transformed into, and only a faint trace of a feral smell clinging to their clothing.

"You look the worse for wear," she teased, hoping to cheer Owen up. "I thought you would be immune to such a human failing as being struck with water sickness."

"I'm not sick from the boat moving," he insisted. "Rewen's spell has caught me short of my stomach. I'm still groggy."

"You were lucky that was all she did. The way you carry on would tempt me to leave you under some binding from now until we reach Eirn Bol."

Owen rolled over and sat up on the edge of his bunk. "You simply amaze me! The one person who has been the most responsible for your having come to harm since we met him at Emerald's wedding has been that upstart braggart from the horse riding! Now you make it seem as though *I* were trying to create trouble with an innocent man!" The young man's exasperation got the best of him, and he could find no more words.

Deros smiled disarmingly and turned to Jeremy. "We seem to be making good way now. I think I will join the others on deck to find out how it stands. Come with me. The open air will make you feel better, I'm sure." She directed her invitation to Jeremy and Hamlin, and left Owen scrambling out of his berth to go with them.

Spindrift

As Owen followed the others onto the deck, the shrieking wind caught him and almost blew him back down the companionway. He could not face the wind, for the blown spray stung his skin and eyes. He heard Coglan shouting but could not make out all the words. As he turned to once more try to locate where Deros had gone, Findlin was suddenly beside him, shouting next to his ear, "They've lost the foretop. We're trying to get all sail off her and steer through the channel to the Roaring! Bear a hand forward here!"

Owen struggled to follow the nimble Archael as he worked his way to the foredeck, but twice had to grab the shrouds to stop himself being washed overboard. He clung on for his life, and his stomach lurched sickeningly as he saw his feet dangling above the angry whitecaps with the deck nowhere in sight. In the next moment, the Thistle Cloud righted herself, and he banged his knee painfully on the railing and found himself scrambling on all fours, following the barely visible form of Findlin.

When he reached the foredeck, he had barely time to grab a fallen boom when an enormous wave crashed aboard, blinding him momentarily. There was the dreadful roaring of the sea, and the agonized protests of the boat, with splintered wood cracking, and canvas ripping, and the hollow, almost inaudible cries of the sailors fighting for their lives. Owen was treading water and clinging with tired arms to the boom. As the wave crested high above the boat, he saw it a stone's throw below him, moving away, and then it was gone in the trough of the sea, lost to sight. When he realized what had happened, he held on tighter to the boom.

There was nothing about him but the roaring and crashing of the water. He kicked, hoping to propel the boom back toward the ship, where he could call out for help.

He gave up that at the next cresting of the wave, for he looked quickly about as he rose near the top of its movement and hung suspended there for a long moment or two; no matter which quarter he turned to, there was nothing before him but the face of the raging, empty waters. The wave flowed on, sinking back to the surface, and Owen's hopes sank with it. The full consequences of what had happened began to dull his consciousness. Memories of his mother and father flashed before his eyes, and he knew immediately the end was near, for he had always heard that a man's life passed before his eyes when he arrived at the moment of his death. He saw the beautiful settlement of Sweet Rock as it was when he was a boy, and would ride the forests and hills that ran alongside the River Line. Deros, dressed in her boy's disguise as she had been when he had first met her, stood beside Stearborn at a campfire on a far-away morning. That picture was replaced by the beautiful young woman he first knew her to be in the underground world of Trew, and when he had first discovered that he felt differently about her than anyone else. A great pain began deep inside him as he floundered on, and a sense of loss that was too much to bear hammered at the lovely memories. He contemplated simply letting go of the boom and sinking on into the deep water, into its peaceful arms.

Then his heart raced, for a dark specter suddenly carried

away all the pleasant thoughts and beautiful visions he had seen. It was the beast within him, the Olgnite curse which slept below the surface of his everyday being, but which could be called up if he were weakened or tired. The old blood-red world came back to him forcefully, making him cry out for Ephinias.

As the raging water carried him on, locked into its powerful grasp, Owen saw, or thought he saw, a flash of light through the darkening twilight, and every time he came up high enough on the crest of a wave, he frantically looked about for the tiny splinter of light wedged into the side of the growing gloom, and in every instance, he caught a momentary glimmer of it, twinkling faintly like a star from the heavens that had been dropped into the angry sea.

At first he thought it was the Thistle Cloud, but soon he realized it wasn't moving, so it could be nothing other than a light onshore. Owen knew there was no hope of those on the boat rescuing him from the dark waters. The Thistle Cloud had been driven on, leaving him behind in the turbulent sea, with nothing to hold on to but the broken boom and whatever courage he could muster. The light that faintly glimmered through the wild night was his beacon, and he imagined himself making progress toward it by kicking his feet. Later, when the clouds had gone and the moon had risen, he saw the first of the ominous triangle-shaped fins cutting through the frothy water, circling about him. Instinctively, his hand let go of his hold to reach for the sword from Skye, and his heart fell and his mind was numbed with fear when he realized that it was still beside his bunk aboard the Thistle Cloud. He had no knowledge of what these things were that were now all about him, but he knew that things dwelled in the vast water that were far beyond his imagination. Something bumped into the boom. Something down there, gliding through the darkness with an evil intent, was testing, torturing him before the attack.

Then the creature surfaced, and he shuddered in horror as he saw the beast. Its large mouth gaping, with row on row of terrible white teeth, smiled a death smile at him. It turned to make another circle about him. Owen felt another hard bump through the sail sling, and a blinding fear overtook him. He tried shouting, but found his voice was hoarse and weak, and he beat the water as vigorously as he could. A mouth, rowed with sharp teeth, suddenly appeared out of the dark water, making straight for his arm, and he was barely able to move it out of harm's way before the great beast flashed by, its black eye rolling and following him until it disappeared beneath the waves again.

Owen's stomach felt full of gray, cold lead. He could think of nothing to combat this horrible beast. The thought of drowning with its peace of simply slipping beneath the waves was suddenly and thoroughly wiped away, and all he could think of was how horrible it would be to die, devoured by this cruel thing which stalked him so relentlessly.

Another large wave lifted the boom up, and as he surfed along the edge of its crest, a faint noise, not of wind or water, but one like the sound of a reed pipe trilling, began to force its way into his awareness. He noticed that the light that had been so far away before was now much closer, and cast out throbbing bands of silver-white light that shimmered over the dark face of the sea and made the whitecaps appear to be dancing with the wind, flowing and coiling away until they were beyond sight.

Without much hope of response, he called out, barely audibly, "Ephinias? Gillerman?" His voice was carried away by the surging roar of the sea, and he felt another bump as the monster patrolled beneath him.

The reed pipe music came again, frayed at the outer edges of his hearing by the wild report of the wind, which blew the spray into a low, white mist, stirring over the wave tops like a sandstorm in the desert. Owen thought of a great, vast wasteland then, dry and drawing the moisture from your body in the heat, the wonderful heat. It would be high midday, and the sun would beat down relentlessly, but he wouldn't complain, for he was so cold now. If only the sun were up, he thought, it wouldn't be so bad to die, even if it was to be devoured by a monster from the depths of the Roaring Sea. At least he would be warm at the last. The sun also might send the beasts back to sleep somewhere at the bottom of the deep waters, to float in their horrible dreams of blood and gore, dreaming whatever a monster from those depths would dream, of eels, and rays, and the skeleton-dancers of long-perished men swaying below in the rhythms of the sea, caught in the seaweed and wreckage of a thousand ships. Owen was sure he was dying now, and that it was all a part of his mind unraveling, dissolving into the madness and illusion that came with death.

"Great Bruinthor's Shield, the lad is babbling! Is this the wart on the log we'll have to work with?" It was a clear voice, strong enough to be heard over the roaring of the wind and sea.

Another voice replied, "It is as written in your journal, if you haven't forgotten. 'The one who comes as spindrift is destined to be the apprentice of the Council.' We shall have to build a fire to dry him out, I suppose. It won't do if he catches his death before we get him properly going."

"It will have been a long time since a fire showed in the old port. That might mark a passage in our journal that could signal a turn in the tides of Atlanton."

"There is already a journal entry that notes changes, since the return of the old terrors that once stalked these Lower Plains. The cycle is growing full, and it is high time our young apprentice has showed up."

"I didn't expect him to arrive this way," replied the

deeper of the two voices. "They could have had the decency to have brought the lad in aboard the boat, rather than dumping him unceremoniously like this."

A laugh, clear and bright, followed, which both surprised and cheered Owen. The wind and waves were still high, and the storm seemed to have grown stronger, rather than abating, but Owen was beyond it now, his mind concentrated on trying to hear the voices. He had hardly noticed that the bumping below him had increased.

The light now penetrated the depths of the dark water, making the sea afire with its white brilliance and turning the spray into tiny candles blown on the wind. It was suddenly as bright as midday, and Owen had to squint against the gleaming, shimmering, terrible beauty of it. He felt the boom he clung to lift, and there was a sensation of skimming over the wave tops. That light followed him, with the brightness of the moving day like torches being carried through a dark valley, until with a shuddering jolt, he felt solid land beneath him and blinked in surprise as he found himself upon a wide, sandy strand, where the waves washed him farther and farther up the beach, beyond the grasp of the huge, looming maw of the frightful monster which had stalked him. He lay still a moment, hardly daring to believe the reality of it, and finally, trembling in every part of his body, he crawled on his hands and knees until he was far enough away from the surf to risk lying down and resting. He only meant to stop to catch his breath and try to see where he had gotten to when the brilliant lights were extinguished as quickly as they had appeared, and he was left once more in a deeper darkness than before. But there was solid earth beneath him, and he could smell the deep, rich texture of the soil, and his hand grasped the tall, thin sea oats which covered the dunes behind the beach.

Man Overboard

Findlin tried to grab hold of Owen as the wave crashed over the bow of the Thistle Cloud, but he was swept roughly across the deck, to crash against the mast. When the Archael regained his feet, the foredeck was swept clean of men and sails, and by the time he was able to find his voice, there were other cries all along the length of the boat, shouting, "Man overboard, man overboard," a call that chilled all mariners to the quick every time it was heard.

Coglan was at the helm of the Thistle Cloud, trying to bring her round to face the next rogue wave. Rewen was beside him, struggling to help him hold the foundering craft. The shuddering blow had knocked the boat sideways and almost flat in the water, but she found her keel and bobbed upright.

Coglan regained control of the helm and looked to see where they were. A vast, whitecapped world stretched away in all directions, and toward the open sea, a solid wall of frothing breakers crashed and rolled on the shallow rocks and ledges. "Stand to, lads! We've got to pinch in a little closer if we're to clear that point!"

The exhausted crew watched with bated breath as they neared the line of white water that marked the breakers at the outer entrance where the broad bay ran on into the open sea. The wind howled and tore through the rigging with such force they knew the ship would not stand much more, even though it was a craft built and launched by the Elboreal. Findlin and Lorimen stood beside Enlid, and all three of the Archaels watched first the tortured ship's motions, and then the terrible white jaws of the rocks that lay stretched out, reaching to devour them.

"She's going to make it!" cried Coglan. "We'll be clear in another gust!"

Ragged cheering went up from the tired crew as they watched the sleek craft claw her way past the waiting rocks, and on into the larger, more even swells of the South Roaring. The darkness was falling rapidly, and the red crack in the clouds along the horizon cast an eerie, ominous shadow of light over the wild sea. Rewen turned to Coglan then to speak, but Findlin hurried to stand beside her, his face pinched and old.

"We hawe had men owerboard, my lady," he said, searching for the words to tell her his terrible news.

"I heard the cry," she replied. "Who have we lost?"

"Owen," said the weary Archael. "He was coming forward to help me secure the foresail. One of the big wawes took him right from under my nose. I looked and he was there, and when the water cleared away the second time, he was gone."

"Are you sure?" asked Rewen. "Is it possible he's made his way back here?"

"We'we had a roll call, and he's gone. So have three of my own lads, rest their souls."

Rewen turned to the dark face of the sea, and shuddered. There would be no hope of surviving a gale of this force without help, and there could be no rescue attempt made until the storm let up and there was daylight to help them. Deros had appeared out of the companionway, and saw the stricken look of her friend.

"What is it? What's happened?"

"It's Owen," replied Rewen, leaning close to make herself heard over the roar and crash of the wind and sea.

"What about him?" Deros saw the distraught looks of Findlin and Lorimen, and guessed the worst.

"He's overboard. We can't go back until the storm lets up and we have light."

"Then you mean we have lost him. There is nothing could survive this." The young woman heard the news numbly.

"We shall come back when we're able," said Coglan. "Now, we must sail for our lives, if any of us are to survive. I know the point is where we lost him. We will come back and crisscross the bay and shore. If he's lasted the night, we'll find him."

There was nothing more they could do. Rewen sent word forward for all hands to batten down what they could and go below. Coglan had the vessel under control, and he was attempting to run before the gale, hoping it would blow itself out during the night. As Deros went down the companionway, Ulen Scarlett appeared beside her.

"There is a rumor that Helwin is gone overside! I see now the injustice he had done me, accusing me as he did! The fates are a better judge of character than mere humans, and I have been vindicated!"

Deros felt the numbness begin to slip out of place, leaving her with an empty spot in her stomach, and there were tears very near. "He would not speak of you in such a way. If you can think of nothing kind to say then don't speak of him."

"That is the best advice I have heard concerning him. The sooner he's dropped from our conversations, the better, my lady."

Ulen's face had hardened, and she sensed something else different with his features, which still retained a familiar

look, although he seemed to have aged greatly since he had
been wearing the ring with the Rhion Stone. McKandles
had come down next, followed by Lofen, and both men
ignored their old leader, going straight for their berths.

The Apprentice

The sound of the reed pipe came again, soft and lilting
over the pounding roar of the surf, and Owen lay with his
head cradled on his arm for a long while, listening. Sometimes it sounded like the steam from the teapot boiling in
the kitchen in his old home, and at others like the wild
drumming of the Line Steward's war drums, when he went
with his father to inspect squadrons. He could almost taste
the oatmeal that he had on those mornings when he went
with his father, and half expecting to be once more in his
own bedroom, he opened his eyes.

Or tried to. They were sealed shut with salt spray that
had dried and crusted on his face, and he could not open
his lips, for they were coated with the salt, too. Sand was
in his nostrils, and he got up with a cough, blindly groping
his way around on the beach, stumbling over a clump of
sea oats and falling painfully onto his knees again. He
managed to rub his eyes clean by taking off his shirt and
using it for a rag, and after ripping away parts of the tender
skin on his lips, he was able to open his mouth.

At first his vision was dim and unfocused, but he at last
could make out that he was on a long stretch of sandy

beach, covered with a waist-high plant that grew everywhere, and that the storm from yesterday was moderating somewhat and there were patches of bright sunlight that shone through the gray cloud cover as it blew away, fluttering on the breeze, where high up, the white tips of the clouds spread across the sky like unspun wool from his mother's wheel. As far as he could see in both directions, there was no other living thing, and no sign of any fresh water to slake the burning thirst he felt. Little by little, he realized that he had been spared death in the sea, only to be washed ashore on this barren spit, where he would surely starve, or die from thirst. He sat on the ground and sobbed. Then he heard the reed pipe again, lilting faintly above the roar of the surf.

He sat very still, trying to detect the notes again, and finally, when he could not hear the soft music, he convinced himself it was his fatigue and hunger which had created the small pipe, and that it was simply a trick his battered senses were playing on him. He had redoubled his crying when the sound came again, this time much more plainly, and much nearer to him. In spite of the pain at doing so, he opened his eyes and glanced about him. He noticed a small dot on the beach near where he had come ashore. It looked to be more flotsam blown up with last night's storm, but he had not seen it earlier, which made it all the stranger. He argued with himself for a full minute or two, debating whether or not to exert the energy in going to explore the thing on the beach, but finally his curiosity got the better of him.

Swarms of nasty, stinging small flies, swirled up from the sand as he walked. He was so preoccupied with slapping the vicious insects that he almost missed the craft, so small it seemed a child's toy, that lay there at his feet, carefully moored to the beach by a line and anchor. He barely avoided stepping on it.

A violent jolt surged through his foot, causing his knees

to buckle in pain, and he looked down. A small man, dressed in a brilliant green shirt and red trousers, and with a yellow cap that sat jauntily on his head, stood by the boat.

"I'll take it off the next time, you dolt," the small man informed him, brandishing his sword again. "It has bitten the life out of larger fellows than you!"

Owen knelt in the sand, leaning down closer to peer at the man, who was no larger than his own hand. "Who are you, friend? Why do you attack me?"

"I attack any who try to squash the life from me! You'd do the same if you were in my boots."

"I'm sorry," said Owen contritely. "I didn't mean to. You can see what shape I'm in. I was washed up here ashore last night in the storm, and my companions are gone, or sunk. That was what was on my mind. I would never go out of my way to hurt you."

"Poor excuse for seamanship, being out in that weather," proclaimed the small man. "We had put up for safe haven, until we heard the call that there was a castaway here. No thanks to you. I would have been away down toward the Easting Isles, and many a happy day I've spent there, too."

"You haven't given me your name, sir," went on Owen politely, hoping that the small man would have water and provisions in large enough quantity to satisfy his growing thirst and hunger.

"My proper title wouldn't fit your tongue, but you may call me Politar. The Welingtron legends are full of the tales of my kinsmen, and there is many an enemy warrior who would wish he had never crossed steel with me."

"Do you have water, Politar? I am very thirsty. I don't think I have had a drink since going overboard."

"Plenty of seawater to slake your thirst," shot the small man. "All you have to do is look about you."

"It's salt," replied Owen. "I can't drink that."

"What? You can't drink perfectly good water? Where do you hail from that you are unable to drink good water?"

"The Line. I am a freshwater man. I am not able to drink brine."

Politar shook his head and removed his cap. "This takes the cheese for anything. They send me off here to lend a hand, and then I find out the great oversized lout doesn't drink brine." He slapped his cap back onto his head angrily, and stalked back to the tiny boat which lay just beyond the surf line. "If it's not one thing, it's another. It's been the same since that firebreath has come out of the east again. I'll swear it's times like these that would send you for a Wallbar, and be glad for the change."

"What's that?" asked Owen.

"Preserve me," shot Politar. "I can't believe you've never heard of the likes of the Wallbar!" He harumphed again, and went on with his search of the boat, tossing things about until he found what he was looking for.

"Here," snapped Politar. "Take this. It doesn't look like it'll fill your craw, but we have had good results with it in the olden days at the Middle Tops. There were louts there even bigger than you, and they seemed to have their fill from it." He held up a tiny flagon of a shiny metal that caught and reflected a fleeting piece of sunlight.

"There couldn't be anything in this," protested Owen, bitterly disappointed for his thirst was growing.

"Just hold your jaw flapper until you've heard me out. Hold to it, and watch!" The tiny man drew a circle in the air with what looked to be a twig, and pointed toward the minute object in Owen's hand.

In the blink of an eye, it was transformed into a large metal flask that forced his hand to work to grasp it. There were odd bits of runes all about the middle of the band. A smell of fragrant flowers came from it, and the soft splash of waterfalls could be heard inside. As Owen lifted it to his lips, he saw there was a brilliant sun in a cloudless sky inside the bottle, almost as though someone had painted a picture on the bottom of the flask. As he held it closer to his eye, he was shocked to see that the sun was real, and a pearl-colored conch shell floated upon the clear blue water there, with another figure much like the one before him standing in the center of it, dressed in a flowing white cape.

"What is this?" Owen gasped, holding it away from him.

"Now he asks what manner of help is being offered," shot Politar. "The nature of you overgrown lugs escapes me. They have confounded me for as long as I've been upon my duties here, but I never cease to find amazement in such new and astounding revelations as I'm faced with on occasion. You said you were thirsty, and now you won't drink. Look at the matter fairly, and cooperate if you can!"

"I'm willing to do so," argued Owen. "You've told me nothing, and offer me something that grows out of a tiny nothing into my hand, and now I see there's something in the bottle that shouldn't be!"

"Shouldn't be? Shouldn't be? Great Jowls of Nebar, don't you know anything at all?"

"Not of this nature. I know of many things that Ephinias and Gillerman have told me of, but I have not seen workings like this before."

"And they told me you were to be the one," groaned Politar. "I should have known before I came it would turn out in this fashion. The Council has had it in for me since I came back upon duty here, and now they're determined to have my wits dulled by pairing me with a dolt as thick as a Gralomite boulder!"

Owen had taken the flask away from his eye, and cautiously put it to his lips. A vision of the tiny form inside slipping into his mouth stopped him, and he held it away again. "If I drink, will I swallow what's inside?"

Politar shook his head in defeat. "It beats me how one can run so contrary to polite rituals. The lout doesn't say thanks and drink in gratitude! He stands there asking questions of his benefactor and dying of thirst."

"I don't want to harm anyone," said Owen defensively. "I only asked to make sure."

"The flask is for drinking, you stubborn lug! Please indulge!"

Owen wanted no further permission, and greedily turned up the shiny bottle and drank until he was quite certain there would be no more liquid left in the flask. "That was good. Thank you, Politar. I feel like I might survive now."

"You'll survive, all right. It's not as likely that I will, being appointed to be your guide for the next while. I've had difficult cases before, but I don't think any of them ever reached these epic proportions of failure that I have standing before me now." The small man harumphed himself into a knot and sat cross-legged on the sand.

"My guide? Where are we going? And how are we to do it? All I see here is the wreckage of a boom and your boat. It's not even as big as a shoe!"

Politar mumbled under his breath and got up, walking stiff-legged to stand at the bow of the tiny vessel. "You'll not call the Wind Rhyme a shoe, you ungrateful lug! You'll taste more of my steel if you persist!"

"I mean no disrespect, Politar. It's as simple as looking at it that will tell you I wouldn't be able to fit aboard!"

"Why do you think I gave you the bottle, my quick-witted friend?"

Owen looked at the shiny object in his hands, and began to feel a queer sensation flowing over him, causing his face to flush, and his heart to pound. "You've poisoned me, you wretch! You won't live to gloat, by my oath! I'll grind you and your vessel into matchsticks!" He struggled to take a step forward to do as he threatened, but abruptly found himself face to face with Politar, who stood back, laughing.

"Now, that's more like it. Down to even keels, and no more to say about grinding anything into splinters, without the fact you'd have to go through my swordplay to do it!"

His head spun, and a thousand hot needles seemed to be puncturing Owen on his arms and legs. The sun seemed to brighten, then dim. His heart raced so fast he couldn't breathe to reply to the man who stood over him, as tall as Stearborn, or Emerald, or Chellin Duchin.

There was no question about it. He had shrunk!

The
Welingtron

A Student Once More

Owen looked in wonder at the size of the boat, which towered above him now. Politar, too, had grown in stature, and looked to him to be the size of Stearborn, standing before him with his hands on his hips. The tall plants that had come only to his knees before now swayed gently in the sea breeze high above his head.

"What's happened, Politar? What have you done?"

"You're a one to ask the questions," replied the man. "First you want drink and food, and then you stop to quiz me about how you've managed to get it. I think what you are going to need most of all, my lad, is a dose of good old-fashioned faith in the knowledge that truth is a simple matter, and if you're looking at it, then don't question it."

"But I've shrunk!"

"Of course, you have! How else would I be able to take you away from here? You said yourself that there was no way you could fit on my boat in your old condition."

"What did you give me?" asked Owen angrily. "Look what's happened to me."

"Exactly! Look what's happened to you. A Welingtron dram, common as flies. Not anything to get your dander up about. Simple to give, simple to take, and easily remedied. Once we're safely away, and snug in a pub in Delon Welsa, we'll see what we shall see about the end of it."

Owen paused. "Where? I've never heard of that. And I need to be with Deros aboard the Thistle Cloud when she goes to Eirn Bol."

Politar shook his head, smiling. "You would have been less than worthless to that expedition in your current state of mind. You are bound for Eirn Bol, but after a stay with us. There are things you must learn before you go on."

"I can't go with you anywhere but back to the Thistle Cloud! We are bound for Eirn Bol! Ulen is still aboard, and we can't leave him alone!"

"The Thistle Cloud is beyond the bay now. They were blown to sea in the storm last night. There wouldn't be much chance of finding them now." Politar softened his tone then, and reached out to touch Owen's arm. "The South Roaring is a treacherous place in the fall gales. It would be harder to find the boat out there than to discover the Malingtar Jewels in a dragon's lair."

"We could try," insisted Owen. "I must be there."

Politar had been watching the sky as they spoke, and he pointed to the horizon. "Look. It is coming up again. I had best find our way out of the bay, and begone. There is another storm brewing."

"Then I shall wait here for them. Give me back my size, and leave me!"

"I can't do that, lad," replied Politar. "The others are waiting for you. It has been a long time in coming, and now I've been appointed by the Council to deliver you, and deliver you I will.

"The Council agreed long ago that you were to join us. Your father was there when the decision was made. You have been too green until now. And all the things of youth had to be gotten through. But Olgnite hordes destroyed Sweet Rock, and now the spawn of the Freolyde Valg roam once more. Our time is short, and we must hurry."

"But can't we even try to find the Thistle Cloud? Rewen and Coglan will know how to get back here. If we wait, I know they'll come." Owen's mind clouded with fear at the idea of being separated from his friends aboard the other vessel. The thought of losing Deros and leaving her in the hands of Ulen Scarlett was unbearable.

"I keep trying to tell you, lad, that we shall reach Eirn Bol alongside the others, but you must first finish your schooling."

"Oh, no!" shot Owen. "I have finished with schoolboy things. I spent my time at books and lore in Sweet Rock, and that is long past!"

"These are not your schoolboy matters that you must attend to now," replied Politar, his face suddenly grown serious. "These are the things you must learn in order to be of help to your friends. Real help, not just some youthful fancy, my boy. These are Council matters, and you are old enough now to be seated with the others."

Owen remembered the fear he'd felt when his father had handed him the Cloak of Elder, and the grave weight that had borne down upon him. Again he thought of Famhart, and knew again the great toll those years his father had given as Elder. "Where is this place we are going?" asked Owen in a more subdued tone.

"Delon Welsa. It is a place you shall come to enjoy. And it is not far from where your heart yearns to be."

"But surely, if it is near Eirn Bol, we might wait upon our way and find the Thistle Cloud again."

"Unless the Lady Rewen is traveling by the same way we are, then we shall be there long before them."

"Wind is wind, Politar. I'm no seaman, but I have the common sense to know that much!"

"Wind is indeed that, my lad, but we shall rely upon the old Welingtron source of motion, and I dare wager you we'll be safe in The Goat's Folly by the sunset no longer than three days hence."

Owen had seen the sea charts from the Thistle Cloud and the Marin Galone, and knew there was no possible way they would be able to cover the distance in the time given by the colorful figure before him.

"How could that be, Politar? The distance is too great, even with winds that blew behind us all the way!"

"You keep speaking of winds, but it is not the wind which will drive us." He spoke a short, curt word, and raised his hand, as though he were going to tip his cap. From the water's edge, there came an army of eels, brilliant green in color and almost as long as a man. They were powerfully built, with thick necks and broad, flat tails that were shaped like the heads of a battle-ax. Owen fell back in fear, remembering he was unarmed, and unsure of what came next.

"You have no need to shy away from the Welingesse Fal. They have been our allies for as long as we have dwelled below the Silent Sea. They have saved your Eirn Bol on more than one occasion. You should be glad to make their acquaintance."

"You said 'below,'" pursued Owen. "Below the Silent Sea!"

"What? Oh, well, of course, my boy. The Welingtron have always been below. That is our country, and our passion. There were others not so lucky, and had to go to the surface, but we have been lucky. It has been difficult in these last turnings, I can tell you."

"And these?" asked Owen, watching the great eels as they moved about in the surf, and at a sign from Politar returned to the sea, disappearing from his sight.

"These are our way home. They will propel us quickly and without interruption to Delon Welsa, where the Council is awaiting your arrival." Politar shielded his eyes and looked away toward the horizon. "We had best make our start. It will be blowing again by this afternoon."

Owen looked away in the direction the strange man was looking, but saw nothing but a line of high, white clouds and a low rim of darkness right at the curve of the sea. "How can you tell?"

"That is a thing you will learn of, Owen. You have gone through much, and have had many tests, yet you lack the knowledge of yourself that will mark you out as a member of the Council. The time has come for your initiation."

"My initiation? Into what?"

"You have carried your youth well, my boy, and have shown yourself to have courage and character. It is time you learned of the rest of the promise, and to take your seat at the Council of Keepers."

At that, Owen's face brightened. "Will Ephinias and Gillerman be there? And Wallach? I haven't seen Gitel or Seravan, either!"

Politar smiled slightly. "I don't know for certain who will be there, but I am sure you will be surprised. It isn't every day that a young man is brought into the inner circle of the Council."

"I would rather stay here, to see if my friends come back for me. If I had my way, that's what I would do."

"Would you say that even if you knew that when it mattered, you would be powerless to help them? If you stayed now and they somehow managed to find you, you would be of no use to them at the first confrontation."

"I could at least die with them! The Steward Code is

strict about that. You don't abandon your friends just because there is danger."

"Foolhardy and brave, lad. Would it not be better to have the time come and be able to step into the breach and deliver when they need it most?"

"That's what I'm saying! If you don't allow me to stay, how will I ever be able to do that? I can't help them if I'm not with them!"

"You can't help them simply by being with them now, Owen. There are too many forces at work now. You have heard news of the firesnakes. One has attacked Fionten and left it in ruins. The fleets are scattered all over the South Roaring, and the Straits of Horinfal. There are other reports of attacks all along the coast in both directions. And you have among you the other Rhion Stone, worn by the horseman from the Gortland Fair. Blor Alhal waits for the moment to strike. Lacon Rie is ill, and he has ambitious lieutenants who have used the old books to call up the Dark One again." Politar's face aged, and he looked out to sea, away in the direction where the bay met the open ocean. "These are times that will demand the best of all of us. Powerful enemies are gathering against us, and you must have all the means at your disposal to combat them."

"My sword is still aboard the Thistle Cloud," reported Owen, hoping that fact would sway the man.

"Just the point, my boy. You have carried one of the swords from Skye, and you know you can call it to you, yet in panic you forget."

Owen was about to protest, when one of the great eels surfaced again and called out in a strange, high voice. Politar listened, then said, "We have to hurry. There are reports of a fireworm not far down the coast."

"Then we shouldn't move from here at all. A thing that large surely couldn't see something as small as we are now!"

"You would be surprised by the notions of the Freolyde Valg. You never can trust their motives, and they will out-guess your best moves every time. I have had a run against one or two of them in my time, and it is my great good fortune to still be here to speak of it."

"How did you escape them? Did you slay them?"

"Slay one of the beasts? Now that would be a dandy piece of work, I can tell you. No, I merely relied on a ruse to escape. Sometimes they are overly greedy and would forgo the pleasure of roasting and eating you for the chance to add a new bauble to their hoard."

"Then there are ways around them?"

"If you think of that as outfoxing them. Not so lucky for those who have given up their secret troves, only to have the snake to return again and have them up, too. They are pure evil, and think in ways that are beyond us. Our natures do not run that deeply into the black arts."

As Politar finished speaking, a distant haze became apparent on the horizon. It was neither natural cloud nor sea mist, yet it seemed to be moving in their direction.

Owen pointed it out to his companion. "What do you make of that?"

As they watched, a great, roiling curl of blackish plumes rose upon the morning air, and a distant thunder rolled and rumbled, barely audible to their hearing. The great eels surfaced then, and beat the water with their tails, making a keening noise that set Owen's hair on end.

The Black Mist

The black cloud grew nearer, and the thunder rolled and rumbled. An inferno of smoke and ash swept over the coastline very close to the ground. In amazement, Owen watched as the terrible wind came ever closer, dipping over the water, where great spouts of steam exploded into the air.

Politar pointed toward the approaching fire and smoke, and the great eels disappeared again beneath the sea. Owen watched their white wakes as the great sea creatures moved straight toward the danger.

"What did you tell them? What will they do?" asked Owen.

"The Welingtron eels are descendants of the High Dragons. They sometimes are able to confuse the fire-worms. They can talk to them. That has come in more than handy once or twice in my past skirmishes with the Scourge."

"Won't they be fried? Does the firesnake really have the ability to breathe flames?"

"You haven't read of them? I'm surprised you don't have more of their history. Yes, they breathe flames. They have discovered the mountains of fire high in the old ranges, and devour the burning slag from there to keep their dangerous talents."

"You mean their bellies are full of fire?"

"It is something akin to that. What they belch out is gases from those fire mountains. I have not seen one myself, but I know well a man who has been there and returned, and lived to tell me about it. It is a terrible place, and nothing could live there but these beasts. They thrive on the blighted land, and travel out to find victims and baubles."

"Who would want to go to a place like that? What could they seek?" asked Owen, carefully watching as the black cloud rolled on toward them.

Politar snorted a short little laugh. "What any man would want if he were tempted to go into a hell's hole like that. Treasure! Pure and simple. There is no other reason for one to go there." His brows knit, and he thought a moment on what he had said. "And to reach nearer to the truth of the matter of all things," he went on. "Sometimes a man would go there for that." Politar turned a piercing look on Owen, studying him for some time.

The darkness of the cloud began to increase. Owen's heart hammered in his tunic, and he longed for the sword of Skye. "I wish you with me," muttered Owen under his breath.

In his mind he saw a deep, black night and a field of stars. As the vision faded from his mind, there was an old, familiar feeling in his hand, and when he opened his eyes to look, there was the sword, humming softly and glowing with a faint, white light. The scabbard was securely belted to his waist, just as if he had put it there himself.

"Just in time," said Politar, smiling. "Our firesnake is becoming interested. Look!" The older man pointed toward the huge winged beast, which was slowly lumbering into a half gliding turn and coming directly down the shoreline toward them. Owen could hear the heavy wing beats plainly now, churning the air into a dull roaring.

"Will the eels be able to turn it?" asked Owen, watching in fascinated horror.

"We shall see," replied Politar. "They have been good in

the past at this business, but I don't know about the spawn of this new Scourge."

Far out from the coastline, Owen saw a circle of the great eels, coiled and lying above the surface of the water, floating in formation. They faced the approaching invader with their heads raised and weaving, as if in time to some unheard music.

"What are they doing?"

"They are preparing to speak to the worm. Can you not hear them?"

Owen shook his head. "All I can hear is the wing beat of that thing, and the rumbling."

"Listen closer. Try to imagine yourself there with the Welingesse Fal. You can see their dance from here."

"I can see it, but what does it mean? Are they trying to appease that thing?"

"The Freolyde Valg are odd beasts. You can never be sure of what they're thinking, or what they'll do. Sometimes it is said you can lull them to sleep by singing a ditty they like, or whistling to them in the dark. Underneath all the fire and claws, their minds are like that of a small child who's been tormented into anger."

As the great leather wings swooped to dive, the beast bellowed out a roar, followed by a scalding black cloud that filled the air with a stench so putrid it almost choked Owen. Its huge talons extended, the beast suddenly halted in midair, its grotesque head turned toward the eels.

"It's heard the Welingesse Fal," whispered Politar. "They have spoken to it."

"Look! It's turning!" cried Owen, seeing the huge beast lumber awkwardly into the air, flying out over the waves to where the eels had their circle.

Another sound beside the leathery wing beats of the beast was heard then, very high in pitch, just on the outside edge of hearing. Owen's ears rang with the sound, and he discovered it was echoed by the sword at his side, which shot bright showers of light from its scabbard, and turned warm against his side. The beast's head began to sway from side to side then, and it lowered itself toward the eels, with its gnarled talons extended, emitting a screech of rage that momentarily deafened Owen. Without falling back, the eels went on with their ritual.

Owen thought the great eels were surely doomed, but the flying snake halted its dive just above the water, hesitant to go farther and looking confused.

"It's worked!" exclaimed Politar. "They've sung him the old Wylch poem about the Pentograf. It will work most of the time."

"What's that? What do you speak of?"

"An old rhyme about dragons by a man who slew many," replied Politar. "He lived in other times, where there were these beasts as thick as hogs in a farmyard. His music became his weapon."

"Was it that bad? Maybe Emerald has heard of him. What was his name?"

"They called him Minstrel, but his proper handle was Wylch, which means 'the seedling' in certain tongues from the olden days."

"His music drove off the beasts? He must have had other ways."

"His music was the key, my boy. Amazing thing, music. You would be surprised at what all it encompasses."

"Emerald always seemed to be sad about it," answered Owen, thinking back to his friend's odd looks at times when he thought no one was looking. "I've never thought much of music, other than as a way to tell a tale, or to put babes to sleep with."

"There is a secret key in the Well of Truth at the Heart of Windameir, and it is to fit that last lock that keeps us from seeing the Most High. It can only be unlocked by a song, sung or played as simply as this tune the Welingesse Fal are using against the snake."

"Can a human learn it?" asked Owen, very anxious to learn of anything that would drive away the monster that now lumbered about clumsily on great leathery wings.

"It is for me to teach you exactly that," replied Politar cheerily. "You ask all the wrong questions before you reach the one that pertains. The Welingesse Fal and I will be your tutors until we reach Delon Welsa."

"That will be well and good, if we survive the dragon," said Owen, still apprehensive. "He doesn't seem to be going away."

"The eels will lull him some more," replied the old man.

Owen noticed for the first time the old man wore a gray tunic beneath his other more colorful clothes, and had an oddly designed pendant that was barely visible at his throat. He was curious about the object, but was stopped in midsentence by a motion of the older man's hand, and he found himself back at his full size, towering over the tiny boat. Politar, however, had grown with Owen.

"We will have need of our other forms for this confrontation," he explained, seeing Owen's bewildered look. "You would not be able to call upon the full powers of the sword if we remained small, and that may well be what you shall have to do. My friends do not seem to be able to send that worm back where he came from." Politar pounded his chest and shouted out in a tongue Owen did not understand, although he saw it had a profound effect on the flying beast.

Whirling in a cumbersome motion of beating wings and belching fire, the cruel monster turned and bore straight down upon them, its jaws opened wide to reveal rows of razor-sharp teeth, and spewing small fires that smelled of sulfur and old places below mountains that had not seen daylight or fresh air since their beginnings. Owen grasped the sword from Skye, and began repeating the names of Gillerman and Ephinias, and in the next instant, the blade burst into its own white-hot flames that scaled his skin and forced him to close his eyes.

"Hold it up, lad," admonished Politar, shouting from somewhere nearby. He called out again, but a savage roar knocked him backward, and a heat so unbearable it forced him to cry out raged all about him. Owen was on the verge of passing out, for he could not get his breath in the blazing oven that exploded all about him, when the sword began another noise, a faint song that reminded him of something that Emerald used to sing.

The last lingering thought he had before the blackness closed upon him was remembering a faraway glade where he would sit and listen to the minstrel singing softly as he looked across the fire at Deros, her deep blue eyes a vast mystery to him.

Another Gale

The sky in the distance continued to blacken, and Coglan stood at the helm, his brow drawn into a worried frown. They had come about after the storm had died down the night before, and attempted to beat back into the gulf where Owen had been lost, but now the threat of a new storm worried him. He turned to Rewen, pointing.

"I see it," she replied. "It does not look to be a short-lived storm."

Findlin, joining them on the afterdeck, agreed loudly. "I'm fond of the lad, and would do anything within my power to see us safely back to search for him, but it won't do Owen any good if we sink ourselves in the wenture! These gales come up like this in the Werges, and I doubt we'll see another two days of good weather running. We'd be better off to put in to White Bird, and bring back an expedition owerland."

Coglan had been gazing at the approaching storm intently, watching it form. "That's not all nature there," he said at last. "There's a look of one of the fireworms to that blackness."

Twig, sitting on a coil of rope beside the helmsman, rose on his powerful forearms. "There is the hot coals of the fire mountains there, good friends! Twig can smell its breath, and hear it hunting!"

"Then it is impossible to think of going back," muttered Lorimen. "If we keep to our course until White Bird, then we can see what's to be done from there."

Stearborn had come up from below, with his lieutenants behind him. He asked Rewen what had happened, and was answered with her pointing in the direction of the storm. "It is one of the Freolyde Valg. It is following us now."

The old warrior gripped the rail of the Thistle Cloud tightly, studying the darkened horizon. "I never thought we'd see their likes again."

"Fire and destruction, that was the promise," chanted Twig, making his face a pale mask against the dark.

Deros stood beside Stearborn. "Aren't we going back to try to find him?"

"Through this, lass? Look for yourself. A storm is brewing again, and now we've got one of the flying snakes to deal with as well!" Stearborn clenched his jaw and shook his head. "No. The lad will have to find his own way this time. There is no help that can come from us."

Deros looked at him steadily for a moment, then snapped angrily, "Are you growing so timid in your old age? I have always heard that Stearborn laughs at danger."

"Mind your manners, lassie," returned the old warrior, his face grown dark. "When you've known the things I've known, we'll sit at table and trade secrets about what is courage, and what is not."

"Twig laughs at danger," muttered the small man. "What is left of Twig to hurt? And he knows the song that will hurt the firebreath!"

"There is no chance to go back now," soothed Rewen, hearing the heated discussion and going to stand beside Twig at the rail. "As soon as we are able, we will send for Owen."

"If we can't go back, then how will we do that?" persisted Deros.

"There are ways," answered Rewen quietly. "The Thistle Cloud doesn't have immunity to gales. We must go on to White Bird, but the Order still has followers all through this country who can help Owen."

Deros's face was flushed. "You speak as if his rescue is just a matter of time, and we haven't even gotten to White Bird or told anyone. And we can't go back, so it's pointless!" She was unable to go on, and Ulen put an arm around her to comfort her.

"He's run clear of other scrapes, my lady, with no more damage to him than an inflated sense of worth. We can't rely on him being gone this easily."

"It would suit your plans well," snapped Jeremy, "but I can't bring myself to believe that anything to further your cause would be so easily won."

"You judge me too harshly, my good Steward. I know you have never been fond of me, but you can't lay off any of this to me. Young Helwin has found his own way overboard."

"He has, at that, and no thanks to me." Lorimen held his hands stiffly at his sides as he spoke.

"It wasn't your fault," assured Rewen. "Any one of us could have gone over in that gale. The sea is generous in her call, and any may find himself in her embrace."

Deros was torn between wanting to reach Eirn Bol as soon as the ship could take her there, and the insistent emptiness that had begun with the news of Owen's disappearance. She had given no thought of going without him, even though she had pretended not to care whenever he talked to her of his going. Ulen still stood beside her, and she came to her senses enough to take his arm from her waist.

"We shall have a good run before this breeze," predicted Findlin. "With any luck left to us at all, we should fetch White Bird before nightfall tomorrow."

"By then it may make no difference to us," cautioned Stearborn. "The black cloud means a fireworm, and to be caught on the open water will only spell disaster for us. I have seen these beasts at their grisly work."

"You forget that the Thistle Cloud has her shelter back," reminded Coglan. "And Twig tells us he has a way to deal with the beast. It has been said a dragon may see things of fire and earth in the dark, but I don't think that vision applies to the things of the sea and air."

As he spoke, the sleek boat heeled over hard as the first gusts of the approaching storm hit. The crew lowered more of the sails.

Ulen followed Deros below, raising a voice of complaint. "We would have been far enough at sea if it hadn't been for that unfortunate Helwin! Even when he's gone, he still is a thorn in our sides."

"Don't speak of him," snapped Deros. "I hate you both! Leave me alone!" She stormed into Rewen's quarters, holding back her tears until she was alone. Once inside the small cabin, she threw herself on the berth and all the torrents of frustration and loss poured forth, until she thought at last she would not ever be able to stem the tide. Owen was lost.

She didn't hear Rewen enter the cabin until she spoke. "Are you all right, little sister? I thought you might be here."

"Oh, Rewen," wailed Deros. "I don't know what to do!" Her shoulders heaved, and she fell sobbing into the older woman's arms.

"We shall all have to do what we shall have to do."

Stearborn poked his grizzled head through the door. "Here, lass, we won't be having any of that now! It won't do Owen any good, and it sets the lads to wondering who will be next. Not a good thing to have going on in a war camp." His voice was gruff, but his eyes were gentle, and he reached out a rough hand to touch her. "And we still have our horseman to deal with, so we must look to our best face."

Rewen handed Deros a brightly colored cloth to dry her eyes, turning to the old Steward. "Our good horseman has been an unwitting aid to us with the Rhion Stone. They are listening in Blor Alhal, if I don't miss my guess. I shall have other information for them soon, which may allow us a clear passage of this beast that's behind us."

"What would rid us of that Scourge? Do those enemies of Deros control the worms?"

"After a fashion. I think they will want no harm to come to one who is wearing one of their Eyes. As long as they think the ring Ulen wears is still on the hand of the Hulin Vipre prince, they will call off the firesnake."

"You hope they can, my lady," replied Stearborn. "From all I know of the Purge, there is only one who controls them entirely, and that's the Dark One."

"She may have her own reasons for holding her spawn in

check. Her ambitious henchmen in Blor Alhal have sought to have the Alberion Novas for their own for so long now, they have forgotten that it is she who is driving them on. With them in her grasp, it would be a sad, lost wilderness here below the Boundaries, with no map or chart to guide any of us here back Home." Rewen looked at Deros sadly. "Our little bird was drawn into this at an early age, and there is no way out, except by defeat of the Darkness. It is the Reawakening."

Stearborn looked puzzled. "I have not heard that before."

"It is the time of the Dark One come again. Some say the Resurrection and Reawakening are one and the same, that it is the coming of Windameir back into the Lower Meadows, but if you study it more closely, it is the coming again of the Dark One, out once more to claim her kingdom below the Boundaries, and to hold all the lost souls here forever."

"I would need Chellin Duchin to spin me those tales, my lady. I am an old warrior, and don't know many of the yarns that there are."

"We all have our parts to play, good captain, and the more we know, the better we shall play them."

"Will you be able to get word to those you spoke of?" asked Deros, drying her eyes. "Would there be someone who could help Owen?"

Rewen nodded. "We have already spread the word to all those who are yet here. If he survived the sea, and is alive somewhere, then he has a chance of being found." Her eyes seemed to darken then, and a slight frown marred her beautiful features. "There will be others who will have heard my call, as well. It seems we all operate within the same heartbeat, although one is bent upon the destruction of the other."

"How do you mean?" asked Deros. "Who else would hear your call for help to the Order?"

"The Rhion Stones are powerful, and were given in good cause long ago, yet look at what use some of them have fallen to. It is the same with the Order, little one. The sisters we met on the river were once a part of our Order, before they fell prey to their powers. It is difficult when you have them."

"I think Owen found that to be true when he took the form of the Olgnite," agreed Stearborn. "And I'd swear by my own shield that lad is as good through and through as any still walking upon Atlanton!"

Coglan shouted down the passageway from the helm, calling for Rewen. Come quickly, we've company!"

His voice was drowned out by the rising wind, and yet there was another sound above that, dangerous and seductive, like a cry of pain or surprise. It came again, more plainly, and all who heard it felt their blood run cold in their veins, for there was no mistaking it, the unique call of the dragon, reaching out to them over the noise of the sea with its sweet promise of death and peace.

The Billows

Steam arose from the sea all about the Thistle Cloud, and a stench of rotten flesh was thick in the air. An unbearable heat had begun to burn through them, until it seemed their very skins would melt away, and the same voice, sickly sweet yet awesome, kept filling their ears. Stearborn, who had heard the voice and felt the beast in the terrible destruction of the Middle Islands, whirled into action, and had Jeremy call all hands to battle stations. Rewen was also familiar with the ancient Purge, and with Twig beside her began a chant which seemed to cool the ovenlike heat and drowned out a portion of the dragon's voice. When it sensed the power of the Daughter of the Altar and the ancient voice of Twig, it let out a deafening roar and belched a terrible stream of flames which licked all about the Thistle Cloud, although it did not set the boat aflame.

Rewen called forth another list of the Bindings of the Order, and the beast redoubled its frenzied attack, although it seemed unable to pinpoint the location of the boat, or to be able to do much more than terrify them with its eerie ability to cast its own thoughts into the minds of those below.

Another voice was raised then, which seemed to come from somewhere inside the depths of the water around the boat, or from the innards of the boat itself, and it seemed to be answering the dragon, and inviting it closer.

"Who is that?" shouted Jeremy, looking wildly about. "That's coming from this ship!"

"Get the horseman," ordered Stearborn. "See where he's gotten to!"

Rewen halted him with her hand, drawing him closer to her so she could speak into his ear. "We want him to let them think there is an ally aboard us. The fireworm can't see us, but he knows we're somewhere here. If he hears a voice, then he will think we are already one of the troves that belong to the Dark One."

Stearborn made a signal to halt the others from searching for Ulen. "Leave him," he whispered harshly. "It goes against everything inside me, but we must not endanger ourselves for nothing. If this stuffed cock can help us, even against his will, then we'll have it."

From above deck, they heard McKandles cry out over the howl of the wind and the compelling call of the dragon. His voice cracked and trailed off into a hoarse whisper.

"We're coming, citizen! Hang on, lad! We'll be to you before you can speak a name of the old Weryin clan," Findlin answered.

Lofen stuck his head out of the hatch long enough to call to Rewen. "I ain't ameanin' to dash no lamps ma'am, but we has Ulen Scarlett acallin' out for that there firesnake, and goin' on like he was shy of his wits! Kandles was atryin' to calm him down, and the beggar has done and stuck him! His own hostler for more turnin's than you could count on both paws!"

"What?" shot Jeremy. "What's he done?"

The frightened Gortlander opened his eyes wide, his face white. "He's done stuck Kandles! I has him out of harm's way, but Scarlett has come plumb aloose of his wits!"

"Bring your friend to me," said Rewen evenly. "We'll have him mended in no time."

"Yes'm," mumbled Lofen, bowing and hurrying away to fetch his friend.

"He's further gone than I thought," said Stearborn. "It seems the power of the red stones is too great to resist."

"For a small mind, or a heart full of greed," replied Rewen. "That is why they were not meant for any but those on the High Council."

"It sounds from your stories that they were too much for even some of those on the High Council," corrected Stearborn, seeing to his weapons.

Rewen nodded sadly. "Gingus Pashon, the Emperor of the Hulin Vipre, was not strong enough. The lure of Astrain was too much for him. It is not often that those things occur, but they do. That was long ago."

"But we still pay for it," added Deros. "They set into motion something that has not seen its end yet. Eirn Bol has been the force that has held the Hulin Vipre in check since then, but Cairn Weal cannot stand in the face of the beast forever."

"No, little sister, it cannot. The underlings of the Dark One have called back the Freolyde Valg. The Old Order called it the casting of the bones."

"Bones is what we'll be if we don't find some way to send this worm back where he's come from! He's scorched the sails, and it's too hot on deck to stay without cower," said Lorimen urgently. "Can we find some way out of here?"

"If the horseman is at his work, then we should see an end of this attack soon," assured Rewen. "Look." She held out her hand, showing the others the gleaming red stone on her finger, glowing white-hot now, and as they peered more closely, they could see the Eye of Blor Alhal searching for the voice that came from the other stone, now worn by Ulen Scarlett. There was a great sheet of fire and smoke across the face of the ring then, and in the next instant, the terrible beast hanging above the Thistle Cloud lifted away abruptly, its leathery wings beating up a dreadful wind that stank of burned flesh and sulfur.

"It's leaving!" shouted Jeremy, dashing up the companionway to stand by the rail. Coglan had returned to the helm, carrying Twig on his back, and they watched as the lumbering beast wheeled slowly away toward the north, fire and smoke trailing behind it in a gray, ashen wake.

"It's headed toward White Bird," he said grimly. "I hope they are ready for it."

"Is there no way to warn them?" asked the young Steward. "That thing is too much to fight without help."

Deros watched the retreating form of the dragon, her face colorless. "You might try to reach Linne," she said at last. "Or Elita. They would be able to hear you."

Rewen nodded. "I shall try to warn them."

"They have faced this spawn from hell before," said Stearborn. "They know what to expect."

The Thistle Cloud's sails still smoked from the malignant heat of the beast, and the decks were hot to the touch. Coglan wrapped his cloak about the tiller, and set the boat back on course.

"The storm is still with us," he reminded them, and a rising wind heeled the boat over, dousing the hot timbers with cold sea spray. A hissing steam went up.

When Stearborn looked again, the grotesque form of the dragon was lost amid the bigger clouds that now began to darken even more, and the wind's howl became a muted shriek through the rigging of the ship. As he turned back to speak to Coglan at the helm, Ulen Scarlett came on deck, his features wreathed with what appeared to be a murky fog, which played about him like a smaller storm within the storm. Twig somersaulted forward to place himself before the young horseman.

"Twig hears the Black Wind here! It blows stronger than this one that tries to sink Twig's boat!"

Ulen kicked viciously at the cripple, but Twig had moved in the blink of an eye, and was out of harm's way. Hamlin, seeing what had happened, moved to grasp Ulen, but Stearborn held him back.

"I see the ghost of an old Emperor," said Rewen, her voice calm. "Have you come to command us?"

Ulen's eyes were hidden, and his voice was strange, as though he were speaking in a stone room. "You are wise enough to prove dangerous, my pretty! Astrain shall have a lovely time, once you are given over to her. That will be a worthy entertainment to see."

Stearborn had drawn his sword and stood panting in anger, held in check by Coglan.

"You will obey me," snarled Ulen. "Or I shall call the Paluge back!"

Twig had moved unseen behind the horseman's back, and stood close to Ulen. In another instant, he had flipped himself into the air and clasped his powerful arms around Ulen in an iron grip. "Take the red stone! Take it quickly!"

Coglan leapt to grasp the horseman's hand, but there was a flash of reddish-green fire and Twig was dumped to the deck, grappling with thin air.

"He's there," shouted Jeremy, pointing to the helm.

Ulen's face was a grotesque mask as he pulled the tiller hard over.

A Voice of Blor Alhal

Ulen had grabbed a handrail next to the companionway and braced himself. An eerie greenish light played at the edges of his eyes, and his voice was that of a stranger. "You have seen the might of the Lost Fire, and now know what you face if you continue on to Eirn Bol. It will be useless to resist."

Deros placed herself defiantly before the horseman. "You may follow your old line of breaking off whenever something becomes too difficult, but I will never cease the fight until I have no life left!" Her eyes blazed.

"It will be a different matter if the Paluge comes back. You will not feel so plucky, my tasty morsel."

Stearborn turned to Coglan. "Who is the Paluge?"

"It seems someone else is speaking through him. He must mean the firesnake."

Rewen quieted Stearborn before he could speak again, and encouraged the young horseman to go on.

His mouth had turned into an ugly sneer, and his voice deepened. "We have the way to the Lost Tomb now. There shall be no stopping us when the gales of winter come calling upon Eirn Bol."

Deros lunged forward. Light reflected off metal clasped in her hand, and Stearborn reached out to stop her at the moment she struck out against the horseman. "Here, here, little bird! Your talons are too sharp for this job." He forced her hand open, and took from her the small knife he had given her so long ago. "My trinket would have found a sorry end if it had urged our good Gortlander's heart out of his tunic!"

"Give it back," Deros breathed haltingly. "He has gone over to the enemy!"

Rewen held out her hand. "Come below with me, sister. We have some things we need to speak of now. You will endanger us all if you continue to attack the horseman."

"He wasn't shy about astickin' old Kandles," shot Lofen shortly. "If I was to be athinkin' about what was agoin' on here, I'd say he's come plumb aloose of his cinch strap."

"Your friend is all right, citizen," assured Hamlin. "If it hadn't been for his thick hide, he might have had more to worry about."

A squall shook the Thistle Cloud, and Coglan brushed roughly by Ulen to take the helm. He ordered the others to get below, but the horseman stayed behind a moment longer before turning to the helmsman. "You would be wise to keep your course wide of White Bird. The Paluge is on his way there now." He let forth a brittle laugh, then disappeared into the hatchway, followed by Twig.

Coglan struggled with the rising wind, and was blinded by the blown spray and rain that washed over the boat's decks in growing waves, feeling the strain of the wind and sea through the tiller. He knew she was a strong boat, as fine as could be built by skill and craft and the special care of the Old Ones who had launched her for the Order of the Sacred Thistle, but there were limits to what even this vessel could take. The deteriorating weather was something that no ship nor crew could change. He ran farther off the wind, threading his way carefully between the canyons of water that rose and slid away beneath his keel.

Findlin and Lorimen had remained on deck to help him, and he called to them now.

"We're seeing one of the worst of the Werges' tricks," said Lorimen. "When the wind shears from south by east to north this way, we're in for a time of it. I've seen blows like this before."

Findlin nodded, helping Coglan steer. "I'we seen ones like this go on for a week running. No good place to be, no matter what your reason to trawel."

Coglan smiled bitterly. "We're in it now, lads, that's cinch sure. No place to run for but open water, and hope we don't find a hard bottom in between."

"There's clear water here, friend. It's not a matter now of ending up aground, but whether or not this wessel will hold together long enough to bring us safely back from a storm like this."

"The Thistle Cloud is as strongly built as a ship can be, good mariner, but you and I both know that most of what we rely on now is more of being in Windameir's hands. There is only so much a sailor or his ship can do."

"We're falling off a bit, mate! Try to keep her head up higher. These wawes are growing by the minute."

Findlin helped Coglan bring the ship's head a bit higher into the wind, and ran off down the back of a long, surging wave full of angry white foam. "We shall need another watch soon," he shouted. "We shall wear ourselwes down, and then that's when the sea snatches you! You can't fight her when you're asleep on your pins!"

"There is no second watch to call," returned his friend. "Ewery hand we hawe is above boards now doing what he can. If it blows out in the night, then we might hawe a chance."

Coglan strained against the helm, holding the boat's head up into another wave. "We'll be lucky if this moderates before morning. Help me tie myself here, and I'll stand this watch. You two try to get below for some rest, if you can. I'll send for you when I need to be relieved."

The two Archaelians surefootedly made their way below, where they were greeted by Stearborn, who was standing at the bottom of the companionway, his jaw locked stubbornly.

"This sets sore against my grain," he muttered as the two joined him. The Thistle Cloud was rolling wildly down the face of a wave, and they all had to grab hold of the railing to keep themselves from pitching forward. "I've seen some craven acts in my time of riding to a Steward banner, but these past days have set my teeth on edge!"

"Easy, friend," comforted Findlin. "According to the Lady Rewen, we hawe our own best interests here to think of. What does it hurt to let the poor misguided soul suffer a bit longer under the web the Dark One has caught him in?"

"If you mean to say we'll just let that fireworm burn and destroy White Bird by making no effort to reach there and warn them, then you've got a different road to walk than Stearborn! I have no quarrel with keeping the poor devil out of our plans for now, but the matter of my friends at White Bird is something else again!" His jaw tightened, and the veins on his forehead stood out as he struggled to control his anger.

Lorimen let out a short laugh that was without humor. "We'll hawe a time finding a road to White Bird in this weather! Ewen if we wanted to reach there, it's not likely this will let up anytime soon. I don't know how far a fire-snake will get in this, either, when it comes down to it."

"They would not be taking lightly to this," said his friend. "All the wet weather dampens their fire. I think ewen our flying stove will be trying to find shelter before this blow."

"They're not of nature," replied Stearborn. "But they may find the going difficult."

"Here's our horseman now! Let's hear what more he has to say of this matter," whispered Findlin. "Or what more from whoewer is doing his talking through him."

The gaunt features of Ulen seemed even more sunken, and his eyes were fevered, and he looked like a man recovering from a long illness. He held a hand to his head, but when he was addressed, he replied in his old voice. The other, from wherever it had come from, was gone for the moment, and Stearborn noticed that the ring was no longer on his finger.

Rewen stood behind the horseman, making a motion with her eyes not to speak to him. "We have McKandles comfortable below. He'll be all right."

"Not no thanks to some one particular here," sneered Lofen, looking hurt. "It wasn't no right thing to be adoin', no matter what. And if abein' stuck don't do him in, all this floppin' around in this here bucket will!"

"Better that we go on flopping around, citizen. Otherwise we'll be fish food. I don't know about you, but I would prefer being a little woozy to full of seawater."

"Well, you don't has to paint me no pictures," replied Lofen. "I hasn't never told no one that I was ahankerin' to be here awashin' around like one of my old dame's shirts in a tub! Why, I hasn't never had no call to be any nearer water than to drink it! I can't find no good use for any of it, 'cept to wash down trail dust, and to splash on after a long ride through rough country."

"Now we have enough of it under us to float us all the way to Eirn Bol, to help our young friend here. All we have to do is make sure we stay on top of it," said Stearborn.

Ulen Scarlett spoke then, in a faint voice. "You would be wiser to forget that plan. I have seen things. They are ready for us." His eyes were cast down, and he picked at his cloak absently.

"Can you remember any of it?" asked Rewen gently. "From the voice, or anything you saw?"

He shook his head. "It was so dark there, and there was something that smothered me! I couldn't see its face, but I felt it! And the voice. It was like facing something very dangerous in a pitch-black night."

"That sounds like his old self," offered Lofen. "What's been ahappenin' to him?"

"The ring," replied Rewen. "He has the fever now, and it won't be burned from him easily. The Rhion Stones take a grip on your soul that's more deadly than the grasp of a hawk. It will never let go once it has you in its power."

"Isn't there anything to be done?" asked Jeremy. "Couldn't you just keep the ring?"

At the mention of the word, Ulen's eyes turned to the woman, widening. "My ring! That infernal cripple has taken my ring!" He began to move weakly toward Twig, but the motion of the boat pitched him forward onto his knees, where he struggled helplessly. "My ring! It's mine!" He tried to regain his feet, but another lurching motion pitched him headfirst into a bunk board, and he fell in a heap. Hamlin and Judge put him roughly into an empty berth, trying to keep from losing their own balance.

"How did you get it from him?" asked Stearborn quietly.

"Twig tripped him when he came below," she replied. "I simply took it from his finger, hoping to revive him."

"Now that you have it, can't you keep it from him for a while?"

"The Eye would soon notice and report to those in Blor Alhal that someone else has taken it."

"But wouldn't they have known that Ulen is now wearing it, and not the Hulin Vipre who had it?"

"Ulen fell so quickly under its spell, it might not have been known by its masters. I think it's possible that they aren't sure about it. Indeed, I pray they aren't, for it is our only hope."

Storm Signals

As Findlin and Lorimen came on deck to stand their watch, the Thistle Cloud swung wildly, and water ran down the companionway. The Archaels managed to keep their footing and hurried to Coglan, still lashed to the wheel. As they made their way forward, the dark form of another vessel loomed close aboard on the starboard side, its sails torn and snapping in the wind, and for a brief moment, a face appeared out of the white spume. The helmsman of the other boat was so close that they could read the fear in his upturned eyes as the Thistle Cloud swept past.

"A boat," spluttered Lorimen. "That's why we nearly foundered. Coglan must hawe turned hard to miss her."

Coglan was drenched and exhausted, hanging on to the tiller with all that was left of his strength. Findlin took the helm as Lorimen helped the spent man to the companionway.

There were others waiting in the cover of the companionway to help Lorimen hand Coglan down, and by the light of the swinging lamps below, he could see the helmsman's drawn features plainly.

"It was the Marin Galone," Coglan managed, coughing. "She's out here, too!"

"How can you be sure it was the Marin Galone?" asked the Archael after telling the others about the ship they'd seen.

"You can't miss a bow shaped like that. Came up out of nowhere, and slid right by us on the starboard side. I thought we'd gone for splinters for sure."

Jeremy brought a mug of hot broth from the galley, and handed it to Coglan. "But they wouldn't have known we were here. I thought the Thistle Cloud wasn't visible to anyone."

"Lanril probably had no idea he came so close to ramming us," replied Rewen. "We must keep a careful watch for the Marin Galone."

"Go topsides, good captain," Coglan urged Lorimen. "Your friend could use your help now. I'll rest below here a moment, and be back."

Rewen had handed her lieutenant a small silver cup, which he took and drained the contents of, and after a short time, the color began to return to his face, and he appeared to feel stronger. He returned the cup to her, and laid his head back against the hull of the boat, closing his eyes. "I feel better now. I seem to feel the storm beginning to ease, too. I'd best go see to our course. I know the good Archaels are brave and willing, but this ship is a handful in these waves." His eyes met Rewen's.

"I shall try again to reach those in White Bird," she replied.

"Can I help?" asked Deros. "I know Elita and Linne well."

Rewen smiled. "You will be of great help, little sister." She beckoned Deros to her, and they went up the companionway quickly, followed by Coglan. In the distance, they could see the white wall of the heavier storm moving on away from them, billowing out upon the open sea like a flower opening against the darkness.

At the mainmast, Rewen stopped, turning to the young woman from Eirn Bol. "Think of your friends now as clearly as you can."

"Is that all I need do?" asked Deros.

"That, and pray that they hear us," replied Rewen. "It shall be a slaughter if they are caught unawares by the Purge."

Deros tried to quickly picture Linne and Elita, but found her concentration was interrupted by both the fear she felt of the hideous beast she had seen, and the loss she felt from Owen's disappearance.

The Welingesse Fal

The wind had shifted again, and a pale autumn sun peeked through the tattered clouds, beaming pale golden rays of light onto the sails of the Wind Rhyme, and turning the gleaming heads of the great eels a burnished green as they pulled the small ship along. A chill was in the air, but it was a promising omen. Owen sat on the foredeck holding a small, neatly bound book open on his lap, but he had not been paying attention to it, so rapt had he been with watching the strange beings who pulled the boat, and enjoying the respite from the storm. Before him, the entire broad gulf was a perfect picture of light blue water with small whitecaps. Politar came forward from the helm and sat down near him, watching the easy, rolling motion the eels made as they swam strongly toward the eastern horizon.

"You have been unseemly quiet, my boy. Do you have something wearing on your mind?" The old man's eyes met Owen's for a moment, then slid away to search out some distant point of interest far out over the gulf. Seabirds, the first they had seen since before the storm, circled above the ship, wheeling and calling loudly.

"I was thinking of my friends. In calm weather like this, we might come across them. The eels are moving us faster than we could sail."

Politar shook his head sadly. "I can see that you insist on

locking yourself into one way of thinking, my lad. That is the bane of this younger generation. I have always said that it is dangerous to know too much. You always manage to convince yourself of something that is not so."

Owen flushed angrily. "Whenever I speak of believing in friendship, or honor, or doing one's duty, I always get the same riddles in reply! Ephinias was a master at that."

"Then your Ephinias was well within bounds, where it comes to dealing with you, my impetuous young whelp. Part of my tutoring shall have to be to teach you to leave your emotions out of your actions. They can get you into deeper trouble than anything else in these Lower Meadows, especially if you follow them blindly."

"And what are we supposed to do with them?" questioned Owen hotly.

"Feel them," replied his teacher. "And do not take action upon what they dictate!"

Owen got up, tossing the book aside, and paced rapidly about the deck. "You and your Council go on about this as though you were ice. I hear what you say, but it is beyond me how you can expect anyone with blood in their veins to simply decide to do or be some way, and not have their heart to do battle with. At least I can understand the Steward's Code."

Politar smiled, looking beyond Owen's shoulder. "Your Steward's Code is an admirable way to live. There is nothing wrong with it, but it must be enlarged upon if you are to be of service."

"It is all I know," insisted the youth.

"And that's why there will be our little sessions. You must know many things that run deeper than these things that you insist upon knowing."

"Like what?"

"Like how you are to survive the Doom Fields, and

where you shall have to go to find out about Wylch, and the Pentograf."

Owen looked at him blankly.

"Those are for later, but they are questions that will surely have to be answered satisfactorily, and which will be critical to your success in bringing effective aid to Alban Ram on Eirn Bol."

The great eels had begun to emit the strange sounds again, and it seemed to Owen that they were raising their voices in a chorus of song, although it was like no music he had ever heard.

"They still hear the Purge," reported Politar. "They are singing a dirge for some poor soul, no doubt."

Owen looked about in apprehension, but saw nothing that would suggest the firesnake was returning. "I don't see anything!"

"The Welingesse Fal don't see it, either. Not as you would. They are watching inside."

"Inside?"

"Exactly. Where have you been, my boy? Didn't this Ephinias teach you even the first things about the levels?"

"The levels?"

Politar huffed himself up in indignation. "You are going to be even more trying than I first thought. I shall have to have a word or two with your tutor."

"I would be glad of that. Then I might find out about Seravan and Gitel, and where Gillerman and Wallach are."

"So they would be able to do your work for you?" The old man shook his head and wagged a finger at Owen. "That shall have to come to an end. They will not be able to keep on protecting you that way. An admirable trait, and they have had their reasons, I'm sure, but it will only make it harder for you in the end. The sooner we're quit of their meddling, the sooner you'll be free to really be of some use."

"I wouldn't call them meddlers," snapped Owen. "I wish they were here now. You might change your tune, then."

"I might, my intemperate pup, but not in a way you might think." Politar pulled a small pouch from his pocket and took a pinch of its contents, which sent him into a bout of sneezing. Owen watched in amazement as his odd companion held out the pouch to Owen. "Would you care for some of the herb, or did your tutors not teach you such foolery?"

"Why would you want to make yourself sneeze?" asked Owen, baffled.

"Why would you not?" countered Politar. "You must think about that, in order to get to the bottom of life, and how it's lived."

"Then it's not a question I would ask," shot Owen. "That's something that you may have time to think about, living as you do."

"And what would you know of that?" asked Politar quietly. "You have shown me so far that you know nothing at all of even the most simple tasks, and aren't aware of any of your power, or how to use it."

"I survived the Olgnite curse!"

Politar looked away, rumpling his face into a disapproving scowl. "Child's play," he grumbled. "More will be needed than that, when it comes to it. You have seen what the stakes are, and who we will be dealing with! You saw the firesnakes." He sighed. "I wonder how the coastal colonies will fare. Poor devils haven't seen nor heard these beasts in so long they may have forgotten how to deal with them."

"And how do they deal with them?"

"Cunning and luck," replied the old man. "And there were once warriors who were schooled in the arts of slaying those things."

"When was that? Would my father be one of them?"

"And your mother. In the Middle Islands, they were taught the why and wherefore of not hearing the beast's voice, for one thing. After its victims have listened to it long enough they are willing to be killed. The Dark One truly has their black hearts beating in time with her own."

"Its voice wasn't so hard to ignore," argued Owen.

"You were in the presence of the Welingesse Fal, and myself, and you have the sword from Skye, my lad. Those are three very powerful things, but only in a very temporary fashion, and we need solutions that will last for more than a day or two. That is why you must be schooled in the Doom Fields, which lay before the Plains of Grief. It is there we shall look for answers."

The names the old man mentioned sent shudders down Owen's back, and he turned away.

"There are no other paths for us now," went on Politar. "Our time is short, and the Dark One has made all her moves more swiftly than we anticipated."

"Will you be with me?" asked Owen hopefully.

Politar shook his head. "I will be at the coast with the boat. I am an old man, and would only slow you down on your journey."

"Will anyone go with me?"

"Whether there is anyone there in the flesh or not is beside the point, Owen. I can say that you won't be going alone, no matter what you see or think."

Owen paced away angrily, stopping amidships to look at the water sliding quietly by. "I ask simple questions, and all I get are riddles."

"They won't be riddles when you are standing on the ground ready to go," assured Politar, smiling faintly. "You will see your answers soon enough."

A faint humming from the sword was heard, and Owen hurried to where he had placed it in its scabbard secured to the mainmast. "Look, Politar! It's trying to signal! See the light?"

The eels hummed the same note as the sword until the hair on the back of Owen's neck stood out, and he was washed over from head to toe with chills and trembling. Politar had gone to the rail and was looking coastward, his face beaming. "So he shall come with us, after all," he muttered.

Owen overheard him. "Who shall? Who shall come with us?"

"The friend I mentioned. The eels are taking us to him now."

The Wind Rhyme turned slightly to port and made for a headland that jutted out into the blue water, leaving a small protected anchorage behind. Owen stood beside Politar as the great eels carried them rapidly shoreward, still filling the air with their eerie, strange song which made his heart race within him, until he was able to see plainly the stretch of beach that marked the shore along the land's outer breakers, and the small dot that was moving along toward the anchorage, leaving tiny dark footprints in the sand.

Torch of Darkness

Linne tossed and turned uneasily in her sleep. She was dreaming of her husband, a vague, disturbing vision of Famhart astride a horse he had ridden long ago, when they had been on the difficult march to the final battle in the

Middle Islands. As she watched, the horse became winged and leapt into the air, pursuing a dark shadow that loomed amid a huge black cloud that was split apart every few seconds by dull green lightning flashes. She tried to call out to warn Famhart, but her voice would not come. Someone else was trying to reach her, to tell her something, but she could not hear clearly what was said.

From somewhere far away, the voice was insistent, pulling at her, and she awakened with a start to look into the troubled face of Elita. "I am sorry to awaken you, my sister, but I have just had a dream! I am afraid we are in great danger."

Linne nodded. "I, too, dreamed of danger. Could you tell what was wrong?"

Elita shook her head. "Not exactly, but we should warn the others. I smell something in the air here, something from long ago. It is coming from the sea." Elita clenched her hands into tight fists. "I have lived in dread that this day would come. I had hoped and prayed it was truly over after Trew, but there has always been a part of me that knew we would face these evil things again."

"It is not likely that the Dark One would simply stay away. When we left the Middle Islands, I had that same feeling. When Owen was born and I settled into a quiet life in Sweet Rock, I had hoped that the troubles wouldn't come again in our time." Linne smiled sadly, holding out a hand to comfort her friend, who was kneeling beside the bed, crying softly.

"I have been burned by the dragonfire, and was healed by the Elboreal, so I have some protection," Elita said after a time. "Are there any others here who will be of use to us?"

"Famhart and I," replied Linne. "Stearborn was with us, but is somewhere on his travels with Owen."

"It's good he has gone with them. They will need a steady hand to see them through."

"The Archaels are good seamen. I have no doubt that they will be of great service." Linne rose, and fanned the banked fire into life and hung a kettle of water over it. The house was small and tidy, with whitewashed walls and a thatched ceiling, and furnished with a gaily painted wooden table, surrounded by comfortable chairs, which were carved with boats under sail. Across the front of the house, a long row of windows ran, opening onto a porch, which overlooked the nearby quays of White Bird. Linne pulled back the blue curtains and stood watching the scene below as she waited for her water to boil for tea. There was movement near one of the vessels moored there, and many torches were seen to come and go, making the area bright with the reflected light off the water.

"The elders of White Bird have been most kind to us since we have come. I hope we haven't brought the same misfortunes to them that we suffered in Sweet Rock."

Elita sat near the hearth, adding wood to the fire. "It seems sometimes that we have always lived in the midst of one terrible battle or another. When we came to Sweet Rock, I thought Emerald and I would build a house, and watch a garden grow, and learn to do those things that other people do. And now we have dreams to trouble us."

Linne poured the tea and handed her young companion a bowl of honey to stir into it. "Drink this. Soon Famhart will return from walking the perimeter, and we can tell him."

The sky outside had brightened, and only a few pale stars shone weakly through a tattered cloud cover. Linne walked to the window again, watching the waves roll in outside the harbor breakwater. She stood for some time that way, silent, and was on the verge of returning to the fire when she noticed something else, far down on the horizon, almost like a late star, glowing dully near where the earth and sky met.

"Come here and see what you make of this," she said finally, turning to her friend.

Elita followed Linne's hand pointing at the distant object, which seemed to move in their direction. A faint echo of horror sounded somewhere in her soul, and she began to tremble. "The Purge," she whispered under her breath, unable to tear her eyes from the fiery object that had grown even closer as they spoke. "We have to sound the alarm."

Linne's face hardened, and she turned back to watch as the firesnake neared White Bird. She remembered watching another of the terrible beasts sweep down from the sky across their armies as they fought to gain an advance toward the Dark Queen's stronghold. There had been so much carnage that day, she thought she would not live to see nightfall, but even against the monstrous firesnake, the forces of the Light had prevailed. She tried desperately to plan what defenses they could put up against this beast from the terrible armies of the Dark One.

Elita sprang for the front door, and ran quickly toward her own shelter, searching for her husband. "Call the others to arms! We must go from the settlement!"

Linne had just dressed and gathered her own weapons, when Famhart rode up at the head of a troop of Stewards and dismounted. "Have you seen the sky to the east?"

She nodded. "I had a dream. Elita, too."

Famhart strode into the small, comfortable room. "It seems we no more than find a dry place to shelter, and a fire to warm us, than the past catches up to us." He took Linne in his arms.

She felt his strength, and the sadness there. "But it is never dull, husband."

A Steward war horn sounded outside his window, and Chellin Duchin clambered noisily up the stairs that led onto the porch. Entering the room, he said, "We've seen it come about again, just as regular as a river tide growing following spring. I don't like the looks of this any too well, but we're going to have to deal with the beast now or later. The Senchal of the settlement has told me of raids up and down the coast by what they first thought were the raiders from the Out Islands."

"It wouldn't be hard to find a firesnake's trail," returned his friend.

"It would be, if you hadn't dealt with one of the brutes before. I don't think these folk have seen any too much of things of a violent nature. Seem pretty tame, by my reckoning."

"Anything short of a sword stroke has you saying the same thing, you old bowhog! That means I suppose we'll have to take them under our wing."

"They said there is a cave not far from here, big enough to hold us all. That might not be such a bad notion. I've no knowledge of this brute," confessed Chellin. "Save what I've heard Stearborn talk of at fire, but he left me no doubt that unless you know what you're about, you're most likely a roasted tidbit for their bellies."

The door opened, and Emerald and Elita came into the room with Port and Starboard behind them. "Have we decided what is to be done?" asked the minstrel.

"We're thinking of a cave," replied Famhart. "If it is big enough for us, and too small for the firesnake, then we may have a shelter."

"I wouldn't want to be roasted alive in a pit without a bottom," shot Port.

Before Famhart could defend his choice, a broadshouldered man in his late fifties blustered into the room. His head was balding, but his beard was bushy and black, and he carried the staff of Senchal. "My greetings, Famhart."

"You have my service, sir. We need guides to your cave, quickly. We have the most dreadful of the Dark One's servants almost upon your settlement!"

"Why can't we drive the beast off?" asked the Senchal, who went by the name of Cache Dunlin. "You have my village routed out of their beds in the middle of the night. Surely, we can put up a fight without a march to the cave!"

Port had stepped closer to the man, his eyes narrowed. "Have you ever seen the hide fried off a horse? Or a man burned and taken at a single bite, by teeth as tall as me and sharper than my blade?"

Starboard joined his brother. "These brutes come from the Doom Fields, and fill their bellies with the fires there. They love to torture anyone they find for the sport of it."

Cache Dunlin turned for support from Famhart. "I have no doubt they are dangerous, but shouldn't we show the thing we're armed, and that it had better find someplace else to forage?"

Linne stepped forward and took the man's hand in her own. "The good brothers do not wish to frighten you, good sir. They are simply saying the truth of these beasts, who are beyond wickedness."

"My wife speaks the truth, Cache Dunlin. If there are caves that we may seek shelter in, then we must be gone quickly. These things are deceptive in their ungainly flight. They appear slow and clumsy, but that is only one of their lures. They can be as fast as a hawk, and as quick as a cat, when they smell blood."

The Senchal of White Bird paled, and his voice trembled. "Then gather your clans. I will meet you in the Round Market as quickly as I can rouse my people." He hesitated a moment. "Could you send someone with me? To tell my followers about the beast? I don't think they will believe me."

"Certainly. Emerald, you have the best tongue for the tale."

"They will only think it is a minstrel's story," he replied. "Better to send Chellin, or one of the Brothers. There is no denying a soldier's report."

"Then Chellin, it falls to you. I hope you convince them soon, for if we wait much longer, that cursed thing is going to be right among us." Famhart strode to the window as he spoke, and watched as the dirty orange globe slowly neared the settlement. A roaring and crackling like the sound of a giant furnace reached them, and fiery sparks shot upward into the dark sky above the horizon, like so many signal torches on a field of battle.

Fire
and
Air

The Chalk Caves

A white scar ran across the face of the cliff, leading toward the small beach at the bottom, where the ocean boomed and rolled onto the jagged outcroppings in frothy white spume blown up from the great waves crashing to their death upon the rocks. Cache Dunlin stood motionless, looking for a long time down the precarious trail, then stepped out timidly onto the path, clinging to the sheer cliff wall for support. He turned to speak to Famhart, his livid features drawn in fear. "I've brought you to this old cave, as I said I would. I hope you're right about the danger from the firesnake."

Famhart had to shout to make himself heard over the wind and sea. "You will be looked upon as the savior of White Bird, good citizen, if you find us safe shelter from the beast."

Linne was behind him, looking over the sea, watching the red glow there become larger each minute.

She heard staccato pulsing of leaden wing beats and the hissing roar of the flames coming from the fiery insides of the beast.

A long line of people wound along the cliff top, and as the dragon came closer, there was a great panic among some of the citizens, who were near to going over the sides of the white chalk heights. The Stewards were there, trying to calm and encourage everyone, but the citizens of White Bird, long unused to warring and danger, were difficult to talk to. Finally Kegin fought his way through the frightened mobs to find Famhart, and to get Cache Dunlin to come back to speak to his own people.

"This has really got their blood up," he reported to his leader. "It looks as though they're going to put half the settlement over the edge of the cliff if they don't settle down."

Famhart called out for the Senchal of White Bird, and explained to the man what they needed. "The last thing we want now is a panic before the beast gets here. Listen, both of you. Do you hear anything? Anything speaking to your mind? It would be very sweet, and very subtle."

"No, sir. Nothing like that."

"You, Senchal?"

"I don't know what you speak of, good soldier. I hear all the obvious, and fret that I may not make my people understand what it shall take to save them. What else can I hear but their poor, pitiful cries?"

Famhart nodded grimly. "Good. It isn't the dragon yet. We'll know that for certain, once it comes close enough to us to speak."

"Speak? Do these monsters speak?" asked Cache Dunlin.

"They speak in a most horrible way, good Senchal. They become your thoughts, and speak in the depths of your soul. It is pure madness they bring, and as awful as the fiery breath they use to sear and burn, for their words keep you still while they devour you."

The man's eyes widened in fear. "Is there no defense? Are we all lost?"

"Not if we can get to cover in the cave before it arrives. If there are no victims ready to hand, it might settle for burning the settlement and torching your fields."

"Can't we do something to stop it? All our winter stores will be lost, and the fall crops will die in the fields!"

"Nothing to be done," said Famhart heavily. "If we might drive him away before he reached White Bird, or could lure him farther away, there might be a chance, but I see no way clear to do that."

"If Ephinias were here, he could do it," suggested Kegin. "I've seen him do as much before."

"Our good master is not among us. All we can do now is try to escape the beast. What happens after will follow, no matter what."

"It's easy to see what will follow if that worm gets here and finds us hanging like ripe fruit on a tree! We have to hurry!" Kegin's voice was tight as he looked over his shoulder to watch the progress of the beast.

From ahead on the trail, there was a cry, and the word was passed back that the cave opening had been found. "It's here, just as they left it in the old days of the Horinfal raiders!" The scout who had delivered the news ducked his head and disappeared into what seemed a sheer wall of rock about sixty paces down the trail below them.

"It looks as though it might work," said Famhart quietly. "The entrance isn't large enough for the beast."

"Large enough for its head," added Chellin dryly. "Roasted like lambs in a pit," he growled. "If there isn't somewhere farther in for us to go, he may not get to nibble our tender parts, but we'll be roasted just the same."

"Good old Chellin, always the one to look at the brightest," chided Famhart, although not without realizing the truth his friend spoke. He turned to his wife. "And you should go ahead now with Elita. There are a few things Emerald and the rest of us have to do aboveground here."

"You should let me come with you. I know as much of the worm as you. It was our combined front that held us through the dangers in the Islands."

"This is not as dire, my dear. We have one firesnake. It can't be as strong as those older beasts, and they were all drawn back to the Doom Fields."

"Bold talk, husband, but you don't fool me. I will take my place beside you, whether you will it or not. If we are to die, then I would as soon be with you. I don't think I would want to go on should anything happen to you."

Famhart hugged his wife. "You make it sound as though this might be the end of the road for the survivors of Sweet Rock, and the Line Stewards! It shall take more than this brute to end all this grand history."

"There's something coming through the Bernolt Wood, sir," reported a young Steward, who stood panting before his elder. "Look away to the north. See the light?"

There were odd flickers of red and blue, with occasional flashing bursts of a brilliant white, all too intense and bright to be cast from rush lamps or torches. Famhart's thoughts immediately turned to their old friend Ephinias, although he knew him to be gone beyond reach.

Emerald paced a step or two in the direction of the odd sight. "That looks to be some doings there. Are there any patrols left out, Steward? Anyone know more of the lights?"

"We're almost all back now, sir. The call was to muster here."

"Send a patrol back," urged Chellin. "I'll lead it myself."

"You won't go without me," snapped Port. "No lad of Trew is going to be left out of this sport."

"Hear, hear," seconded Starboard, rattling his sword up and down in its scabbard.

"Whichever one of you louts go, do it without any more mouthing about it! If it will keep you all quiet, then have at it. But look to it! The worm is making good time now." Famhart turned back to the Senchal. "If you can spare a lad or two, it would be good if my men had a guide."

Cache Dunlin called out two names, and the men hastily joined their elder. They listened to their instructions briefly and turned to the group of Stewards. "If you want to get to where the strange lights are, we must cross out through the Plower's Gate. It will take us out through the grain fields, and then we'll hit the Bernolt Wood. That's where the light is coming from."

"Hop to it, my lad," growled Chellin. "We'll have unwanted company if we don't step lively. I don't think we want to dance a line or two with that brute who's coming to try to cinch us up for his supper."

"I've heard that the worm will sometimes keep prisoners alive for entertainment," offered Port. "Play with them like a cat with a mouse."

The two citizens of White Bird turned pale. "If this beast is so dangerous, shouldn't we get to the shelter of the cavern?" asked one of them.

"Plenty of time, lads. The thought of the snake will keep us fleet of foot," laughed Starboard.

Cache Dunlin interrupted the men, pointing excitedly. "Look! See what's happened in the wood!"

Famhart studied the new development intently, his arm around Linne. "It's moved farther back," he observed aloud. "It seems to be drawing away from White Bird."

"I think that may be the purpose of whoever it is in the wood," said Emerald. "It's making fireworks that are sure to attract the snake. See how it's changed course since we've been here gabbing?"

The dragon seemed to be homing in on the spectacular lights that were growing still more brilliant and shooting high up into the night sky above the Bernolt Wood.

The companions stood still, watching for a moment longer. Then Famhart made his decision. "Let's get to the cave, good Senchal. Whoever or whatever is in the wood will distract our fireworm for a while. It might even be that your settlement and crops will be spared. Those lights seem to be getting farther off now."

Famhart moved down the path toward the opening of the cave below them. A steady line of settlers from White Bird, followed by Stewards and citizens from Sweet Rock, filed into the dark opening. Above them, and veering steadily away now, was the dragon, carving a fiery hole through the darkness, following on toward the brilliant lights that now were deep into the Bernolt Wood, moving steadily away to the west.

A Visitor from the Sea

As the Wind Rhyme neared the smooth stretch of white beach, the great eels leapt above the wave crests, performing an intricate dance of greeting for the small figure that waited there on shore. Owen saw the creature hurry toward the surf with an awkward gallop. "What is it?" he asked.

"Who is it, you mean, my boy! Who, indeed, but the

very act of kindness himself, and a talented storyteller, as well. I have spent many an hour with him on occasion, and every time our paths have crossed, I've always come away the wiser."

"That animal?"

"Yes! Exactly that! A remarkable likeness, don't you think?"

Owen, growing more confused by the moment, stared in amazement as the great eels of Welingtron performed their intricate rituals, and sent up the eerie, oddly moving music. The small animal was in their midst, frolicking and cavorting, and he felt an overwhelming desire to laugh out loud. His feelings bubbled inside him like a teakettle at boil, and he found himself at the rail of the Wind Rhyme, waiting to help the mysterious being aboard.

"Who is he?" asked Owen again, turning to Politar.

"You wouldn't know any of the names I might tell you," replied the older man. "It would be like naming the wind. You can't see it, yet you always know it's there, whether it has a name or not."

Owen snorted in disgust. "You sound more like Ephinias than ever."

"There are no straight answers to give, young man," said Politar rather stiffly. "If you would open up that cage you call your mind, you would be able to see beyond your own nose for a change!"

They had no further time to argue, for the small animal swam beside the boat, peering up from the sea through large round eyes, behind a slightly gray muzzle. Owen knelt to pull the otter aboard.

"Thank you," came the words, and Owen was slightly taken aback by the voice. "May your seas be kind, and your home fires warm."

Owen hauled the wriggling animal aboard, and was

thanked for his trouble by being thoroughly drenched as the otter shook himself.

After a hard scamper around the deck, the new arrival stopped to speak. "I've had a hard time finding you, old friend. I was south for a bit, but there was nothing there but rumors of the Purge. I came this way on a gamble that the Wind Rhyme might be exploring about for flotsam." The gray otter stood on his hind paws, looking directly at Owen. "Never underestimate the nature of water," stated the small animal cheerfully. "It might save your thirst, or be the cause of your crossing the Boundaries."

He scampered between Owen's legs, then perched next to Politar on the rail. "There'd be no crops without rain, no food to eat, no seas to sail or rivers to explore!" His whiskers bunched up, making him look serious. "And come to think of it, we drink it, and swim in it, and float on it, and when we cry, that's tears!"

"You certainly make a roundabout point, Beran, but you could properly introduce yourself to the lad before he begins to think you've lost your wits."

"Are you a friend of Ephinias?" asked Owen suddenly. "Do you look like this all the time?"

"He has mentioned this Ephinias in an endless string of accusations," explained Politar. "It sounds as if he's from the Council, but I don't know of anyone who goes by that name. It may be the one he uses below the Boundaries."

"He was fond of turning me into all sorts of animals," Owen went on. "Usually when I had no desire at all to do so!"

"Then he must be a very wise man to know so much," said Beran. "It isn't often you find a human with so much good sense." Suddenly he was a handsome man in his middle years, with salt and pepper hair and a mustache that had gone gray. He was dressed in simple clothes, fashioned of a cloth Owen had not seen before. There was a coat of arms sewn upon the chest. It was so brilliant, Owen would have sworn that the threads were real gold.

"So you do change into animals," muttered Owen.

Beran's eyes twinkled a light blue-gray, and his laugh was kindly. "Sometimes it is the other way about, my good pup. You may not have heard, but there are those who are true animals, but take on the human form when they need a mask."

"Well, Beran," Politar asked, "have you news for us?"

"The young one's friends are safely on the way to where they need to be," said Beran softly. "And you're to take him to where he should be quickly."

"If that's not Eirn Bol," said Owen peevishly, "then it will be far from where I should be. Politar has told me I would be of no use there, but we have already driven away one of the firesnakes."

"The Purge is held at bay for now by the strength of the Alberion Novas."

"You mean they are attacking Eirn Bol?" asked Owen, his color drained.

"Listen, the Dark One has found a way she thinks will allow her to keep everyone prisoner here without release. She has found new allies, and is strong again. Although she attacks Eirn Bol, you must believe me. You will do your friends, and all who follow the Light, the most good by taking Politar's advice."

"What am I going to have to do? He mentioned something about a fire somewhere, and having to put my sword into it."

Beran nodded. "The Doom Fields. It shall be up to you to reach the three peaks which mark it. The sword you carry must be touched by that fire if you are to be of help to your young friend and her father on Eirn Bol."

Owen nodded. "Politar had been telling me much the

same. I trust you, though it is hard to see what good it will do."

"You have not seen all there is to this, my young friend. In time, you'll see that it falls into a pattern as intricate as a rainbow, but you have to be standing in a place you can see all the colors."

The Welingesse Fal called out in rhythmic chords, drawing Politar to the rail. "We're making good time, Beran. With luck, we'll put Owen ashore in two days. They are singing now of the great depths of the sea, and how it speeds us along."

"Then you must put me off when I say, Politar. I have another stop to make along this coast."

Owen looked perplexed. "Aren't you coming along? I thought you were to teach me about the Doom Fields."

Beran laughed a short chuckle. "You'll learn about those without any trouble, lad. Never fear for that."

A Light in the Forest

The wind through the trees shook down the dying leaves, sending them swirling and flying through the air with a clattering racket that was deafening under the broad eaves of the wood. The air had a definite chill to it which promised winter, and the dawn that was visible through the ragged clouds was distant and cold. In an ancient grove, a lone figure stood beside an oak, watching and listening to the wind. A cloak of rough brown wool covered the man from head to toe, and although it was finely made, it had seen much hard wear. At that instant, a new sound rose above the chorus of other noises in the wood, and the man pulled back his hood and stood listening intently for a moment, then raised his heavy staff.

A single, brilliantly green ball formed in the air before the man, and ignited. Balls of red and orange and bright silver followed, flowing into a circle, whirling faster and faster, until at last they shot upward into the deeper shadows above the Bernolt Wood, blazing and sparkling in dazzling rainbows of colors. The man raised his staff again, and a blinding white light shot upward. He stopped then, resting and listening.

From far off, he heard the reply he wanted, and pulling his hood back up, he began walking at a great pace, deeper into the wood. He began to hear the enticing call of the dragon then, lilting and soft at first, then more demanding and dangerous. A great bat of darkness crept nearer to the man's thoughts, slowly spreading across his vision, and touching his heart with its icy claw. He sent forth another shower of the flaring colored lights against the cruel assassin and felt the harshness of the guiding hand of the beast reaching out to crush his resistance.

Abruptly, the frightening thoughts were gone, replaced by the sight of a cool, green grove beneath a clear blue sky. A pool, deep and inviting, beckoned to him to lie down to rest, where all was safe and tranquil.

"You are good, my friend," said the man aloud. "This has all the comforts of home here. I might be tempted to lie down for a nap, but I fear it would be my last one." His hand moved slightly beneath his cloak, and a small yellow bee buzzed upon the air, moving toward the pool as though to drink from its coolness. It began to grow, darting in every direction with such quick movements it was hard for the eye to follow. "Be wary of its sting, my friend," warned the man. "It has been known to stun even a fellow as large as you!"

The peaceful setting dissolved into an inferno of scalding steam and leaping flames, and the beast roared in defiance. The man felt the heat, and heard the harsh voice inside, willing him to surrender to death.

"You are much too kind, my good fellow. Your promises are never kept, yet you tell me that if I surrender to you now, you will kill me quickly. I have seen the work of your brothers, and know who your teachers have been. You aren't as strong as they were, and if I have my way about it, you won't have the chance to learn."

The shriek of anger that greeted his speech rocked the trees into motion, and flames erupted from the blackness. As the horrifying outline of the beast crept closer, its huge talons poised to grasp and crush its paltry enemy. As it neared the man, he raised his staff, and a blinding sheet of light erupted, and the whirlwind of colored lights spun about him faster and faster. The dragon crashed heavily to the ground on the spot where the man had been but an instant before. It ground its wings into the earth, and knocked down trees with its slashing tail. Lumbering aloft again, it sought the man, casting its monstrous gaze about for the sight of anything it might torture and kill. Its anger was great, and now it wanted only to kill and burn, to grind up a puny human and slay his cattle and crops. It took great pleasure from remembering those things. The only other joy it got was from the many precious things it took from its victims, which it lined its nest with, and slept on. There were dark dreams, full of blood and shiny metals, and jewels from the crowns of powerful kingdoms which the dragon hordes had destroyed. Those tales were told to it by its mother from the time it came from its egg and the Protector began to speak.

That was another voice which demanded loyalty and

obedience. The Dark One ruled over them with a fearsome terror that even the dragon feared. There were others who called them from the Doom Fields, but they were mere mortals, empowered only by the ancient writings of those who believed they could harness the Purge to suit their needs. This beast had been called forth from its rest by humans, and turned loose upon a fresh feeding ground as reward for aiding them. And always the feeding had been easy.

Now the beast felt a faint tingle of unease. No prey had turned on it before. It knew that where the colored lights were, the hateful enemy lurked, so with a blast from its fiery breath, the dragon's fire scoured the wood below, leaving black scorched earth and smoldering tree stumps.

There were no more colored lights, and the irritating globes which shot around and past with so much force ceased. It smelled its victory, and clumsily landed to rake the blackened earth with its harsh claws. Just as the beast landed, another string of the brightly lit globes rose on the other side of the town it had planned to raze.

The beast was infuriated. Bellowing fire, it raised itself aloft once more. He sought the man's mind, but to no avail. Calling out in its most alluring voice, the dragon told of the many riches it had taken from settlements and kingdoms it had destroyed, and the many deaths it had caused. It promised a special horror for the man.

From a distance, the man saw the beast lift awkwardly into the air, and the rage it went into. He heard the dragon's song, and felt the great temptation to stand and wait for death. Instead he kept walking. A few steps farther, and he found the hidden stairs beneath the gnarled oak. He stepped quickly into the darkness beneath the stone that guarded the opening, whistling an almost cheerful tune that echoed back from the damp walls as he went farther into the shaft. He held up his staff, and the brilliant colored lights jumped into life, showing him the intricate runes that marked the walls.

Before him was a clever mosaic of a winged beast attacking a coastal town. "We have been here before, my good fellow. Now it seems we're repeating ourselves." The fine inlay reflected the colored lights, making the fire from the monster's mouth appear almost real.

A signal, faint and from somewhere farther belowground sounded then, and the man put a small horn carved in the shape of a goat to his mouth and blew a short reply.

The Gray Wastes

Another full two days at sea had passed since Owen last saw Beran. Politar watched as the great eels brought the Wind Rhyme close in to the rocky coast, making for a break which led in to a small, protected lagoon. The rocks were gray, and the entire stretch of land was dull and lifeless, as though it had been weathered by sun and wind until all color was bleached from the earth.

"Not a hospitable piece of rock," proclaimed Politar, gazing at the wasteland. "It has been this way for so long, I sometimes wonder why it doesn't sink beneath the sea. It would be a kinder end."

"Where are we?" asked Owen, his heart deadened by the sight of the wind-racked coast.

"The Gray Wastes, we call it now, though there were other names for it in the past. In the olden days, it was once called Dalorina, and was known for the beauty of its people and settlements. There were great keeps up and down the countryside that held wise men, and secrets of great worth to all who came on pilgrimages of the spirit."

Owen shook his head, staring out at the blighted land. For as far as he could see, the coming winter seemed to already grip the vast waste in its frigid hold, and even the clouds that hung above the coast were cold and gray.

"In the middle years, there were great men who accumulated wealth and made many allies across the Silent Sea. There were not many who did not deal with the Dalorinians. Many strange and wonderful things were seen in some of those keeps and fortresses. It was said there was a man near the outer boarders who rode upon a carpet he had tricked from a caliphohan."

"A what?"

"Caliphohan. They were commonly known as wirdochs, or magicians as you might know. No one could say for certain where they came by their wares or knowledge, but their magic was no secret among the Council. Gingus Pashon, when he betrayed the Circle, was not one to keep back goods that might win him power or wealth, and he sold off some of the lesser pieces of the knowledge he took with him when he left us."

"Like the Rhion Stones," added Owen, unable to pull his eyes away from the lifeless land.

Politar nodded grimly. "Exactly. Those were to prove the most dangerous to us, and still plague us to this very day."

"There is one aboard the Thistle Cloud who has one of the rings he took from a Hulin Vipre prince. I tried to get Rewen and Coglan to take it from him, but they wouldn't." Owen flushed angrily, remembering the arrogant sneer Ulen had leveled upon him.

"There will be another chapter to Rewen's story," explained the older man, pausing to call out something to the great eels, and motioning Owen to lower the anchor. It dropped with a muted splash into waters as gray and murky as the land, and a silence followed, broken only by the slight humming of the wind through the rigging.

"Sit down here a bit, Owen. We have to fashion out a plan of putting you ashore. It's not going to be easy, and I don't want you to go off half notched into something that could well spell your doom."

"Putting me off? Here?" Owen's eyes widened, and he forgot about Ulen. "Surely you are jesting!"

"I'm afraid not, my boy. This is one part of my duty that I do not relish, no matter how often I may be called upon to do it."

"And I can see why, if it is to murder a friend by leaving him stranded on a wasted piece of land like this! If you had an idea of leaving me anywhere, you should have left me back where you found me! At least there was a chance of my friends returning for me!"

"You are not deserted here. This is the first part of your lessons."

"Then they are lessons I don't care to learn! Look at this place, Politar! There is nothing here but certain death!"

"Certain death, if you see it that way. Yet this is not the worst, my young friend. Inland are the mountains where the Freolyde Valg make their foul nests. It is there that your journey will take you."

Owen shook his head in disbelief. "You expect me to go overland through this barren place, find a spot where the fireworms nest, and then come back to you safe and sound." He laughed bitterly. "Sometimes I think it would have been kinder if I had not come back from the Olgnite spell."

"It is that very spell that will give you the strength to complete this task, my boy. You carry within you the seeds of evil, which is a very powerful force. It is the one strength you have that marks you fit for this journey. You have been to the heart of the darkness, and returned. It is more than can be said for most."

"It was not an easy thing," returned Owen. "Ephinias didn't know how deeply that spell would take me. They almost weren't able to bring me back."

"I know that. The Olgnite curse is one of the strongest of the banes that can be cast upon a human. The Dark One is clever in her handiwork, and she does not make many mistakes."

"Sometimes I still feel that other way. I know it's still inside me."

"The Elboreal and the Dwarlich would be able to speak to you of those feelings. So can the old Keepers from the animal clans. Beran knows what you have felt."

"I wish we could find the elves again," admitted Owen, his voice full of longing.

"How can you be so sure they aren't about?" asked Politar.

Owen scowled. "It isn't hard to see they aren't."

"It depends upon the way we're looking," went on the older man. "That's what I was saying before. You make your mind up one way, then everything that happens can only be seen one way. It has taken me a long time to break that ugly habit, and I can't say I've missed it."

"You speak in riddles. Things can't be changed by wishing they were different. I may be young, Politar, but I recognize that much."

"Isn't that why you decided to make the trip to Eirn Bol instead of staying to take the Elder's Cloak from your father? To see things as you wished to see them, rather than as duty dictated?"

Owen flushed hotly. "I am too young yet for those duties and my father is not yet too old. He has many good years left before him."

The old man paced back and forth across the deck of the Wind Rhyme, his hands clasped behind his back. "When I was your age, I believed as you do, my boy. The world was in its golden time, and it spread out before me in an endless feast. I could not stay in one place long enough to finish what I needed to, and I rushed from here to there like a butterfly racing from one blossom to the next without thought."

"I hardly think of myself like that. The only reason I'm moving at all is because of the Olgnite and Hulin Vipre. And Deros and her father need all the help they can for their cause."

"The Line is in grave danger, too, Owen. Your father and mother have guided their followers well, and served bravely in every campaign they were called to."

"Are you saying I am not acting properly because I chose to go with Deros rather than stay at my father's side?"

Politar shook his head. "I did not say that. I merely gave you an example. You cannot use a yardstick to measure a barrel of water. You must learn to see that."

Owen, growing more confused, looked away at the bleak landscape stretched out before him. A faint movement near a great outcropping caught his eye. As he watched, a great, black shape lifted slowly into the gray sky, flying away toward the north.

"Look! What is it?"

Politar frowned, his eyes narrowed. "Not news of a nature good to us. I'm afraid our presence will be known before long. You had best make a start, and see if you can't get to the flows before dark. If you reach them, you'll have a better chance of going the rest of the way undetected."

The old man removed a much-worn and -folded map from inside his tunic and spread it out carefully on the deck. "We are here, at the spot called The Claw. You will make your way straight north until you hit the flows, where the fire mountain spilled its molten rock. That's a good day's march, if you're quick on your feet."

"A day's march! How can I make a day's march in a place I don't know, and which is full of things that intend me no good?"

"Sometimes that is the very thing that gives us speed," said Politar lightly. "But you will have your sword, and Beran said to give you this, as well." He placed a small leather pouch in Owen's reluctant hand. "It is something that will help guide you."

Owen drew open the small object, and pulled out what appeared to be a carved stone with a notch in the top. "What is this supposed to do?"

"It will guide you straight and true to the Fire Pit."

He pointed to the worn map again. "You see these peaks —Spindle Rock, Devil's Cap, and Roshagel? Each has a pathfinder rock at its summit. In the days when the lands were first mapped, the surveyors left these guide stones for use as markers. Even though these lands have been barren and lifeless most of this time since the Dalorinians were driven out, those peaks are still standing. Beran has traveled here before, and made sure of them." Taking the small rock from Owen's hand, he held it out at arm's length before him and sighted at a distant mountain. "Look at this. You'll see your way true with the use of this."

"And what if I have to travel after dark?"

"You aren't to travel after sunset," said Politar firmly. His features darkened into a worried scowl. "Under no circumstances are you to travel by night. When you reach the Fire Pit, you must stay there until daybreak. Remember that, my boy. You must not travel in the darkness for any reason."

"Where is this Fire Pit?"

"It's here on the map. Between Roshagel and Devil's Cap."

Owen peered at the thin lines that formed the two peaks, and the ominous valley that lay in between. "Is it really a pit of fire?"

Politar nodded slowly. "It is, and it isn't. To an eye not accustomed to looking at such things, it might seem to be nothing more than a great hole filled with smoke, but there is fire there, below the surface. It is there you must plunge the sword of Skye. After that, it will sear the Freolyde Valg if it touches them, and drive them back to their foul nesting place here in this blighted land." He was silent as he folded the map. Then he stood and spoke again.

"The morning is well on now, and you have a need to make time toward your first point. Just remember to mark your way by Spindle Rock, Devil's Cap, and Roshagel. And once you've reached your destination, you must spend the night there. You will be safe enough. Don't pay attention to anything you may see or hear. Watch the sword."

"It would be nice to have Seravan now," lamented Owen. "I could make better time, and be back before dark."

"You will find something else you need toinght," replied the older man. "It would not do so well if you were there and back before dark."

"What else do I need beyond the sword put into the fire?"

"A riddle. You'll find your clues and all the answer you need if you stay where you are supposed to."

"I don't see how I'll be able to do anything other than that," snapped Owen. "This doesn't sound like a task I'm going to look forward to. Even if Beran couldn't, you might at least go with me."

Politar laughed. "That would be like leaving the back door to your house open with an invitation to the thieves to come in. If anyone found the Wind Rhyme with no one aboard, it would be a sad day indeed for all of us."

"No one could fit aboard unless they were small."

"There is such a thing as picking up something you want."

Owen, seeing his arguments were futile, sighed and looked away at the distant humps of the three mountains. "Will I have food and water, or do I have to find my own on the way?" His tone was resigned.

"You'll have plenty of both," answered Politar, handing Owen another small pouch. "These are the pride of my ancient clan's art. There is food enough to feed an army for months there, and water to supply both the soldiers and mounts."

Owen smiled. "I would settle for a knapsack and a canteen."

"You have no need with this. Watch closely, and listen to me." He opened the small pouch and produced two small bottles. Laying them both upon a cloth he had placed at Owen's feet, he spoke a quick word over each, and touched the bottles with his hand. A small wisp of smoke began to rise from both, and Owen had to jump back to make room for the camp table that appeared spread before him with cheeses and hardtack that reminded him of the saddle fare of the Stewards. There was fruit, too, and small piles of nuts, which surrounded a jar of a deep golden honey.

"What shall I drink?" he asked in a much subdued tone.

"Your choice," replied Politar. "Here is mulled wine from the Crosiant Vale, or springwater from the headwaters of the Tybo."

"How do I get all this back into the bottles?"

Politar spoke another word, and then had Owen repeat both commands over again to his satisfaction. "Now you won't have to worry about starving on the way."

"I may not have to worry about starving if there's anything else there waiting."

"There is another trick to the bottles," confessed Politar.

"If you should run afoul on one of the beasts there, or should any other danger force you to it, you may take refuge by speaking the word while you hold it."

"You mean I would go inside it?"

"Exactly. But there is nothing to keep an enemy from picking the bottle up and carrying it away. So you have to be very cautious about using it that way."

"How do you come out?"

"Touch the side of the bottle, and repeat the word twice."

Owen studied his new gifts thoughtfully, full of questions about them.

A long, black shadow glided over the Wind Rhyme, bringing a chill across the early morning air, and Politar stood. "You must go now, Owen. You have your instructions, and know what to do. Good luck, and may Windameir bless you, my boy. Hurry!"

The old man's face was drawn with worry, and he kept looking upward at the empty sky. There was no sign of whatever had cast the shadow, and the wind carried nothing but the lonely sound of the boat's rigging humming, and the slight bumping noise as the small skiff was lowered over the side. Politar rowed Owen swiftly ashore, and pushed off as soon as the young man's feet were on dry ground. "Watch yourself," he admonished. "And on no account must you move after dark."

The Sons of Aranas

Pale golden light lit the shaft as the man moved downward. The sounds of soft music filled the air, and pictures appeared on the inlaid walls. The air smelled of sweet spring flowers, and a salty tang made promises of the sea. In the distance, the man heard the ebb and flow of the waves pounding and crashing against the chalk cliffs of White Bird. He blew his horn again, and this time it was answered with a call as several men came into sight.

"Hail, good Parson! You have reached us at a moment of much action! It seems the Colvages lizards are awing again."

"I have lured it this far, Fabin Farthrower. What we need now are some of your family's old tricks."

The men, who were all dressed in pale blue jerkins with yellow trousers tucked into polished black boots, were silent a moment. Then the one called Fabin asked, "How came you to know my family?"

"How would I not know the deeds of Aranas Farthrower and his sons?" The Parson laughed a deep, booming laugh, and sat down upon a low stone stool. "It is a long time since I have seen your brothers. When your father crossed the Boundaries, it was a sad day for all left here to carry on without him."

"It was indeed, Parson. There has been much trial and pain heaped upon our kingdom. The Dwarlich and Elboreal have long gone over, leaving the Aranas clans to hold and protect as best we're able. But a time has come when we shall not endure, and there will be no more of the Aranas Col, or a timbrehorn to sound through these shafts. No music, no pretty pictures in the stone! It will be a sad and fallen time, my friend."

The Parson nodded. "My good friend Tirhan spoke much the same. He has been and gone a hundred times. The sadness of it all, he says, is that your kind remembers the times from before, when the Golden Age was still upon us, and Atlanton was new."

One of the strange band leapt upon another stone stool and pulled an oddly shaped silver and mithra horn from his tunic. When he put it to his lips, even the Parson halted his speech and sat enthralled in the haunting tune the small man played. A dazzling change came over the carved walls of the shaft, and the figures there almost seemed alive. Time stood still, and a sweet-smelling wind blew from a spring meadow, making the mind drowsy, and there were bird songs that joined with the lilting horn in joyful celebration of some early morning sunrise.

As the music faded, tears glistened in the eyes of Fabin and his men, and they stood silently for a time, lost in their own memories. The Parson touched the smaller man's shoulder.

"You have followed your father's footsteps well, my friend. The sons of Aranas Col have kept a light burning in this country, even if no one else has known it."

"There are some that have known it," replied one of the other men. "White Bird and all this part of the coast have had guardians watching over them while they've slept. There are more than a few who can attest to that!"

"If dead men told tales," laughed another grimly.

"There will be dead stacked like cordwood before all this is over," said Fabin. "If the Colvages curse is upon us once more, then it means we have come to the crossroads the old Matre told us of when she cast the stones."

"We can start the game by using your passages to our best advantage. If we draw our rude guest here and there through the wood, he'll be ready to attack anything."

"You mean the great Salt Pit?" asked Fabin. "True, if we tease the beast enough, we may lure it to the Salt Pit, and before it realizes what it's in for, it will be scalded and scaled, but even though it is easy to bait the lizards, it is another thing once you have their interest."

"Then we have to work swiftly. Are your tunnels still well kept and ready for use? Do you have the numbers here to make it seem we are an army?"

"More in the shaft that borders White Bird." Fabin motioned for one of his followers to step forward. "This is my cousin Albin, our signaler."

"My service, Albin. I wish you well. We will need to coordinate before we call the beast. Any mistakes on our part will spell disaster for us, as well as those left in the settlement."

"We can throw out a tidy lure for the lizard in the heart of the wood," said Fabin, "and draw it out of the valley that runs down to White Bird."

"Some extra fireworks might be in order as well," added the Parson. "I think we should try calling out to the beast. He may be waiting to speak, if we sit quietly to listen."

The Parson motioned for silence among the small band of Aranas Col, and sat down cross-legged among them. He drew out a cloth bag from inside his cloak, and took out a small harp and began to strum softly. "This is a relic from the Middle Islands. It belonged to a great minstrel there, who was slain by one of the beasts. He told me of its powers, and how to use it best. It strikes a note that is painful for those of the Purge to bear. It is said to be the notes struck by the High Dragons."

"Then it will make this lizard angry?"

"Very angry, Fabin. We should be able to get him near the Salt Pit easily. Send forth your men, and I shall begin to harp."

Fabin called his followers into a small circle, and they knelt on one knee around their leader, heads bowed. After a murmured prayer in their own high tongue, they rose with a resounding battlecry, and quickly disappeared into the tunnels which led away into the underground maze they called home.

The Great Salt Pit

The silvery reflection of the moon shone on the great stretches of the salt flats that ran behind White Bird. The Parson watched for signs of the dragon, and looked away to where the settlement now stood dark and deserted, barely visible against the night sky. Fabin waited beside him, a small horn poised at his lips.

"Shall we signal the others?" he asked.

"We must first find out where our firesnake is. They sit and wait sometimes."

"Like big cats. I have heard that of them."

Fabin was looking far out over the salt flat, toward the coast, when he detected the slight movement. The Parson followed his glance without speaking. A thin finger of flames rose up, flickering against the shadow of night.

"That devil's burned the fishing boats below the settlement," Fabin hissed.

"So he's found something to torch, has he? Let's give him something a little more tempting!" The big man laid his cloak on the white ground. He placed the harp upon it, and motioned for his companion to leave. "I'm going to strike a chord or two now. You'd best find your shelter. Tell the others to be ready."

Fabin nodded and disappeared into the tunnels. The Parson heard the faint signal and waited for the first diversions to appear. He had not long to wait, for almost at once the faint glow of another fire began to his left. As the Parson turned back to the coast, he saw the grotesque form of the great beast rise from behind the cliffs, sparks trailing in a fiery wake.

"Come along to the dance, my pretty," hummed the big man, striking another chord on the delicate harp. The dragon hesitated, pausing as though it had heard the soft notes. The Parson became aware then of the beast's mind, then as a solid sheet of flames roared and crackled, and the sight of men being devoured spread across the Parson's vision. A cold, hard voice promised him a slow and painful death. In another moment, the full face of the creature was revealed, a horrible red maw with rows of yellowed, razor-sharp teeth, and eyes that pierced through the gloom like daggers, and plunged into the living heart of any who saw.

The Parson struck another chord on the small instrument, and spoke a rhyme to himself. There was nothing left upon the great white flats then but the man and the harp calling out in its soft voice to the dreadful beast.

The fires in the wood caught the beast's eye, but the thing that tormented it like a thorn beneath its thick scales was the music which burned its dark heart with a white light and drove it into a frenzy. The beast dropped from the sky and leveled the trees for a hundred feet in a circle around where the fires had been. Lashing out with its tail, it ripped and burned everything that caught its eye, but there were no humans.

Fabin had signaled again, and another fire was set, just beyond the wood where the beast now sat leveling the clearing and scorching what was left with its fiery breath. It saw the distant light flickering, and heaved itself into the air once more, its mind filled with horrors. The Parson saw the new promises of the dragon, and felt the pulse of the dark heart. There were no sweet lures offered now, only a slow and terrible death.

From high above, the firesnake blasted wood and field alike, leaving a burning wake behind it. Nearing the wood where it had seen the signal fire, it swooped down like a hawk, slashing and uprooting trees, and landed with a thundering crash the Parson felt through the earth. A moment later, the dragon's terrible cry of rage roared out, setting the ground trembling again. Rising slowly and sending out searing sheets of flame, the beast lifted once more, now a ball of flames that lit the night with a blazing roar. The heat from it touched the Parson's cheek, and he set a thought into motion which would be sure to lure the dragon nearer the trap that had been set for it. On the cloak before him now lay a sparkling heap of jewels and precious stones, twinkling invitingly in greens and golds and reds, with the silver and mithra reflecting the dragonfire. The harp still thrummed with its maddening chord. The beast turned toward the Parson's snare, but it seemed to sense danger.

"Come along, my foul friend," whispered the Parson. "I shall make it sweeter for you yet." He gestured, and next to the pile of treasures stood a member of the dwarfish clans, clad in full armor. The stocky figure set about counting the precious jewels, not once stopping to search the sky for the great danger that lurked not far away. At the sight of its ancient enemy, one of the dwarfish clans were ever the ones responsible for the death of the dragons and the robbers of their treasures.

Blazing across the sky like a meteor, the dragon made straight for the hated dwarf, all thoughts forgotten save watching his fragile skin fry beneath the fiery breath, and tasting the sweetness of an enemy devoured. The beast put out a gnarled talon to grasp his victim, but instead of precious stones and metal and the softness of a body, there was nothing but a searing, burning pain that racked the beast. A sound, high-pitched and terrible, tore the air, and flames erupted from the dragon's mouth, turning the surrounding earth into black, molten rock. The ground shook and trembled as the huge creature turned and thrashed.

Fabin, hearing the monster's dreadful racket, signaled the others. The clan of Aranas started their victory chant as they gathered to try to strike the death blow. As Fabin raced forward, he saw a huge gray-flecked bear darting about between the foreclaws of the beast, striking savage blows. A booming voice that Fabin recognized as the Parson's warned, "Stay clear. This is not done yet!"

The dragon, although blinded by the whirlwind of salt churned up by the Parson, was far from helpless. He lunged toward the sound of the voice, and came within a hairsbreadth of crushing the Parson with its great talons, but the bear was too fast. Thundering blows were exchanged as the two struggled, and the ground shuddered all about the beast as its tail and foreclaws slashed and smashed at empty air. But the bear was quicker, worrying the great beast with blows and bites. In a last flurry of rage, the dragon leapt into the cloud of dust and smoke, and flew awkwardly away, showering everything in its path with a blazing hail of fire that smoldered and burned long after the creature was gone.

"You've done it!" cried Fabin. "The lizard has turned

tail!" The sons of Aranas put their timbrehorns to their lips and blew joyous notes that rang in the night.

Fabin looked for the bear he'd seen struggling with the dragon, but saw no sign of it. "Did the beast slay the bear?" he asked, much saddened by the thought.

"Was there a bear?" asked the Parson, smiling slightly.

"A great bear with a silver-gray coat! Couldn't you see him?"

"That may have been some illusion the firesnake made."

Fabin shook his head. "It wasn't making this. It was trying to kill the bear." He looked over the emptiness of the great salt flat, now deserted again in the moonlight. "I know he was here," he insisted. "I felt him."

"Let's see to the fires," said the Parson gently. "They'll need some help in White Bird if the town is not to burn, and it will take some time to rebuild the fishery."

"We shall help them with that. My father and his companions were masters of the wood and sea. There shall be another fleet inside a year."

"The people of White Bird will need allies now. The Purge is a sign that the Dark One has her armies on the march again." The Parson watched the retreating monster flee toward the dark horizon in the north. "I wonder where the creature is making for."

"Away from here," replied Fabin. "And if it's blinded, it won't be much danger to anyone else."

"I wouldn't be so sure of that. Even without sight, it still has the uncanny ability of casting its thought into others."

Fabin looked earnestly at the big man. "Will you be staying with us awhile?"

Shaking his head, the big man laughed. "I could find no better companions, Fabin Farthrower, but I have a wounded dragon to tend to, and if I'm not mistaken, a rendezvous with my old friend Twig somewhere in the Sea of Silence not long from now." He picked up a small, glowing shard of dragon scale. "Keep this with your clan for a reminder of a brave time. Your father would be proud of you all."

In the distance, a great flash of dirty orange light lit the night sky. "Even blinded, the dragon is still capable of terrible destruction. I must take my leave now. Carry me kindly in your thoughts, Fabin. Windameir be with you and your men." After shaking hands with each of the clan, the Parson stepped into the darkness and vanished without a trace. A horn sounded, calling farewell. The eldest son of Aranas took his own horn out and returned the call, then turned his mind to the people of White Bird, who had begun coming from their underground shelter to see what had become of the dragon.

That night, another storm began to blow up, and the wind howled through the ruined fleet as the sailors made their way to look at the damage the terrible beast had wrought upon their peaceful coast. By dawn, the storm had intensified, and the citizens sought shelter once more, as the howling wind tore at the walls and roofs of the settlement, and by noon, the skeletons of the ships in the protected harbor of White Bird had been washed ashore, like the bones of some ancient tragedy.

A Messenger of Doom

Walking as fast as he was able, Owen soon found himself at some distance from the Wind Rhyme, and was barely able to see her masts above the slight rise in the wasted land. That disturbed him, and caused him to hurry his pace even more. Politar's parting words to him did nothing to lay his fears to rest, and Beran's sudden departure only convinced him further that if there was anything to do with wizards, they simply vanished at the very instant you might need them most. Far ahead, he could see the jagged peaks rising gray against a gray sky, and just to reassure himself, he raised the notched stone out before him and looked through it. As before, the tops of the hills lined up within the notch of the stone he held, so he knew he was traveling in the right direction. The idea that he must stay the night at the Pit of Fire turned his blood to ice, and his thoughts churned with ways he might avoid it. He was so preoccupied that he failed to notice the slight shadow that fell over his own, keeping pace with him until, after a long period of steady walking, he glanced downward to check his footing on a steep incline and saw the huge winged shadow float across a lighter-colored fall of rocks. Looking upward quickly, his heart in his throat, he caught sight of a large, black bird with a red crop on its head, and an ugly, drooping beak.

Relieved that it wasn't what he had feared, he picked up

a stone and hurled it at the ungainly bird. "Get away from me, you filthy thing! Go on!" He threw another stone, which the bird easily evaded. "If I had my bow, you'd be a rotting carcass to match this blighted place!"

The huge bird flew out of reach of Owen's stones, and hung against the breeze, waiting, taunting him.

"Well," Owen said aloud, "at least I know where you are. Stearborn and Chellin Duchin and the brothers always agree that it's better to have an enemy in sight, than to have him at your back."

He set off at an even greater pace. "There's nowhere for you to perch here, so I hope you're a strong flyer! And if you land, I may see to it you don't take off again!" His empty threats didn't improve his anxiety, for he knew without a bow he would never be able to reach the ugly bird, no matter how slow or awkward it appeared.

"Now I could stand the use of some of Ephinias's little tricks." He smiled to himself.

His desire to skewer the bird began to tickle his fancy, and he spent the next long period of doggedly plodding along thinking of how good it would feel to kill the bird and leave it to rot in the vast, gray land.

A cold finger of fear came from a place deep inside him, where the dreadful echo of the Olgnite lay entombed in the frozen dungeons of his memory. All the terrible moments from Trew came back in vivid detail, and a dark sense of despair slowly settled over his heart, slowing his step. The thoughts of Deros and Rewen, and all his friends aboard the Thistle Cloud crowded in upon him, bringing him very near tears.

As he slowed, the bird altered its pace to his own then dived close to the youth.

Owen forgot himself for a moment in his rage at the infuriating gall of the hideous bird, and gave chase for a short distance, thinking only of killing the horrible thing and being rid of its mocking calls.

He pulled himself up and looked around, trying to calm his pounding heart. When he looked at the three peaks, they seemed different, and after taking out his guide stone, he confirmed that the bird had drawn him off his course.

Owen smiled bitterly. "So that's your game," he muttered. He resolutely marched back in the direction he had come, stopping now and again to sight the notched stone toward the peaks.

He saw a trail of smoke rising above the low mountains in long, black spirals. Owen stopped, peering intently at the new mystery. After studying it a short while, he drew himself up and continued his march, which led directly toward the columns of smoke.

"Politar said the place I was to seek had fires, so it's reasonable there would be smoke as well," he said, trying to cheer himself.

A great plume of fire and smoke rose up into the gray sky, darkening the sun for a moment and making the three peaks stand out in stark contrast. The sword at his side began to hum softly, and was warm to his touch, although there was nothing to see in any direction but the bleak sameness. After another few paces, Owen heard the faint thunder from a distance, but thought it was no more than a storm, until the ground began to shake, sending a tremor from the soles of his feet up through the top of his head.

When the next rumbling jolt came, it knocked him off his feet, and he lay, unable to rise again until the horrifying shaking subsided.

And then the voices began.

In Norith Tal

From the high windows in the south wall, Jatal Ra saw the shadow of the great beast, and heard the sound of its breath roaring like an inferno. He ran for the door just as he heard the crumbling of the stones as a huge gnarled talon smashed through, grappling about in search of a victim. His mind was full of the beast's thoughts, and he could feel death very near. It took him a few moments of paralyzing fear to realize that the illusion was all in his mind, and that the wall before him was still intact. His hands were sweaty, and he had to seat himself hurriedly to keep his knees from collapsing beneath him.

"Salun Am! You are wanted! Heed me, my friend, heed me well!" He waited with held breath for a reply, but there was nothing but echoes to greet him, and his chamber, which faced the great tower of Norith Tal, remained silent and foreboding, flooded with the distinct odor of death. Jatal Ra reached into his robe and brought out the small bit of charcoal that he kept for the most desperate of moments.

He called out again for his companion, but got no reply. The palace guards had found the body of Lacon Rie, and the alarm bells in Blor Alhal had been ringing since. At first, he was terrified they would come straight for him, accusing him of Lacon Rie's murder. He listened to every footfall which came and went beyond his door, the beads of sweat breaking out on his forehead. Every sound seemed to foretoken a troop of the Emperor's guard marching down the empty corridors to drag him away to the ugly crossed tree, where a victim's neck would be brutally broken for his crimes. He alternately felt terror-stricken and arrogant, remembering the Nod and the power it gave him. There would be no one who would be able to confront him, a Conductor of Quineth Rel, and a most feared and respected member of the Mardin Council. Only Mortus Blan would dare to raise a hand against him, and Jatal Ra heard from his spies at court that the old man had become dotty.

Salun Am had suggested once that they could destroy Mortus Blan through the bone-caster who traveled with the gypsies. The old man's weakness as he grew more forgetful was an obsession with young women, and it was a known joke around Blor Alhal that the Emperor's advisor was never without a golden coin or a sweetmeat to try to tempt some lass.

There were things Mortus Blan knew which disturbed Jatal Ra. He had never let his ridicule of the man get in the way of the knowledge that he was a dangerous enemy, one who would have to be eventually reckoned with. Now, with Lacon Rie dead, would be the time, he thought.

And then his heart slipped into his throat as he heard armed men coming down the hallway toward the door to his rooms. A heavy pounding sent him staggering backward into a chair, and he held the small bit of charcoal out before him in trembling hands. He was ready to speak the words which would release the Nod, when the voice of Salun Am carried through the heavy walls, calling out urgently. "Jatal Ra! Open the door! They've found the Emperor and there are some volumes of the Warl Book spread about. Do you hear me? We must work quickly, or there will be much damage done!"

He rearranged his robes about him, and still clinging

tightly to the small black object in his hand, he drew open the outer door which opened onto the Emperor's own courtyard and portico. "What is all this racket?" demanded Jatal Ra, as though he had just been rousted from a deep slumber.

Salun Am bowed gravely, turning to the Court Guard. "The Commander of the Guard has just come from the Emperor. He is dead. But there are volumes of the Warl which are left open, and shall need our hand to close! If you ever moved quickly, then let it be now, Jatal Ra. Our Emperor needs us in this moment as never before! They have sent parties to find Mortus Blan, but no one knows his whereabouts!" Salun Am spoke with urgency, his eyes sending other secret messages that were not seen by the members of the House Guard.

"You will come with me, please," urged the commander. "I do not like leaving the dangerous books out! The Emperor must have taken them from the Wall, for they were spread out in the Norith Tal. It bodes not well for us."

"He may have been trying to call our old allies," suggested Jatal Ra, remembering with a shudder the terrifying vision of the beast tearing down the wall of his apartment. He had said nothing of the dreadful images to Salun Am, although it had happened from the very first time he took the Books of Warl from their sacred hiding place in Norith Tal, and began the readings that would command the Freolyde Valg.

"Whether he was or no, we cannot leave those volumes about for someone to find and destroy, or steal," said Salun Am. "The Commander has left a sentry to watch until we can once again seal the books into their sacred altar."

"Then come along quickly! We have wasted enough precious time." Jatal Ra put the small lump of charcoal back into his cloak and followed the small troop of guardsmen up the winding stairs, until they at last reached the high tower of the Norith Tal.

Rush lamps and torches cast dark shadows over the faces of the men who stood back uncertainly, awaiting the orders of the two Conductors. The Emperor's body had been removed, but the large book lay where they had placed it, open to the page which was covered with the monstrous picture of one of the dragons of Warl. Jatal Ra's mind once more filled with the horrible vision of a great black talon with razor-sharp claws reaching to grasp his soul, but he took a deep breath and marched resolutely forward, flipping the heavy tome closed. "There! Now help me place it back into its hiding," he said, motioning for Salun Am to join him.

They burned incense and made a show of parading about the chamber with a long mithra vase that contained seawater, sprinkling it over the frightened guardsmen, who fell back quaking and averting their eyes.

Jatal Ra leaned close to his friend's ear and whispered something that made the man grow pale.

"I have no visions such as that," replied Salun Am. "It is said to be a part of the curse when you draw back those old bindings from the forbidden knowledge."

"We are the Conductors of Quineth Rel, you fool! There is no knowledge that is forbidden to us!"

Salun Am shook his head, motioning toward the doorwall to the hall. "Look who has arrived!" His voice was tight, and his eyes were slits.

Jatal Ra turned to see Baryloran limp into the great chamber of Norith Tal. Behind him was the Emperor's High Chancellor, the man called Mortus Blan. He was old, but with quick movements he stepped forward with a bounding rush, his gray beard flung over his shoulders like an outspread cloak.

"Greetings, Chancellor," said Jatal Ra smoothly. "We

had word that you were nowhere to be found, and we took the liberty of putting back the Book into its sacred altar."

The old man cackled, "My good Jatal Ra! How convenient you should be here. Baryloran has spoken to me, filling my head with such nonsense that a man wouldn't be able to walk and keep his cap on straight! Such things I've heard! Of you, too, Salun Am, my redoubtable fellow." Mortus Blan shifted his beard and dug into the folds of his cloak, as if searching for something.

Jatal Ra's hand closed around the small black object hidden next to his chest. He was on the verge of speaking the words to free the wraith, when the old man pulled forth a wooden comb and tried to brush out the tangles in his long gray beard.

"What things have caught your ear, Chancellor? There are many things that float about that have no basis in fact, sir. You have been around these good many turnings to know a thing or two of that."

Baryloran was standing next to the old man, his eyes red from weeping, and his fists clenched. He made as though to speak, but he could manage no words, and Jatal Ra turned to him, bowing his head. "I offer my condolences on this untimely death of your father. He will be missed by all."

The youth trembled from head to foot. Mortus Blan reached out a hand to touch him, but Baryloran drew away violently. "Leave me with these assassins!" he was able to gasp at last, finally managing to gain control of himself long enough to utter a few words. The guardsmen looked at one another in confusion, but stood still. Salun Am had begun to measure the distance to the door where the Book was kept, for he knew there was a secret way from there to the keep far below.

Jatal Ra did not change his sympathetic tone. "I realize you are upset by the death of your father, the Emperor. You go to the heart of old disagreements Lacon Rie and I had over the waging of war against Eirn Bol, but you have overlooked our good standing with him. He saw fit to keep an opposite view upon his Council, and his wisdom has proven itself time and again. Neither Salun Am nor myself would have wished your father ill. In fact, we were both against his meddling with the Book of Warl. Our last disagreement came when we knew he was once more trying to call back the Lost Fire."

"Liars! Murdering dogs!" hissed Baryloran, being held in check by the old man's iron grip. "You will pay for your treachery!"

Mortus Blan spoke in a soothing low tone. "You have your opinions, my boy, as we all do. There is a time and place to go into these things, but it is not now. Now control yourself, and fetch the rest of the Mardin Council. We must inform your subjects your father is dead, and that you are now Emperor in Hulingaad."

The lame young man hesitated, trying to find more words to express his venom. His mentor shoved him toward the door, and motioned for one of the guard to escort him. "He is the Emperor now. You are entrusted with his life."

The House Guard saluted smartly with a resounding note as he clapped his gauntleted hand against his chest, and opened the tall, heavy door that led into the hallway beyond.

"I shall find a way," promised the young man, his eyes blazing with unconcealed hatred. "My brother shall return with the wench, and I will give my father's crown to him. Tien Cal will know how to deal with such traitors and thieves."

Salun Am and Jatal Ra both bowed low, murmuring words of obedience to their new Emperor, all the while looking about to see if the young man's words were having any effect on the House Guard. The men were wide-eyed and wanted no part of the argument, but Mortus Blan sidled closer, brushing back his beard so he could speak to the two without being overheard. "So now we have just the three of us in this cozy tower. It is a delightful place, to my recollection. I can think of a time or two we had here arguing about the safety of using the Warl Books. Nasty and uncontrollable they are. Not to be tampered with again."

"It seems your Emperor thought better. If only he had seen the wisdom of pursuing his course for another short time, we would be sitting snugly in Cairn Weal at this moment, thumbing through the Alberion Novas at our leisure."

A creaking laugh echoed somewhere in the folds of the old man's beard, and he moved away toward the diamond-shaped windows of the tower. "I have always had a fondness for this wing of the keep. It has the best views of the harbor, and on nights with storms, the lightning always comes to roost on this roof." He drew open one of the colored panes and pushed his head through to peer about.

"We all have a fondness for this place, Mortus Blan. It was well loved by our late Emperor, as well."

"There have been odd comings and going here of late," said the old man over his shoulder. He suddenly turned and stood facing the two Conductors with his beard standing out about him like a wild gray mane. "I know you have the Nod, Jatal Ra. I myself have felt it move in these very chambers not many nights since. I was with Lacon Rie when you loosed it, and he knew well enough who was at work."

Jatal Ra's eyes narrowed to slits, and his hand was on the small black fragment in his cloak, but he held his move until he could be sure of what the old man intended to do. Salun Am stepped forward with outspread palms.

"I beseech you, sir, to think of what you're saying! There has been no one of us who would still risk the wrath of Lacon Rie by keeping such trifles of the old ways. We voted among ourselves long ago to forgo those dangerous relations before they would destroy us. After it was proven there was no way to keep them from continuing to grow stronger if they were once released, we needed no further proofs that they were a power too dangerous to use."

"That's what was agreed," said the ancient man, placing one fold of his cloak in his hands and pacing back toward the dying fire. "Guard! This poor excuse for a blaze could use some help. This always was one of the coldest of the rooms in the keep."

A startled House Guard roused himself from his position against the doorpost, and hurried to stoke up the embers of the fire. As he knelt to add another log, a strange vision began to play out in the flames, which Jatal Ra and Salun Am recognized at once and hurried to move closer to watch.

There before them in the orange shadows of the renewed fire was the same strange face in the eye of the Rhion Stone, and next to it, the soft features of a young woman, standing beside a man at the rail of a ship beneath the familiar stars of the Sea of Silence.

"What do you make of that?" asked Jatal Ra. "It is the same faces we have seen from the Eye on more than one occasion."

Salun Am stood transfixed, watching. "The stone answers no riddles, but it yet answers our call. It is the wench who belongs to Eirn Bol, as I stand here, but I cannot find the other's face in my memory."

The old man poked at the burning logs with a poker, and muttered into his beard. The focus of the Rhion Stone wavered for a moment, then clearly shone on the man's face as he stood next to the young woman. Mortus Blan spoke again, and a faint voice replied through the hiss and roar of the fire. "I hear. Command me."

"You've reached him!" uttered Salun Am. "The stone is still under our power!"

"Very much so, my good fellow. All you need do is recall the strings to play. He will be our puppet, whoever he is, so long as he wears our Eye. Now Baryloran will have his lever to pry off the lid of Cairn Weal. They are most likely on their way home to Eirn Bol, or I miss my guess. With the right preparation, we can have a proper reception for them." Mortus Blan cackled into his beard. "She is a pretty dainty."

Jatal Ra knew it was futile to free the Nod as long as Mortus Blan was about, for Mortus Blan had also studied the forbidden knowledge and could know the words to thwart the spell. "It seems as though our best-laid plan would be to ring Eirn Bol with our scout ships, and keep watch for the wench's arrival. Alert all our spies to be on the lookout for a ship coming from the west."

"A sound plan, Jatal Ra. I will instruct this young ally with the Eye to inform us of his whereabouts, so that we may make ready to receive them properly." The old man paced away from the fire, almost upsetting the startled sentry. "I must tell Baryloran to alert the troops, though I shall not tell him all. It will be well to celebrate a victory over Cairn Weal as a fitting salute to our fallen Emperor." He paused at the door, turning to face the two. "You have done well for yourselves, my devoted friends. I would suggest you keep up your good work, and report the findings to the Council. I hear the call going out for them now." A low signal horn, deep and melodious, sounded through the keep, repeating itself at intervals.

Jatal Ra bowed to the older man. "Our services, sir. We will be at table."

Salun Am bowed also, looking sideways at his companion. When he turned to speak, Mortus Blan was gone.

"You may go now," ordered Jatal Ra, turning to the sentry. "You won't be needed here now that the Book is safely away. Good night!"

The soldier saluted and retired, leaving the two men alone in the great chamber of Norith Tal.

"That meddling old fool," snapped Jatal Ra, placing his hands behind his back and striding about in great agitation. "Now we shall have to hold our plans until we can find what he will do next!"

"He knows," said Salun Am. "He knows everything."

"Not as much as he thinks. We shall still have our little surprises for him, no matter how smug he gets."

"They will ask us at Council about the Eye, and the Warl Books."

"And we will tell them everything, of course," went on Jatal Ra. "How Lacon Rie despaired of finding a short end to the war that has been dragging the Black Hood down all these turnings, and his secret decision to call back the Lost Fire. We came upon him at his work, and tried to dissuade him, but he turned on us and drove us from Norith Tal. It must have been too much for him in his weakened state, and that's when he was found."

"And the Eye? Mortus Blan knows of it, too."

Jatal Ra studied the fire, standing before the great stone hearth. "That may be to our best interests, as well. We must make certain we are with the ships when they go greet our new ally, whoever he is. If we are with him when he finds his way to our shores, then we shall make our impression upon him, which all the others will have trouble breaking. And by then, we will have already been to Cairn Weal, and secured the Alberion Novas for ourselves."

"How shall we do all that?" asked his companion. "There still are the armies of Eirn Bol to contend with."

"Alban Ram will find it best to comply with our demands, if he wishes to keep his daughter from becoming the mistress of Mortus Blan. I think he will see matters in that light, and help us to accomplish our little feat. And we will leave him as head of Eirn Bol. We will set up a new Council to rule, and he will simply carry out our wishes."

"And we will be the new Council? What of Mortus Blan, and Baryloran? Our new Emperor will not be pleased with our arrangement."

"Undoubtedly. He will rule Hulingaad, and the Black Hood, as is written by law. The Conductors of Quineth Rel will become Ministers to Eirn Bol."

Salun Am wrapped his hands in his cloak, lost in thought. "Those are grand plans. Mortus Blan may not agree with the outcome."

"He will be occupied. I saw the look he wore when he looked at the wench in the Eye. She will serve as our hold over him until he dies."

"*If* he dies, you mean. It is said he is over four hundred now. He has a potion he takes, or some such."

"He will die. The wench will help us there. She is the daughter of Alban Ram, and her hatred for all of the Black Hood is a powerful weapon."

Salun Am concealed a hooded smile from his companion. "You are a most clever man, Jatal Ra. I think great challenge brings out your best."

"Indeed it does," returned his friend, staring into the fire, then straightening. "I think the Mardin Council shall have need of our presence now. Come. Let us give them what we know, and offer our services. Long live the Emperor."

Teachings of the Master

The Curtain of Fear

"Turn back! There is death for you at Roshagel!"

The voice came as clearly as a bell rung in a silent hall, and Owen jumped to his feet. The sword of Skye made a steady humming sound.

He drew the blade. The sword was glimmering a pale silver-white, and the current that always ran through his hand when danger was present merely tickled. He searched the sky in every direction, but the huge black bird was nowhere to be found. "That should encourage me, yet I find it worrisome," he muttered. Then, trying to make his voice steady, he called loudly, "Who are you?"

There was no immediate reply, so Owen moved forward.

"You will die by the fire," came the voice again, in a lower, almost confidential tone.

Owen remembered how he had felt as a young child when he would awaken from a bad dream and call out in the darkness for his parents. The terror that gripped him then was always driven away by the light of the rush lamp as his mother or father came to hold him, but the shadow of it always returned once they had gone to their own bed. It simply waited, as it was waiting now.

The thin veil that held back the terrible Olgnite curse was weakening, and Owen could feel the powerful urges he had felt when he had been changed into the grotesque form of the bloodthirsty monsters who had destroyed Sweet Rock.

His walk had slowed to a stumbling pace, yet he was drawn on toward the smoke he saw in the distance. A faint vision of Politar flicked at his senses, drawing his attention away from the darkness that clouded his mind. He was aware of the sword, pulsing in his hand, and other faces which flickered by his inner eye with a dizzying speed. People called his name, but before he could tell who they were, they had vanished. The soft, deadly tone spoke to him again, this time almost in a whisper. The quietness of it made it even more menacing. "You were a fool to listen to those who would send you to your death! They lie safely now, while you will die for their greed and folly!"

"Who are you?" Owen struggled to free himself from the paralysis of fear which gripped him.

An icy laugh rang hollowly. "Can't you see me, good warrior? Haven't you guessed yet who you deal with?" The laughter came again, like dry leaves in a frozen wind.

The gray day began to dissolve into darkness before Owen's eyes. He watched in motionless horror as the mountains transformed themselves into great coiled winged snakes, and made straight for where he stood rooted to the earth. Owen's hand trembled, but he held his sword unflinchingly. He called to Politar and Beran. "You have left me here alone, so you must help me now! I can't hold off three beasts by myself!"

The voice that answered him was the same soft voice,

oily smooth and maddening in its contempt. "When will you realize there is no one here to help you? Your friends are gone, and you face the Purge alone!"

Owen grew angry. His blood boiled, and the lurking Olgnite spell filled his mind with gory visions of slaughter. The sword from Skye blazed forth in fiery white light that blinded even Owen, so he could not see his enemies, although he could feel their chilling presence and began to hear the dreadful wing beat of the beasts.

As Owen prepared to die, for he knew he had no chances of surviving, he thought of his father and mother, and then of Deros. His rage flared more violently when he remembered Ulen. He braced himself for the attack, holding to the white-hot sword with both hands. "Come on! I have your death in my hands! Come on, damn you!"

He stepped forward, slashing with deadly blows that cut left and right, moving forward to close with one of the beasts, but nothing was there to confront him except the same cold gray sky and the faceless land.

Enraged by the enemy's flight, Owen began to run toward the three peaks. "Now you shall feel the blade that carries your death," he shouted aloud.

The noise of his voice seemed to bring him to his senses, and he slowed his pace, looking about him in confusion. There was the slow voice of the wind over the barren face of the wilderness, but no other sound or being was there. He was alone.

In the distance, he could see the peaks were the same, and had not moved, although the smoke that rose up on the gray back of the sky had increased, and there was another slight tremor of the ground.

"It's the dragon," he said aloud. "I've been dealing with the dragon!" Walking more quickly now, he tried to remember exactly what had happened and what his father and mother had said of the worms and how they had fought them.

As soon as he had prepared to die and gone for his enemy, the dragon's hold had been broken. It seemed that the black terror the beast used to paralyze its victim was one of its most deadly weapons, and if one could break that, there was a chance.

The Death of Master Flit

Sitting in the intricately carved camp stool before his food, Owen studied the two small objects which had produced his feast. They were both of the same deep opaque green glass, so that he could not see what was inside. When he held the bottle that produced the food so that he could peer into the opening, he was surprised to see a hallway lined with armor and weapons. Beyond, there was a kitchen, with barrels of apples and other fruit, and wheels of cheese and sides of bacon hanging from the ceiling. As he peered more closely at this strange sight, he noticed great longbows resting against a wall beside a quiver of arrows that were at least as long as Stearborn's feared Leech shafts.

Looking up quickly, he searched the sky for the bird which had haunted him since he had begun his journey to find the Valley of Fire. He laughed aloud. "All I need do is repeat the words Politar taught me, and I can bring out that bow. Come along now, Master Flit! I promise you a surprise!"

He carefully scanned the sky again, and seeing it was empty, he repeated the word while grasping the bottle tightly to his chest.

The change was not immediately apparent. The gray lands surrounding him slowly formed stone walls, and as he rose to stand from the camp stool, he found himself in a hallway lit by muted brown light that came through the very stone itself.

He took a few tentative steps, for he thought the floor might crack. He took one of the longbows and found it was made of cool, smooth wood. One of the arrows was sharp enough to draw blood when he touched its point. At the end of the hallway, another archway led to a second long, narrow passageway with a staircase at the end. There was enough weaponry in the two passages to completely equip a squadron of Stewards.

He went to the staircase, and saw with surprise that it led to floors both above and below. Owen looked up and down, then decided to save those explorations until he'd examined the kitchen.

The apples and pears tasted as fresh as if he had just picked them in the orchard behind his old home in Sweet Rock. The cheeses were heady and filling, and along the cabinets in rough sacks, were all manner of shelled nuts, which spilled onto the floor with a clattering noise as he opened one.

The sound was the first he'd heard since he'd entered the bottle. He realized he could spend the rest of the day there, so he took a bow and the quiver of arrows, then touched the side of the wall as his mentor had instructed, and repeated the word he had been taught.

The light slowly changed, and Owen blinked wide in amazement to find himself seated once more astride the camp stool, sitting before his table. In his hands were the bow and quiver, and he put them aside to look into the bottle again. In the place where the weapons had been, there were new ones of exactly the same size and color.

Owen placed the small bottle back on the table before him, and picked up its mate. Inside, a green lawn ran down to the edge of a rippling stream; there were bright colored canopies set up beside the water, and behind there stretched before him a thick ash grove in full summer glory. He repeated the words to enter the bottle, planning to remain there just a moment before continuing his journey.

He'd just had time to slip into one of the canopies when the ground suddenly shook violently. Owen fell backward as the calm scene turned upside down. He shouted the word he had been taught and slowly became aware that he was sprawled upon the ground outside the bottle. The huge black bird was perched on the table, feasting on the cheese and fruit, and had knocked the bottles onto the ground.

Owen grabbed the bow and had notched one of the long arrows before the bird noticed him. As it rose into the air, Owen sent the shaft straight into the chest of the fleeing bird.

A horrendous screech of pain tore the air, and flapping wildly, the stricken bird crashed to earth. Owen notched another arrow and cautiously approached the fallen creature, feeling remorse at having actually struck it in his fit of anger.

As he neared the dying bird, he heard a high thin voice unlike that of the dragon. "You have killed me! I would have taken you to the one you seek, but you've killed me for my trouble!"

As the bird struggled, its shape became hazy and indistinct, and Owen watched in disbelief as the form of a man began to emerge. His features were vague at first, but soon Owen saw a closely shaven man with pale eyes, almost the color the bird's had been. He was dressed in a tunic of black and gray cloth, and wore a silver chain about his neck with a pendant in the form of a strange animal.

An arm which had been a wing a moment before beckoned to Owen. "Come closer, murderer! I wish to deliver a message to you, even though you are guilty of such a cruel blow!"

"Who are you?" asked Owen, keeping his distance from the strange apparition.

"I have no name, and now you have none, either. Whoever slays me loses his powers and his property!"

Owen's heart missed a beat. "If you hadn't taunted me so, and driven me to it, I would not have shot you!"

"You can make excuses as you will, but you won't escape my curse. It will plague you from this moment on."

"Who were you taking me to?"

The man's eyes closed, as though the effort of speaking exhausted him. He pointed feebly toward the crown of Roshagel.

"That's where I was bound without you," replied Owen.

"I was taking you to the one whom you really wanted to meet," croaked the odd man. "The greatest of all beings who yet scour this frail and worthless world. His is the final curse, but mine will last as long as his."

The dying man's eyes opened, revealing an empty stare that chilled Owen as though a freezing wind had blown through his very marrow. "You will have to take my place, since you have slain me."

"How can you be freed?"

"I can never be free. I belong to the master." A look of fear flickered through the pale eyes.

On an impulse Owen slipped his sword from its scabbard, and laid it on the man's chest. He screamed pitifully as it touched him, and tried to writhe away, but was too weak. After a brief struggle, he ceased moving, and a long sigh escaped his lips. Owen watched as the body relaxed, then tensed, then relaxed again, and a calm peace settled over the racked, pain-ridden face of the man, and the pale eyes opened wide for one last time, free from the terror which had bound the man for so long.

A breath of wind touched Owen's face, and the dying man's spirit slipped from the corpse, and vanished into the sullen grayness of the day. He replaced the sword into its sheath, and looked for something to cover the body of the slain man. He began to gather stones for the task, but soon realized he wouldn't have time to spend completing the sorrowful work.

He hurriedly repeated the words to return the contents of the bottles to their place, and turning his face toward the three peaks, set off once more. The red curtain that contained the splinter of the Olgnite within him stirred, but Owen thought of Ephinias and Politar and Beran. A vision passed before his eyes then of the small gray otter signaling Owen to hurry his march. Beyond the small animal burned a huge fire, making a reddish-orange slash that hung like a great wound across the horizon.

Flames of Baluven

It took Owen the rest of the gray afternoon to reach the foot of the three peaks. He studied each one carefully: Roshagel, Spindle Rock and Devil's Cap, rising up from the dull gray earth. The ground he stood upon gave way beneath his boots like snow, and when he looked to see what it was he found it was layers and layers of gray ash.

"The Freolyde Valg," he muttered. The darker smoke he had seen earlier was gone now, but he was anxious about its absence. Politar and Beran had given him the directions to the monsters' nest, but they had not told him enough of their wiles or cunning, and he felt exposed and vulnerable.

"It was easy enough for them to talk of their exploits while we were safe on the Wind Rhyme, but when it has finally come down to it, here I am, and there they are!" He kept trying to whistle the songs he could remember Emerald singing, but his mind leapt back constantly to the grim fact that he was in the very heart of the wasted country of the dragons. Every step he took brought him closer to discovery. At any moment, he might look up to see the terrifying shadow of one of the beasts, and there would be no place to hide.

Toward the waning part of the afternoon, he reached a stone outcropping that resembled a man lying on his side, and sheltered in its cover to drink from Politar's bottle and rest his aching body. He sat with his back against the stone ledge, peering out over the landscape below. His attention was drawn to the peak next to him, Roshagel. A shower of red-hot stones flew into the air, accompanied by a shock wave that vibrated the ground about him until he almost dropped the small bottle. A column of gray smoke and ash darkened the sky even more, forcing Owen to shield his face from the choking cloud that was slowly descending on him like black snow. He covered his nose and mouth with his cloak, and turning to rise, saw the opening in the stone wall not more than a few feet away. He hurriedly gathered his kit and scrambled inside the dark cave door.

His foot dislodged something that went skittering across the dim cavern floor and came to rest not far away. Kneeling, Owen picked up the object and examined it by holding it in the light that came from outside. He recoiled when he discovered he was holding a human skull. The entire cavern seemed to be filled with more of the grisly objects, scattered about in careless disarray. His hand clasped tightly about the sword, he slowly drew it from its scabbard and held it out before him. The blade was a dim golden color, but it began to brighten as he stood transfixed, knowing without doubt that he was in the outer shafts of one of the beasts' lairs, where they had slaughtered their helpless victims, and gorged themselves on the terrible feast. He turned to leave when the wind stirred up the gray ash at the entranceway and it became dark as a great shadow loomed outside.

Without another thought, Owen sprang for the inner shaft. Moving as quickly as his legs would carry him, he raced madly, holding the sword from Skye before him. Its glow had grown more intense and now cast enough light for him to see his way. He soon slowed to a walk, pausing to catch his breath and listen for any sign of pursuit.

He noticed odd carvings on the wall of the shafts, and thought they must be some sort of runes or markings done by the poor unfortunates who inhabited the caverns before the beasts. The tunnel was wide and tall, but Owen consoled himself with the thought that the opening he had used was not big enough for anything much larger than him.

And then there was the breathing, a noise like a huge fire being fed. He stopped, hardly daring to move, and his heart hammered so loudly he was sure it must be heard by the terrible things that lived in the monstrous shafts. His hand sweated on the sword hilt until he had to dry it on his cloak.

The heavy smell of sulfur overpowered Owen, and he coughed violently. He knew one of the beasts could be in any of the dark tunnels that surrounded him. A sliver of fear embedded itself in his heart, making it hard for him to walk forward, but he doused his cloak with water from his bottle and held it over his nose so he could breathe in the foul chambers where the great firesnakes had been. Flickering reddish-orange lights came from some of the shafts that he stopped to peer down, and a faint, persistent rumble reached his ears, just on the very edge of hearing. He thought of the light, and forced himself forward. A thread of an old tune Emerald used to sing about the crossings at the River Silver ran through his head, and he began to hum it, softly at first, then more strongly as he went along.

After another few steps, the voice, which had been silent since that morning, began again, this time in a kindly, soft tone which reminded him of Ephinias. "There are pretties here. Nice pretties to tempt your eye. You must have a sweetheart. O brave one, who would like to have one of my baubles to wear about her soft neck."

Owen sought to keep his thoughts centered on the song he was humming, and clasped the sword from Skye even tighter. He paced ahead resolutely, following the sweltering shaft ever downward, and closer in to the very heart of the peak of Roshagel.

Partings on the Quay

The once proud settlement of White Bird was bustling with activity, as the inhabitants worked to rebuild the destruction brought by the dragon. Chellin Duchin and his squadron were scouring the forests at the north end of the village for unburned timber, and the Brothers had their men set to the task of pulling down burned structures so the rebuilding could begin. All hands stopped to stare in wonder as the Marin Galone ghosted into the ruined harbor, flying her flag of friendship.

"Ahoy, the vessel!" cried Emerald, who with Elita, Linne, Famhart, and many others had seen the ship and hurried to the wrecked quays to hail her. "Where are you bound from?"

"Marin Galone, outbound eighty days from Pan Dorsla, on the Delos Sound. Permission to land for water and provisions. We also have wounded aboard. Do you have healers?"

"Come ashore, and welcome," replied Cache Dunlin. "I am Senchal of White Bird. Welcome you are to what poor fare we have left. We were attacked by one of the Purge night before last, and you can see the results plainly enough for yourselves."

Lanril had lowered a boat, and four men rowed him ashore. He extended his hand to all, and bowed low to the Senchal. "My greetings, sir. We saw the worm as he passed. No good comes of their foul kind. We were lucky it was dark and stormy, or we most likely would be sweetmeats for its appetite."

"Which way have you come, captain?" asked Famhart. "We have friends that we are expecting, aboard two boats that were captured from our enemies. I thought perhaps you might have raised them." His features were drawn, and he stood with his arm about Linne.

"Did any aboard answer to the names of Stearborn and Owen?" Lanril called. "We had a gam with the crew of the Thistle Cloud, and there were those aboard who hailed from Sweet Rock." He grew more grave then. "And there were those from Fionten who heard my news of their home port with a sad heart."

Famhart shook his head. "That would have been the Archaels. The name of the boat is strange, but she seems to hold those we left aboard two Hulin Vipre vessels when we split our forces. Did you say Thistle Cloud?"

"Aye, sir. The Thistle Cloud, as pretty a ship as you've ever laid your running lights to. Her master went by name of Coglan, and there were two ladies aboard, Rewen and Deros."

"How long back since you have seen the Thistle Cloud?" asked Famhart. "Were they on their way here?"

"They were," affirmed Lanril. "We got caught in a blow on the Broads off the old settlement of Great Bend, and had to fetch back to wait out the storm. The Thistle Cloud was a better boat in a breeze, and she made for the open sea. That was the last we saw of her."

"You saw nothing of her after the gale?" pursued Emerald. "Surely they wouldn't have been blown so far to sea they would have missed you afterward!"

Lanril shook his head. "They could have been blown very far. In that sort of storm you run with the wind."

Port and his brother joined the others on the quay. "Do you think there's a chance you might catch up to this vessel you're speaking of, captain?" he asked.

Lanril laughed good-naturedly. "The Marin Galone is as fleet a vessel as you'll find on any ocean, but she can't sail if she's sunk, which is what's more likely if we try to venture out in this late part of the season."

"But if you were careful," pressed Famhart, holding Linne close to his side and feeling her pounding heart. "If you could find the Thistle Cloud and put some of us aboard, we might find a way to make it worth your while."

The ship's captain let out another laugh, although it was without humor. "Making a commission on drowning at sea doesn't appeal to me, citizen. We would be wiser to wait out the foul weather here in this safe port, and try in the spring."

Cache Dunlin broke in to suggest they all retire to his temporary shelter, where they could talk more comfortably.

As Famhart led the way into the Senchal's shelter, Lanril Tarben recounted what he had learned of the party from the Thistle Cloud as they visited ashore before the gale. "They told me they left the Hulin Vipre vessels to go aboard the Thistle Cloud," concluded the seaman. "More than that, I know not."

When they reached the shelter, Cache Dunlin's wife brought food and drink. Once they were seated at the long table, Famhart asked, "Is there a chance your ship could reach Eirn Bol at this time of year?"

Lanril nodded. "It could be done safely, if you picked your time. There is a world of difference between making for a known harbor and following the guessed-at course of a storm-driven ship. We would find rough weather now, but it wouldn't be as bad as what you could expect after this. I would say, have your kit packed and on the vessel within the day, and you would be likely to reach that fair isle somewhere in the days we mark on our calendars as the ceremonies of Lachlamas."

Lanril took a tightly furled chart from a leather bag slung over his shoulder, and moved a tray of fruit and cheese so he could unroll it on the table. He anchored the edges with apples. "We sailed from here, in the Delos Sound, to White Bird. All the settlements between have been attacked by the same devils that set upon you." He drew a line with his finger. "It is going to make a voyage extremely risky, knowing we may run into one of the beasts between here and Eirn Bol."

The Senchal of White Bird spoke up next. "Are there any survivors of those other settlements? Are there vessels left intact anywhere?"

Lanril Tarben nodded. "As I told the two seamen from Fionten, there is a fleet of survivors at sea now, but it's dangerous to band together, for it only draws the beasts."

"Then they should go straight for the very nest of the devils," offered Starboard gruffly.

Port nodded. "Give them a start! Nothing like running up the middle with cold steel."

Emerald pointed to the chain of islands that made up a curved finger of land across the chart. "Eirn Bol is within the heart of the Silent Sea, and it seems to be secure from the firesnake. What if we took your ship, gathered all the others, and formed up at Eirn Bol?"

Lanril studied his chart, his features drawn into a mask of concentration. "You know, no one we met has ever mentioned an attack on the island."

"It is because of the Alberion Novas," said Elita. "Devos has told us of the scroll which her father guards and his father's father before him."

"And all this other business has been diversions to cut off aid to her father." Famhart smiled sadly. "That would please the Dark One, to be given so much power. She is certainly capable of it, and I see she has gathered her forces again. I had hoped to simply meet here in White Bird and reorganize our settlements in The Line, but the more I hear of the dragon, and the battles that are as yet unfought, the more I see that Eirn Bol, and the girl who came to us seeking aid, are but a single thread in a tapestry that's only begun to be revealed. It's taken longer for me to see, for there has been no word from Ephinias. I had thought that anything of import would be announced by him." He paused. "Now it appears the biggest news is proclaimed by his silence."

"Are we to try to reach Eirn Bol?" asked Chellin Duchin, who had arrived at the meeting late. He picked up one of the apples holding the chart and devoured it.

"Leave it to you to smell trouble," laughed Famhart. "Yes, we shall if the good captain sees his way clear to do it."

"We shall need stores, and it wouldn't hurt to have the Marin Galone hauled and her bottom scrubbed, if we're going to be baiting the worm. Best if we have a turn of speed at hand sailing those waters. I could use the time to round up what vessels are still afloat hereabouts," suggested Lanril.

"We still have a few ships that aren't too badly damaged," said Cache Dunlin. "They aren't so large, but they're seaworthy."

There was much discussion then. Cache Dunlin and Lanril worked out the most likely places to search for other ships. The Brothers and Chellin, bored with inactivity, offered to find an overland route to the Straits of Horinfal. They could look to survivors along the way and meet the ships there.

Famhart frowned, putting his hand to his eyes and rubbing his temples, suddenly appearing very tired. "I think we shall do first things first here. We'll load Lanril's boat, and send him on his way to fetch what other ships he can. We'll rest and order ourselves for a voyage. There's nothing else we can do for now. Chellin, you see to the chores you were upon, and you Brothers tend to what you were doing. Rebuilding a town is not to a fighting man's taste, but for now I do not want to divide our forces."

The Steward captains grumbled loudly, but ducked out of the shelter when they saw the look Famhart gave them. Emerald stooped to study the chart once more. "It might be of worth to have Elita and me aboard the Marin Galone when she puts out in the morning. She and Linne can send messages the same way Deros sent her warning."

Famhart reached out to take hold of his friend. "You might find word of Owen," he said softly.

Elita looked at Linne. There was such pain in her friend's eyes that Elita knew she couldn't refuse to help in the search for Owen. Emerald took her hand, and they left to pack what they would need for the trip, and to say good-bye to their companions.

The rest of the day and most of the night was spent provisioning the Marin Galone, and readying her for the morning tide she would sail with. Famhart and Linne spent the evening with the minstrel and his new bride, talking until the last bright stars had grown pale in the new dawn. As Emerald rose to take his leave, Famhart gave him a bear hug that took his breath. "I don't think I've ever properly thanked you for taking care of Owen before," he said, searching for words.

"There's no need."

Famhart's eyes were half closed, and he seemed to be looking over Emerald's head, toward one of the late stars, now almost extinguished in the pale dawn light. "I know, my friend. Remember that I tried to say what can't be said. My heart speaks, so you must listen for that."

Linne, still seated by the hearth, turned her beautiful face to the minstrel. The firelight was reflected off the tears that flowed quietly down her cheeks. "When we meet again, it will be beyond the places we've known here. May Windameir guide you always."

Emerald was about to question her further, but a seaman from the Marin Galone knocked loudly and announced that they were sailing within the half hour. Famhart and Linne accompanied Emerald and Elita to the quay, but were silent and spoke no more of the disturbing thought of parting with no reunion. As the minstrel helped Elita aboard the Marin Galone, Famhart held him back and spoke softly into his ear. He placed a bundle in his hands, making Emerald promise to deliver it to Owen.

"What is it that won't wait for you to do it?" asked Emerald, uneasy at his friend's insistence.

"Just promise me you'll do it."

"You have my word, Famhart, if I live to carry it out."

"You shall have a long and illustrious life, my friend. It will please me greatly to hear the brilliant songs you will make of our adventures."

"That's the line of thought! We'll have a wonderful time laughing at these exploits."

"And promise me you'll not let that son of mine stray too far from how he was brought up."

Linne hugged Emerald, wetting his cloak with her tears, and was gone. The crew of the Marin Galone were pulling up the gangplank, so the minstrel had to hurry, jumping from the quay to reach the ship.

Elita joined him at the rail as the ship was rowed away from the slip. Torches and rush lamps burned in bright golden halos over the quay, beginning to melt into the streak of sunlight that was growing across the horizon. The Brothers and Chellin Duchin stood next to Famhart and Linne, waving and pounding their gloved hands against their mail shirts. Elita sobbed against his shoulder and held tightly to him.

The sense that he would never see them again grew stronger when he opened the bundle Famhart had given him to deliver to Owen.

Inside was the Cloak of Elder of The Line, and a thick letter directed to Owen in the fine, broad hand of his father. Emerald looked up again, his heart full, and watched as the faces of his friends on the quay slowly grew dimmer and smaller, as faces dim in memory, and at last were gone, swallowed by time and distance.

The River's Edge

A blast of scalding wind brushed past Owen's cheek. At the end of the shaft the orange shadows of the flames leaped against the darkness at the top of the chamber ahead, and the sword from Skye was now a blood-red color, throbbing painfully in his hand. His entire arm ached with the effort of holding the blade, and it seemed to take on a life of its own, drawing him stumbling forward toward the flames.

He shielded his eyes with his arm, and tried to pierce the fiery curtain ahead, but the heat forced him to duck away. His skin felt as though it would be burned from his body, and his lungs rebelled at drawing in the choking air.

The voice spoke once more in a soft, almost inaudible tone. "You will find what you seek at the end of this path, my young friend. It may not be to your liking." Visions of a fiery inferno blazed through Owen's mind, searing away all thought for a moment. "It is a place that no one returns from. You'll smell your skin frying, and your bones will melt."

Another voice answered. "This is the forge, and my blade will be run into its heart! Its fire will be your doom, Baluven." It was the blade which had spoken.

A searing wall of flames leapt up from the very floor, leaving his clothes smoldering and his hair smoking on his head. He slapped out the sparks with his free hand, still holding tightly to the sword.

A savage gust of fire licked around Owen, and he was blown off his feet and sent tumbling along the floor like a leaf blown in a fiery wind. When he finally managed to stop himself, he had to crawl back to retrieve the pouch which contained the bottles Politar had given him. As he grasped the leather bag, a great talon formed by the flames reached out to slash his hand.

"You shall pay for this invasion of the holy mountain of Roshagel!" boomed the voice. "It is not for the weak toads of the sons of Hamen to cross over into the sacred realms of the Freolyde Valg! It is written that the Protector shall rule, and her Purge shall serve as her Palace Guard. Now you shall feel her wrath as punishment for breaking the law of the Warl!" The great talon snatched at Owen, but missed, and he touched the sword of Skye to the fiery flesh of the beast, which caused it to withdraw, shrieking in pain and rage.

The floor of the chamber trembled, and there was a roar thundering and rolling against his ears as the mountain shuddered on its foundations. Owen saw some horrible form begin to take shape as he watched. His knees were rubbery, and his heart hammered in his chest with such force he was afraid it might tear his ribs apart, but he clutched the sword more tightly still, watching for what the cunning beast might do next.

"Think of the High Dragons, Owen," sang the voice of the sword. "Remember the High Dragon."

As Owen's thoughts turned, seeking the memory, a solid inferno blew down the shaft toward him, setting his clothes afire. The metal locket he wore beneath his shirt grew so fiercely hot that he ripped it from his throat and flung it in the direction of the advancing monster. Then Owen pulled one of Politar's bottles from the bag, peering inside it quickly to determine which one he held. As soon as he saw the green lawn that led down to the river, he spoke the words Politar had taught him, just as the gaunt talon reached out to crush him once more. There was a dreadful moment when he thought he had mistaken the spell, but in the last instant before he was crushed in the grasp of the dragon, he found himself standing on the green lawn by the cool river, all alone and watching in amazement as his cloak lay still smoldering at his feet. The blade of the sword had turned a misty silver, but pulsed strongly in his hand, and the voice spoke again, clear and high.

"You must take water from this river to the beast. It will allow you to plunge my blade into the fire it guards, and will cut the cord that holds the High Dragons from returning to take their brothers."

Owen sat suddenly, clutching his knees to his chest. "I never thought I'd escape. Do I have to go back?"

"The bottle is in the shaft. It will be found and hoarded. That will be the chance we need, for the Freolyde Valg will take it to the Fire Pit."

As the voice fell silent, Owen was thrown onto his side, and everything turned and spun crazily for a moment. "We are being carried there now," the sword explained. "We had best make ourselves ready."

Owen could see the roaring inferno beyond the enchanted walls of the bottle, but he did not feel the heat. He searched through his pouch for something to carry the water from the river and found the small mithra flask that had once held water from the Wells of Trona. As his hands touched the surface of the river, a smooth surge of energy rippled up his arm, and his tiredness slipped away, leaving him refreshed. He bent over and drank a long draft, feeling the terror fade as though it had all been but a dream.

The sword from Skye lay beside him on the green lawn, humming faintly, and Owen took comfort in knowing that

Politar waited. As soon as he'd completed his task here in the heart of the mountain, he would return to the Wind Rhyme as quickly as his legs would carry him.

Under no circumstances are you to travel by night. Politar's words came back to him and Owen frowned.

It had been dayfail when he entered the cavern and must now be well into the watch before midnight, which meant he had many hours to endure before he could begin his journey to his friend.

Owen wondered also how long it would take the dragon to return to its hoard in the heart of the mountain called Roshagel. The dragon might be caught sleeping when Owen again left the bottle. As he turned that attractive thought over in his mind, he became aware of someone standing behind him.

The Forge of Roshagel

"Peace," said a man dressed as a minstrel. "I mean you no harm."

Owen, who had leapt to his feet, looked carefully to make sure the man carried no weapons. Then he replied, "I hope I am not trespassing, but I have fallen upon desperate times indeed, and now find myself here, lying at the bottom of a firesnake's lair, waiting for daylight."

"A wise decision that," agreed the man, nodding. "You will not go far in the dark. The Harlachts roam the wastes after sunset, and feed on any they find out of cover or beyond a fire."

"What manner of beings are they?" asked Owen, growing angry at Politar once again for not warning him more exactly about his dangers.

"Beings? I know not if they are beings, but they do have life, and seem to breed and grow on the unfortunate ones they may snare. They dwelled here long ago, before the beasts came to nest in this desolation. They are useful to the dragons, for they need not fear being ambushed in the dark."

"I thought a firesnake had no fear of anything."

The man laughed. "They have fears, like you or I, and I shall teach you which of those fears might be useful to you. I am Wylich, at your service."

Owen bowed.

"Many say the dragons are no more than a pile of meat and bones. Long ago I learned that the old songs make the life which drives the beasts and they long for redemption." He took a small mithra mouth harp and played a tune on it before handing it to Owen. "Here, take it. Its music is better than a shield to protect you against what you cannot see, or have never heard of."

"What could that be?"

"You will have cause to find out, my lad. Politar said you would be a dense one, and I have to agree. But I like your spirit, my boy. That makes up for much."

"Are the Harlachts outside the cave now?"

"They roam at will over this gray land. The desolation you see is part of their handiwork. No living thing can survive them."

"Then they are like the Rogen in Trew."

"So you have met others like them! Your education shall be complete when you are called to help fight against their kind. There will be men who have found the old lore, and who follow it. The Dark One promises great power that way, and all who fall to her wiles become willing slaves to it."

"Are the Harlachts her slaves?" asked Owen.

"In a way. They were once captives of the dragon, and lived as humans until the beasts found another way to amuse themselves. Now the poor devils are caught in the dragons' web, and exist only to serve them."

"If I could kill this beast, will they be freed?" asked Owen, though the idea filled him with fear.

"If you could kill the beast, more than a few unfortunate souls here would be freed. That may not be for you to do, my boy. The sword has yet to be run into the Forge, and the one who guards it is only sleeping, not dead. There is much we have left to do."

"Are you coming with me?" asked Owen hopefully.

"This is as far as I shall come. My own duties lie elsewhere." The minstrel unstrapped a harp from his back and lay back in the soft grass at the river's edge, plucking a chord or two.

"So you will join Politar and Beran! 'Run ahead, lad, it won't be much! We'll be waiting for you when you've done the job!' Now they're sitting somewhere safely aboard the Wind Rhyme, and you'll be with them no doubt, while I stumble about in the dragon's gullet."

Wylich put down his harp, looking earnestly at Owen. "You have everything you will need, my lad. You have the sword from Skye, and I have given you my mouth harp. The only thing missing is what you find in your heart. Neither Politar nor Beran, nor I, can place something there that is not there already."

"Will you help me find Deros and my friends? And will I be able to do something then?"

The minstrel's eyes softened, and he nodded. "You will be

able to be of more than help, Owen. You will bring them hope when there is none left."

Owen was poised to ask another question of his new friend, but was cut short by another rough jolt that sent him sprawling on the grass by the river's edge. He called out to Wylich, but no reply came, and when he had regained his balance, he was alone by the water. He looked about helplessly, then threw his hands up in frustration, and noticed the object still in his hand. It was the minstrel's mouth harp. He put it to his mouth and strummed a short note, which echoed sharply, then created small waves upon the river. A sharp jolt shook him roughly to the ground, and the bottle spun violently, as though tossed by a great upheaval. Owen put the mouth harp inside his cloak and grabbed hold of the sword with both hands, hanging on tightly. The jolts grew stronger, and Owen, fearing that the bottle might be broken, shouted out the words Politar had given him, holding the sword out before him and trying to ready himself for whatever might await.

As the soft light of the bottle began to harden into a harsh, reddish-orange glare, Owen became aware of another presence, out of sight but very much there. He stumbled over something at his feet, and out of the corner of his eye saw the chests filled with sparkling stones and the brilliant neckbands and wristlets that reflected the fiery walls. Holding the sword out before him, he saw it had turned a blood-red once more, and grew so hot to hold he could hardly bear the pain. He stepped carefully forward, and the very floor of the cave seemed to shoot hot flames up through the soles of his boots. He saw more skeletons, and in a chamber directly before him, he could make out what appeared to be a larger space, one that ran completely through the heart of the mountain.

The heat grew more intense as he neared the entrance to the next chamber. A stench of sulfur began to choke him again, and the cavern shook slightly as he paused at the tall stone archway. Behind him was another sound, like the almost silent feet of a cat stalking its prey, and he whirled.

Standing not ten paces from him was the beast, its eyes burning like smoking coal in its grotesque head, partly hidden behind layers of steely plates, and a great snout full of gleaming, razor-sharp teeth that reflected back the mounds of shining jewels and gold and silver and mithra. Smoke oozed from the nostrils of the monster. Beneath its front feet, there appeared a dozen or more men and women walking in a daze toward Owen. "It is sad for one of our Order to be without the blood of the Hamen." The dragon's voice was soft and compelling. "The harmony of our nests is broken when we are forced to go too long in the turmoil of such fasts. We have been long held beyond the ripeness of your kind, O brave one." It snatched up two of the helpless victims at its feet. The pitiful screams shocked Owen from his trance.

"You should not harm them," he said, noticing that his voice was squeaky. "They have not done you any hurt." He managed the last with more force, in a lower tone.

The smoldering eyes of the beast went from its victims to Owen, and a small flame licked briefly from its dreadful snout. "They have committed the most foul of crimes, my brash young morsel! They dared to breathe the same air as the Chosen Ones! It is their fate, as it is yours, to sacrifice themselves so that we may scour these lands clear of all who would oppose us." In a single gulp, the monster had devoured its victims and spit out the bloody bones onto the floor at Owen's feet. The dragon coiled about the other captives, and lay back down, placing its head on the floor of the cavern.

Rage built in Owen, rage at his own fear, and at the black heart of the monster before him. All the evil that had sought out the innocent men and women of his homeland,

and all the other lands across Atlanton, suddenly was present before him in the hideous beast that now gazed contentedly at the mountain of treasures the dragons had stolen from their victims.

"You were wrong to think no one would one day find you," began Owen, testing his voice.

The heavy lids of the beast's eyes opened a bit wider, although its look was still sleepy and without interest. "Oh, but I always thought my door was open to all! I have made no secret of my whereabouts. My brothers are gracious as well, and have always let it be known where they were to be sought."

"You are great in size and malice, yet there are ways and means to end you. It was done already, in the Middle Islands. The Dark One has been called upon to follow the Law again, and to release her allies to their own fates." Owen's voice held a slight tremor at first, but it vanished as he went on.

The huge beast lay still, listening as though it were bothered by a pesky fly making irritating noises to detract it from its nap.

"I think you have not met many of the Order of the Freolyde Valg, or you would not banter your words so foolishly. A child of Hamen cannot know the power of our race, or the depths of the terror we can bestow. It would serve me ill to destroy you so quickly, before I have had my fill of this small sport." As the beast finished speaking, Owen's vision began to dim, and he could only make out a faint outline of the monster before him. In his mind's eye he saw Deros, horribly disfigured by fire. A loud crackling roar sent the dream vision spinning away.

"Your thoughts give me new inspiration, child of Hamen! I will take great pleasure in finding this one you hold in your thoughts. It will be exquisite for the Scourge to take the beauty of one so young."

Owen's hands clutched the sword from Skye tightly, and he raised it to strike at the foul monster before him, but was struck down by a blast of fiery breath before he could close with his enemy. Desperation kept him from dropping the blade. As he stumbled away, he lurched through an archway directly into a vault that blasted his skin with a raging inferno. When he opened his eyes, he was teetering only a few inches away from the edge of a sheer drop that fell away into a boiling caldron of fire and molten rock. When he turned, he saw the head of the beast shoving its way into the archway, eyes dark and lidded. There was no intent to torment or tease in them now, and Owen read his own death in the smoldering darkness.

Owen searched for the mouth harp that Wylich had given him, but he dug frantically about for the object without finding it. With all the bravado he could muster, Owen yelled, "Stop! My teacher is Wylich, and he taught me songs which will crack your eardrums, and make your invincible armor no more than a candy shell on a child's sweetmeat." While Owen spoke, he backed carefully down the narrow edge of the trail. He had no way of knowing if this was the place where Politar and Beran said he must bring the sword from Skye, yet Owen had no alternative but to hope it was.

A Thread of Light

A voice from the fire called Owen's name, beckoning him straight into the maw of the raging inferno. His sword blistered his hands, and his clothing was singed and smoking, and his hair felt as if he was scorching the top of his head. He was beyond being frightened. He turned his back on the dragon and advanced toward the fiery pit. He had no idea how he was to place the blade into the flames, but that did not matter.

The dragon sent into his mind horrifying promises of a lingering death which would go on forever, and the dreadful vision of Deros badly burnt and pleading with Owen to surrender to the power of the monster. Nothing was keeping him on his feet now but the momentum of his own forward movement, and the tiny shadow of a splinter that lingered in the dark part of his being where the Olgnite curse had been.

A stabbing, searing pain tore at Owen's body, and he was certain he had been devoured by the fire of the beast, yet there was a blurred image of something before him, as though a blazing curtain had been drawn, and there below him was the yawning furnace of doom, bubbling and raging in a white-hot vat that sent showers of crackling sparks and steam all the way up through the crown of Roshagel. The sword of Skye seemed to explode into shards as he teetered on the brink of the fiery caldron, and the voice of the dragon was booming in his ears. He fought free of the leaden weight that crushed his mind into submission. He called out feebly to Ephinias and Beran, and just as he neared the end of his strength, he found the mouth harp of Wylich in his hand. He brought the small object to his lips, but his mouth was so dry and cracked, it seemed as though he wouldn't be able to make any sound. Then the dragon bellowed again, and in a final burst of desperation, the youth managed to force a note from the harp.

As the echo of it reverberated through the mountain, Owen felt a cooling wind. A carpet of soft clouds swept him from his feet and propelled him into the vast, deep hole where the caldron of fire roared below him, and he cried out in a choked voice as he fell straight down into certain destruction. He waited in horror for his flesh to melt, but only the sword grew hot to the touch, and just as he entered the billowing flames, another note sounded from the harp, and he found himself sprawled upon a stone floor as smooth and cool to the touch as snow. The sword from Skye glimmered with a pale golden-white sheen, and he looked around him in shocked surprise. His clothing was singed and blackened, but he still had the leather bag Politar had given him, and the two bottles were safe inside. Above him, he heard the noise of the horrible beast, but there was no more fear in his heart. Owen called out to the dragon in a high, clear voice.

"You are done with your old ways. The harp of Wylich commands you to be free, and come to the fire! It will burn the blackness from your heart, and allow you to go back to wherever the Dark One found you."

There was a silence then, and the beast seemed to hesitate. "I have no place to go back to. I would rather die by your hand in the cellar of this mountain. It is the only home I have known since the Protector called us. They have made the signs again from Blor Alhal, but the fools know nothing of us. Come up and give me peace."

Owen could not see the monster over the fire and smoke above him, but sensed he was there, at the edge of the pit. "Come down here. You will have to come to me."

There was a silence then, as the dragon grew quiet. All Owen could hear was the noise of the fire crackling about him.

"Will you put away that thing that hurts my ears? And the sword? If I come down, there will be no need of them. You have won."

The sword was a pale golden color in Owen's hand, and a brilliant blue flame flickered faintly about the keen edge. "I will hold my hand. If you are truly giving up, you have nothing to fear from me." He pulled the small mithra flask from his vest and put it where he could reach it easily.

"That's what they have always said to the Purge," purred the beast. "No matter what time or place I have been, it has always been the same. They either fear us and try to slay us, or use treachery to trap us. The filth of the Council have long tried to betray us. No one has given us our fair due since we have been upon the Meadows. It is not surprising to find we have finally resorted to our strength to make our way in this cruel life that we are forced to lead."

"Why did you come here? Did someone call you back?"

"We have all been promised a new awakening. The Conductors of Quineth Rel have made the signs, and read the words from the Book of Warl. It is the voice of the new coming."

"Then your new coming is finished."

"You see? You speak as they all have spoken! What did I tell you? My history is full of treachery and deceit, but not mine! It is your own conscience you will have to search for right or wrong."

Owen blew another soft note on the mouth harp of Wylich. It was a bare murmur of a sound, but it brought an explosion of pain and anger from the beast at the top of the fiery pit. A rasping noise was heard next, as though something rough was being scraped against a solid surface. He could not imagine what would produce such a sound, but just at that moment, he saw the dragon on its back, flailing about wildly, lashing out with its talons and long, powerful tail. He remembered the strange marks in the tunnel and knew what had made them. Then the dragon regained its footing and moved away from the pit.

Owen knew he could not lure it down. He peered about for an escape from the deep pit, but could see no exits that would allow him to leave. "If no way out, then up," he said, and found the bottle which held arms and provisions.

Soon he was in the familiar hallway, seeking a grapple with a three-pronged hook, and a length of rope attached to it. Owen had learned from Kegin how to swing it about until enough rope was let out to reach high up into a tree, and then to shinny up the rope like a squirrel. He brought his treasure out of the bottle, put the bottle and the flask away, and gauged the distance to the top of the pit.

When Owen hoisted himself over the edge, he found he was staring directly into the clouded slits of eyes of the huge monster, now laying upon its back on the cavern floor, trying to cover its head with its leathery wings. He doused the dragon with the water from the flask and waited.

Owen cautiously watched it, unsure of what to make of the subdued monster. The small curl of smoke from its nostrils had trickled away to almost nothing, and the black shroud of terror which had smothered Owen was gone. The sword from Skye pulsed powerfully in his hands, and the mouth harp of Wylich felt warm in its pocket next to his heart.

"Leave this place with me now," Owen said.

The beast shook its great head. "The Harlacht clans roam there now. You couldn't pass them."

Owen walked forward and stood before the dragon. "You could have lied to me, but you didn't. You warned me of the Harlachts. Something has happened to you. Your old world is gone. Don't you remember another time, before the Book of Warl?"

"Was there a time before Warl?"

"Think on it for a moment. You were tricked. The minstrel left me with that thought. There was a time when you were somewhere else, and you lived beyond these lairs with your murdered victims and their plundered riches."

He felt the strength of the sword pulse through his arm again, and he reached out to pour the sacred water from the river onto the dragon's scaly hide just below its eye.

There was what sounded like a child's sobbing, lost in a hollow hall which would echo the pitiful cries, until it seemed there were a hundred times that number wailing in such a forlorn, anguished way that Owen could stand no more.

"Come back from the darkness," said Owen in a low, gentle voice. "You can see the light here in my blade! Come back to it. Forget Warl and the Dark One. She cannot find you now."

The shrieking began again, and the huge beast thrashed about wildly on the cavern floor, threatening to knock Owen back into the pit. He leapt nimbly over the flailing tail, and found a safe place among a cluster of channels carved into the walls by molten stone. The beast neared the rim of the fiery caldron, and in another heartbeat it was gone into the roaring flames and smoke. He waited to hear the screams of the doomed monster, but there was nothing. The roaring increased for a time, but that soon died away.

Owen crawled carefully to the pit's edge and peered down into the depths. There was no sign of the monster, and even the fire had dwindled into nothing more than a small memory of itself, leaving a tall doorway showing plainly against the right-hand wall. His rope was unburned, so Owen gathered his courage, slid down it and was soon standing before the great archway, which would have towered even above one so tall as Stearborn. Letters outlined in a smoky fire ran across the top of the entrance, and the heavy metal door was hot enough to the touch for Owen to snatch his hand away quickly, blowing on his burned fingers.

As he watched in amazement, the red-hot door began to slowly dim to a dull gray, and with a grinding noise that shook the ground beneath him, a crack began to steadily open, until the archway stood open. Other sounds grew stronger then; of birds and animals, and a faint music he could not quite grasp, but which sounded familiar, like an old lullabye he had heard long before. There were voices there, too, speaking in tongues he could not make out, but which a part of him recognized. Olgnite and the Hulin Vipre were there, their speech harsh against the ear, followed by the softer sounds of water flowing over sand and the wind through the ash trees that guarded the Sacred Grove on the cliffs of the Sea of Silence. A single call rang out again and again, and at last Owen recognized it as his own name being called. He looked through the great door which had rolled open, revealing such an astonishing sight. Owen sank to his knees in wonder.

Beyond the archway, there spread a green land rolling away to a distant sea, sparkling blue in afternoon sunlight. Looking down, Owen could see whitecapped mountains which formed a range that ran all the way into the silver-blue distance, glinting in the light with such intensity he was forced to turn his eyes away. His name was called again, but he could still see no speaker. "Who are you?" he managed at last, looking about.

"Colvages Domel," came the voice. "I am the dragon."

Owen's hand gripped the sword, and he readied himself for a renewed attack, cursing himself for being so lax when he dealt with the cunning beast.

"You won't need your weapons. You are to come with me now."

"Go with you? Where?" asked Owen incredulously, searching for sight of the speaker.

"You are to go before the Coram Mont."

"I'll go nowhere with you until I can see who speaks. I have heard of the tricks of the dragon."

A brilliant flash of light appeared at Owen's side, and there before his disbelieving eyes was a young man not much older than himself, dressed in glittering armor of mithra and gold, braced with silver and precious stones which formed an intricate pattern of stars on the breastplate.

Owen's hand lowered the sword, now pulsing with a strength that was almost unbearable. "Who are you?"

"I am Colvages Domel," repeated the young man. "I have been imprisoned for many lifetimes by the Dark One."

"How did you come to this?" Owen asked hesitantly, studying the young man's face, which reminded him of the Lame Parson's friend, Twig. He had seen the same look in the young—ancient eyes of the Dreamers.

"I was a younger son who yearned to rule after my father's death. I slew my brother to claim this piece of metal I wear." He removed the dull crown, which was blackened and unadorned. "On the night of his burial, the Dark One came to me and I listened to her weave her spell of death and disaster, with all her promises of power and riches."

Owen's blood chilled as he listened to the young man, whose face hardened as he spoke.

"She kept every promise she made me. I ended my time as a human by slaying all my family and kinsmen, and ruled over my unfortunate countrymen. As the seasons came and went, there were fewer and fewer of my subjects left. The young woman I was pledged to wed was horrified by what I had become, and fled to the isle of Eirn Bol."

"That's where I was bound," cried Owen. "I was aboard the Thistle Cloud with Lady Deros, and got washed overboard in a storm."

Colvages Domel smiled sadly. "You were fortunate, my friend."

Owen laughed bitterly. "I would not go so far as that. You see me here with you, and I don't know where she or my friends are! Politar said we could not go on to Eirn Bol with the Wind Rhyme, even though the Welingesse Fal were there to help."

Colvages Domel sighed. "It seems there are some things that remain the same. That scoundrel was at his worst with me when I succumbed to the Dark One. He has been hounding me forever."

"Are these Gray Wastes your old country?" asked Owen.

The young man in the bright armor raised an arm to the vast green land with the powerful mountains and bordered by the gleaming blue sea beyond the doorway in Roshagel. "This is my country as it was before the Protector came, but it is an illusion. The past is beyond redeeming, but I have been freed from the bond to the Dark One. I owe you my life for that."

"Are the Harlachts still out?"

The young man nodded. "They are out still, and there is darkness beyond Roshagel, if you go back the way you came."

"How else would I go? I must return to Politar. We are bound for Eirn Bol."

"He is on his way now to ready the gathering that was to

take place when Roshagel should fall. You will find another way to Eirn Bol."

"But how will we find our way from here if Politar is already gone?"

"You have seen the terror of the Purge. Now you shall see what the true dragon is capable of. We have our journey to make now. It is a long way to the halls where you shall find your answers. Politar will be anxious for you to tend to your lessons."

"They will all be anxious for that," replied Owen shortly. "Ephinias and Gillerman, and Beran and Politar. They all said I would have a long time to absorb what I would need to be of help to my friends."

"We must go now, Owen Helwin. Look to the east!" Colvages Domel pointed to the window above the arch. A great fleet of ships crowded the ocean's face with blood-red sails. A cloud of fire flowed over the vast scene, and stopped on a quay beneath a high, white cliff.

"What are we seeing? Is this something that has already happened?"

"Will happen," corrected the young man. "You are almost at the point of being able to see where you will be. The Walengaad is never opened to any but the ones who will be able to stand what they see there."

"What is the Walengaad? What do people see there?"

"You might call it the Sight, although others call it the Dragon's Eye."

"Like the Rhion Stones?" asked Owen. "Ulen Scarlett carries one that has turned him against us all."

"If you look again, you will find much that troubles your heart has an ending here." He paused briefly, studying his companion. "There is also a chance you will find things come to pass that will cause the great pain. It is for you to decide whether you will look out over the world from Walengaad. No one can force your hand."

Owen hesitated. "What if I choose to pass it by?"

"Then you will be ignorant of your pain for a time. And you will miss your chance to be useful to your friends."

"You force me to look, then. There is no real choice."

"None, my friend. If you choose not to go through the Walengaad, you will be turning away from your destiny upon Atlanton."

"Will I see what happens to us all on Eirn Bol?" Owen was torn between his fear and a burning desire to know what would be.

"You will see as much as you are capable of seeing."

"I must find out," said Owen resolutely.

"Look at the window."

Owen stared at the brightness of the sea far beyond the rim of the green land, and soon the water began to churn itself into a fierce storm, with howling winds and white-capped waves that rose higher and higher until he was once more in the heart of the gale that had swept him from the Thistle Cloud. Then he saw a tranquil winter sea lapping softly at the pillars of the quays of a city dressed in white, with a long strand of salt flats which ran behind. There were people gathered on the stone landings, and as his vision grew clearer, he began to recognize faces there, and his heart grew glad. There were his old friends Kegin Thornby and Chellin Duchin, talking with the minstrel Emerald. Elita was with him, and just beside her, his mother and father were locked in earnest conversation with a stranger who seemed to be an Elder.

A cloud descended then, with fire and ash, and the white settlement was gone, replaced with a sea full of ships of all size and kind sailing toward a crimson sunrise. Owen cried out then to Colvages Domel, for he did not wish to see further, but one of the ships in the vision loomed larger, as though he were falling upon it from a great height. He closed his eyes to shut out the sight, but he still saw what was there; it was the Thistle Cloud under full sail, making for an island straight ahead, where seabirds whirled and circled in the sky above. Soon he saw that they weren't birds at all, but many dragons, scorching the land with their fiery breath and crushing ships with their powerful talons and deadly tails.

At the rail of the familiar ship, he saw Deros next to Ulen Scarlett, who stood rigidly gazing away at the carnage, his ringed hand calmly grasping the young woman's shoulder. Owen cried out desperately, calling for the terrible dream to end. "I knew he would have been better left! He will betray us all!"

Colvages Domel appeared before him again, and the window of the Walengaad grew dark, as though its mind were asleep. "You have seen what you need to know to help your friends. The Walengaad does not give answers, but asks questions. Did you find what you sought?"

Owen shook his head, suddenly very weary. "I saw more than I wanted. Most I already knew."

"Then we must go now. There is little time. The others await us." Colvages Domel drew a hand across his face, and the air about them seemed to split into thousands of moonbeams, each glimmering and reflecting the others until the very floor of the mountain was lighter than a breath. They rose through the roof of Roshagel, straight up into the cloak of night, deep and silent, except for the tiny bright echoes of stars, spread away in a thick carpet toward the south, where Owen heard the small, high voice of his heart calling to him.

In the great hall of the High Dragon that night were many old friends gathered to meet him in the soft grace of wisdom and love th his dream to come again, so that the Master's breath back to the Dark One were gathered to strike a fatal blow to the followers of Windameir. The halls of heaven were silent, and far below the wind's meadows, no one danced to the ancient song of the sea, nor laughed to hear the Heart of Windameir beat in time to their own.

A great darkness had begun to fall, and all who yet dwelled upon Atlanton waited to see if there would be another dawn.

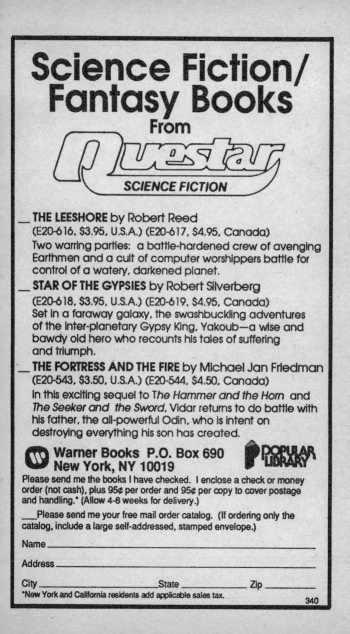